**IN PHILLY AND PHOENIX,
IN NASHVILLE AND THE APPLE,
IN MEMPHIS AND ON THE LEFT COAST,
THEY'RE LAUGHING OUT LOUD AT—**

"If you like to laugh, you'll cover *Baja Oklahoma* with grateful kisses."

—*Los Angeles Times*

"Good enough to 'make you hit your grandma,' as they say down south."

—Liz Smith, *New York Daily News*

"Bright . . . crisp . . . irreverent . . . a great ride."

—*Memphis Commercial Appeal*

"The bawdiest, raunchiest, most hair-raising novel of the season . . . entertaining too."

—*The Asheville Citizen*

"Makes you laugh out loud."

—*Philadelphia Inquirer*

"*Guaranteed* to make you laugh out loud."

—*Phoenix Gazette*

AND *BAJA OKLAHOMA'S* BREAKING UP THE WHOLE COUNTRY— WITH LAUGHTER!

"Jenkins is the only author I know who is guaranteed to provide his reader with that one irrefutable measure of greatness: fifteen or twenty times while you're reading, you'll pick up the telephone to call a friend and read a paragraph out loud so you can laugh together."

—Bob Greene, syndicated columnist

"*BAJA OKLAHOMA* ALMOST MADE ME ASHAMED THAT I WAS BORN IN NEW ENGLAND, NEVER ATTENDED TCU, HAVE SMALL BREASTS, DON'T SMOKE AND DRINK WHITE WINE."

—Nancy Dowd, author of *Slapshot*

"Jenkins at his raunchy best—good-humored, foul-mouthed, wonderfully funny."

—Jane Clapperton, *Cosmopolitan*

"DAN JENKINS KNOWS HIS TEXAS . . .
A MARVELOUS CAST OF CHARACTERS
. . . THE DIALOGUE IS AS STRAIGHT
ATCHA AS A SEMI-TRAILER ON A ONE
LANE ROAD."

—*Jacksonville Times Union*

"CLASSIC JENKINS. THE CHARACTERS
BECOME COMPANIONS, THEIR
DIALOGUE PART OF YOUR LIFE. FORT
WORTH, I LOVE YOU."

—Peter Gent, author of *North Dallas Forty*

"A gallery of hilariously foul dudes . . . alive
with that peculiar Jenkins two-step: raw and
mean one minute, warm and sweet the
next."

—*Kirkus Reviews*

BAJA OKLAHOMA

DAN JENKINS

PUBLISHED BY POCKET BOOKS NEW YORK

Lyrics from "Bob Wills Is Still the King," written by Waylon
Jennings, © 1974 by the Baron Music Publishing Company, are
quoted by permission.

POCKET BOOKS, a Simon & Schuster division of
GULF & WESTERN CORPORATION
1230 Avenue of the Americas, New York, N.Y. 10020

This book is totally dedicated to the former June Burrage, homecoming queen, lifelong love interest, exemplary mother of children and grownups, nurse, bookkeeper, handyperson—and not a bad little chef.

. . . It's a roundup stirring mem'ries
Of the rough-and-tumble days.
It's a detour off the freeway
To see where you were raised.
It's the laughter you can carry
Through the years that turn you old.
It's "Baja Oklahoma,"
But it's Texas in your soul!

from "Baja Oklahoma,"
a song by JUANITA HUTCHINS

Lord, I hate to let you go.
Your body drives me wild.
. . . But I'm a smoking window,
And you're a non-smoking aisle.

LONNIE SLOCUM,
from an unfinished song

Her bluejeans weren't as dirty as
The thoughts that crossed his mind.

JUANITA HUTCHINS,
from a work in progress

Contents

Prologue

The sound was born on a summer night at the old Crystal Springs pavilion in Fort Worth, Texas, when Bob Wills and his string band were entertaining the cowboys and their ladies from 9 till Fist Fight.

In those early 1930's, Bob Wills had already begun to add a barrelhouse piano, drums, even horns, to his fiddle, guitars and banjos, and he was always fooling around with the popular music of the era, slowing down or doubling the tempo on standards like *Darktown Strutters' Ball* and *St. Louis Blues*.

One evening at Crystal Springs the cowboys and their ladies suddenly heard a music they could truly feel as they two-stepped around the dance floor.

Bob Wills and the band were playing roadhouse music, country style, a Lone Star rag, and they called it "Western Swing."

A cowboy grinned at his lady and said, "Them Benny Goodmans don't have to play *St. Louis Blues* no more. It just got done!"

Thereafter, Bob Wills and his followers began writing their own two-steps and ballads about honky-tonk blues, cheating women, hard luck, and the price of stew meat during the Depression.

Western Swing swept across Texas, and far beyond,

when a powerful Fort Worth radio station WBAP, turned over its prime air time to Bob Wills and the Light Crust Doughboys from Burrus Mill.

Bob Wills soon tired of selling biscuits, but he never stopped selling his music. He organized the Texas Playboys and met a San Antonio Rose, fiddled a Cotton-Eyed Joe, stayed all night and stayed a little longer, and cried, "Take me back to Tulsa, I'm too young to marry!"

Now, almost half a century after that night at Crystal Springs, a whole nation was enamored of Western Swing—and a new lie had slipped into barroom dialogue: "I've always worn boots."

The man primarily responsible for these modern occurrences was another Texan, Willie Nelson.

The music had changed a bit. Thanks to Willie, a profound sophistication and humor had crept in. But most of the urban buckaroos who discovered Willie Nelson in the 1970's were unaware that Willie, with his poet's soul, mournful voice and low-C guitar, was only carrying on for Bob Wills as he told America about rejected love, whisky rivers, Bloody Mary mornings, going on the road again—and ain't it funny how time slips away?

Today, in the same Fort Worth where it all started, a lady named Juanita Hutchins, a music lover, took immense pride in the fact that her hometown was the cradle of Western Swing. She would recite this history of the honky-tonk sound to anyone who cared to listen, although she often remarked:

"It's the kind of music I prefer, but I guess you'd have to say it's caused a few problems for life itself."

PART ONE

*Up to Here with All That Corn Whisky,
Smoky Mountain, Bluegrass, Jesus Saves,
Momma-Done-Good Bullshit*

Chapter One

The scrub oaks looked like twisted wrought iron, and everybody's front yard had turned the color of a corn tortilla. It was October in that part of Texas. The north wind had already begun to sling carving knives at the city, even when preachers and doctors were outdoors. A north wind in Texas didn't care whose ass it stung just like a sad song didn't care whose heart it broke. But this was only a crisp day. The sky was bluer than a bathroom wall.

As the days came and went for Juanita Hutchins, she called it a keeper. "I guess I'd choose it over glaucoma," was the way she actually put it. Juanita's optimism had a tendency to get out of hand like that.

Juanita saw the day through the big casement window in the bar of Herb's Cafe. She was charmed as usual by the panorama of Herb's asphalt parking lot, a few of the compacts and pickups that rendezvoused there, a telephone pole, a store across the street with the absorbing name of WALLPAPER TO GO, Slick Henderson's Exxon station, and the side of a laundromat on which a clever old romantic had alerted the world to "Fuck Melissa Ann Webster."

The truth is, Juanita saw the day as she worked

behind the bar in Herb's Cafe, which was how it went, she said, if you were born under the sign of polyester.

It was around three o'clock in the afternoon on that bright autumn Wednesday in Fort Worth.

The luncheon for the South Side B & PW was over, but some of the Business and Professional Women were still around. They were drinking strawberry Daiquiris, discussing the Christmas tree skirts they were making out of felt and sequins, and trying to think of something good to say about their dead husbands.

A fresh batch of Daiquiris was blending. Juanita trifled with the dial of a Panosonic radio. It sat on a shelf near a photograph of her daughter, Candy, a ravishing girl in her twenties. The radio was usually tuned to stations programming Country & Western music. Willie Nelson, Waylon Jennings and Loretta Lynn were necessary to Juanita's work. So were Winstons and coffee—and Anacin, which gave the benediction.

As the blender purred to a stop, Juanita spoke to one of the South Side B & PW's.

"Vera, you don't want any more of this strawberry crap, do you? Switch to Pearl?"

Vera Satterwhite looked around from a table where she was vigorously combating a hot flash with an Oriental fan.

"Thank you, honey," Vera said, "I'd hold me a Pearl in abeyance, if it's real cold."

"Colder than the other side of your bed."

Juanita poured three strawberry Daiquiris and put them on a tray with the Pearl beer. She carried the drinks to the table of Business and Professional Women. Vera Satterwhite sold real estate, Josephine McClure owned a pet shop, Alma Roberts managed a garden and gift store, and LuAnn Hodges was a secretary for a chiropractor. The women all had powder-blue beehives. With their red daiquiris and blue hair, they looked like campaign posters.

Juanita placed the last strawberry Daiquiri in front of

6

the last beehive. "If it was me, I wouldn't know whether to drink this shit or take it over to All Saints Hospital and donate it."

"Now I remember my favorite day in here," Vera said to the other ladies. "Juanita had laryngitis."

Josephine, Alma and LuAnn began combating their own hot flashes with menus and newspapers.

Slick Henderson sat on a barstool in his regular corner. His Exxon patch and partly bald head rested against the wall near a calendar. The calendar gave a special prominence to TCU's Southwest Conference football schedule and advertised O.R. Boynton's Poultry & Meats.

Robert (Slick) Henderson was a strong-looking man of fifty-two. A layer of weather covered his face and there was a glint in his eye. In the hours when he wasn't replacing another vacuum modulator valve on another Volkswagen, Slick worked on his fluorescent tan in Herb's.

Next to Slick, a younger man was slumped over, dozing. He wore a hand-crumpled calf-roper's hat, shredded coveralls, a week's travail of whiskers. Lonnie Slocum was the leader of Dog Track Gravy, a Western band not widely known outside of high school gymnasiums and Holiday Inns. Scrubbed up, Lonnie was an appealing fellow, shaggy-haired and innocent-eyed, but he was scrubbed up about as often as Europe.

Juanita opened a Budweiser for Slick. The Exxon dealer lifted up the brim of Lonnie Slocum's well-aged black hat.

"I think Hank Williams is dead."

"Yeah, old Hank's dead," Juanita said, without looking. "Still dead . . . after all these years."

She warmed a mug of coffee for herself and did something else to the radio.

"Time for Old Jeemy."

Juanita Hutchins was a fervent listener of Old Jeemy's Music for Mourners, 3 to 7 weekdays. Old Jimmy Williams of KOXX in Fort Worth, "Cowtown,

USA," was a Country & Western disc jockey who rarely allowed any tunes by John Denver or Johnny Cash to pollute his airwaves.

Juanita approved of Old Jeemy's prejudice in the matter, although more and more these days special-interest groups were giving prejudice a bad name. John Denver was no closer to Western Swing than jelly beans were to chili, and Johnny Cash had become an example of what could happen to a big talent when Nashville franchised something.

"Old Jeemy played Loretta's new one yesterday," Juanita said, singing a line for Slick:

"He's behind on the rent to my body."

"You could have written that," Slick said.

"I did," said Juanita. "It was just a test."

Lonnie Slocum stirred. He shuddered, groaned, raised his face out of his cupped hands and rubbed his eyes.

"Beat me," Lonnie muttered. "Beat me, fuck me . . . make me write hot checks."

Lonnie was quoting from the graffiti in Herb's rest room.

From the radio came a drawling voice:

"This is Old Jeemy comin' at you, friends. If I don't sound the same today, it's because I got me one of them colds that'd give a headache to a Communist tractor. My throat's dryer than the oil stick on a '57 Chevy. But Old Jeemy's here with you. I'm hangin' in there like stink on a stockyard boot."

Old Jeemy played a Waylon Jennings number and Juanita idly made it a duet. She sang:

"Well, the honky-tonks in Texas were my nat'ral second home . . . where you tip your hat to the ladies . . . and the Rose of San Antone. Well, I grew up on music that we call Western Swing. . . . It don't matter who's in Austin . . . Bob Wills is still the king."

Lonnie Slocum pushed around on his heart to see if he had one.

"Old Jeemy," he said. "Shit. That fucker would steal lice."

"He plays good records," Juanita said, squirting J & B into Lonnie's glass.

"If you pay him enough."

Lonnie used a nasal spray. He looked up at the round Bulova clock above the cashier's window. The clock was on a wall separating the bar from the dining room in Herb Macklin's Bar & Cafe Restaurant. The white stucco building with the red tile roof had been a fixture on the same South Side corner since Bonnie and Clyde. Once it had been a night club. Then it became a drive-in where chunky girls in campaign hats and Eleanor Powell shorts came out to the cars and took orders for frozen malts and pig sandwiches. Herb Macklin became the owner after World War II and he turned it into a popular saloon and eatery with a big neon sign that normally had only two letters broken.

Lonnie was displeased with the time of day. He said, "If Toby Painter ain't here in thirty more minutes, I'm goin' to Waco without him. Fuck rhythm players, anyhow. You only need 'em to play chords."

Toby Painter was the rhythm guitarist for Dog Track Gravy. Lonnie Slocum put together the group in the early 1970's when he and Toby were students at Texas Christian University. The TCU campus was only five minutes from Herb's and reasonably close to downtown, its vanilla-brick buildings ambling across the gusty hill of a neighborhood primarily known as "out there around TCU."

Juanita named the band. One day Lonnie and Toby staggered into Herb's after picking all night at a Chi Omega orgy. Juanita had watched Lonnie and Toby slop a bowl of cream gravy over their chins, sleeves, chests, boots, and part of their chicken-fried steaks.

"There they are, folks," Juanita had said. "Would you give a real Grand Ole Opry welcome, please, to Lonnie Slocum and Dog Track Gravy?"

The name stuck, as the gravy would have if Lonnie and Toby hadn't lapped it up before it hardened.

Slick Henderson said to the bandleader, "Where you headed after Waco?"

"We got a debutante party in Houston. Barbecue convention in Conroe. Back to Nashville after that, if Jesus is still my buddy. I'd sure like to get our album finished."

Lonnie accidentally dumped half a Scotch down his shirt.

"God damn, never let a rhythm player run off in your limousine. Toby better show up with a life sentence of cocaine on him! He's been gone long enough."

"I'm worried about you over there in Nashville," Juanita said, giving the entertainer a serious look. "I hope you don't get Grand Ole Opry'd. You may come home with a rhinestone growth on your collar bone."

"I'm a disciplined performer," Lonnie said, applying the nasal spray again.

"Uh-huh," Juanita said. "Another year in Nashville and you'll be up to your ass in all that corn whisky, Smoky Mountain, bluegrass, Jesus Saves, Momma-done-good bullshit."

Lonnie looked around. "Damn, I hope Acuff-Rose don't have this room bugged."

Slick Henderson pushed an empty Budweiser toward Juanita and got back a cold one.

"There's one good thing about you living in Nashville, though, Lonnie," the barmaid said. "By the time I write a good song, you may have sucked enough cock to help me get it published."

"Juanita!"

The cry came from Josephine McClure at the table of B & PW's.

"I do believe your mouth is the most serious enemy Listerine ever had," Josephine said. "We would all admire another strawberry Daiquiri just the same."

Lonnie Slocum stood up.

"I better go see if there's any more blood."

He shuffled painfully toward the men's room.

Juanita was rinsing out the blender when Slick said, "Where's old Doris today?"

Doris was Mrs. Lee Steadman, the assitant manager

of Wickley's Drug, a regular in Herb's Cafe, a pillar of the South Side B & PW, and Juanita's closest friend.

"She was here for the luncheon. She'll be back after work."

"That old boy been in again?"

"The one she picked up last week? If he had, you'd have smelled my can of Lysol air-freshener by now."

"He's probably dead in a motel somewhere."

Juanita said, "Doris doesn't hurt 'em if they come up with one of those burgundy bulbs on a blue veiner."

"Jesus God, Juanita!"

That cry came from LuAnn Hodges at the B & PW's table.

"How'd you know what I was referring to?" Juanita grinned at LuAnn Hodges.

Vera Satterwhite said, "Juanita, it's a shame Herb Macklin doesn't have any candelabra to go with the rest of the atmosphere in here."

To Juanita, Slick said, "Well, it was true love, anybody could see that."

"Oh, it always is," Juanita said. "Doris is my best friend but I swear when that woman's in the mood, she'd fuck an old boy in a caterpillar cap."

Juanita ignored two glares from the hot-flash crowd.

On the radio the voice of Old Jeemy said:

"Friends, here's a public-service announcement from the Texas Highway Safety Department. This weekend, when you're rollin' along the freeway, think about rollin' over. Thankee."

Lonnie Slocum seemed a little more chipper when he came back from the men's room. He examined himself in the mirror behind the bar and wiped off his nose.

A half-hour later Doris Steadman arrived. Nothing could have prepared Juanita for Doris waltzing into Herb's wearing a brand new full-length mink coat.

A mink coat was not often seen in the vicinity of South Fort Worth, least of all in Herb's Cafe. Minks didn't often escape from the good side of town, the West Side, and seek refuge in a cave of chicken-fried steaks.

Not mouton. Mink. Softer, thicker, and more expensive than the sideburns on the man who followed Doris through the door.

The man was Roy Simmons, independent trucker, a person not to be confused with Lee Steadman, carpet sales, Doris' husband. The men with Doris were seldom to be confused with her husband. Doris' companion was the Lysol gentleman of a week before. Roy Simmons' sideburns were unforgettable. They were shaped like Africa.

Doris and the independent trucker took seats at the bar, at the opposite end from Slick and Lonnie.

"What do you think?" Doris beamed at Juanita. "Have you ever seen anything as pretty in your whole life?"

"What would Mrs. Neiman and Mr. Marcus care to drink?"

In the Blackglama mink and with her hair worn in the style of an oversized gold helmet, Doris Steadman looked pretty much like a Pittsburgh Steeler.

Without expression, Slick Henderson said, "Lady in a coat like that ought to have a longneck Dom Perignon."

"Rusty Nail," Doris said.

Juanita smiled. Doris ordinarily drank vodka or beer.

"What do you care if I like the way it sounds?" Doris frowned at Juanita. "I want a Rusty Nail, damn it."

Roy Simmons ordered a Sperm-off vodka and a pur-year.

Juanita laughed.

"Why's that funny?" Roy Simmons asked.

Juanita replied, "I was thinking about a man crawling across the desert, dying of thirst, saying, 'Perrier . . . Perrier.' I can't remember which came first, can you, Slick? Was it Perrier or jogging?"

Vera Satterwhite had a request.

"Stand up, Doris. Is it really full-length?"

Doris modeled the coat. She glided from the bar to

the cigarette machine. She twirled from the cigarette machine to the jukebox, an old bulging Wurlitzer adding a glow of purple, red and yellow to the paneled room. Doris slunk from the Wurlitzer back to the bar.

"I guess you can say it's full-length." Juanita exhaled a Winston. "Damn thing goes from her knees up to her knockers."

"Is that your coat, Doris?" Alma Roberts asked. "Lee must have made a big carpet sale."

"Lee?" Doris blurted out. "Lee Steadman wouldn't buy me a coat like this if I went home every night and put on a garter belt and a sailor hat."

Doris turned to the barmaid. "Juanita, you won't believe what happened. Roy made this haul to Houston. They unloaded everything in his truck but this coat. They flat overlooked it, can you imagine? It was underneath a quilt or something. They signed the invoice and everything. They are just out one mink coat, is all they are, and it is right here on my back!"

"Pretty coat for a pretty lady," said Roy Simmons.

Doris snuggled up to the independent trucker. She kissed him near the African continent and tenderly squeezed his forearm where a tattoo said: TOJO IS A DWARF.

"Doris, I do admire your coat," Juanita said, relaxing in a tall chair behind the bar. Juanita's chair differed from the rotating Naugahydes on which the customers sat. Her chair had a red cushion and a back. "It's a good deal—you've got a mink coat and none of the rest of us do. Where you plan to wear it mostly—to the A & P?"

Juanita was willing to bet her collection of record albums, even the 78's, that Roy Simmons had not given Doris the mink coat for merely slipping out of her Dr. Dentons.

As the assistant manager of Wickley's Drug, Doris had easy access to all the pharmaceuticals in the store, and Doris liked her capsules and pills. She was not a junkie by any means. But she did like her little pinks

13

and reds for guaranteed sleep, and she liked her little greens and whites and oranges for guaranteed spunk.

Somewhere along the way, Roy Simmons had noticed the inside of Doris' purse. It looked like Moroccan jewelry.

Truckdrivers need pills the way vampires need blood or generals need wars. The screwing was incidental.

Juanita considered herself something of an authority on truckdrivers. She had opened her share of beer for truckdrivers, made her share of small talk with them. Once, in another life, she had even been married to a truckdriver.

Weldon Taylor qualified, Juanita would argue, although Weldon had only driven a delivery truck.

Actually, if Juanita brought up Weldon's name at all these days, she referred to him as the crowd-pleasing Weldon Taylor. Weldon had disappeared long, long ago, leaving nothing behind but a fetus and some fingerprints.

Juanita's daughter by Weldon Taylor, Candy, had grown up a luscious thing and very sweet, but rather adventurous.

At the age of twenty-three, Candy had run off with her second dope dealer.

Candy had once gone to an Oregon commune on the back of a Honda with a skeleton who braided his hair. The skeleton's name was Skylab. This time, Candy had driven to Aspen in a Mark VI with a young man who called himself Dove Christian.

Dove was a former wide receiver at the University of Texas whose given name was Ronnie Lee Dickerson. He had changed his name to Dove Christian, believing it to be more suitable for the humanitarian deeds he performed.

Only the day before, Candy had phoned her mother at Herb's and reported with breathless excitement that Dove had come up with a revolutionary method for smuggling cocaine into the country.

Dove's "mule" had used the method in returning

from a buying trip to Bolivia and it worked better than diplomatic immunity.

The mule, following Dove's orders, had dissolved the cocaine in pure alcohol and poured it over his cotton clothing. When the clothing dried, the mule wore it through customs. After safely clearing the customs inspection, the mule soaked the clothing in a solvent for fifteen minutes. The liquid filtered off and the crystals dried. Dove's cocaine had been restored.

"Dove's a genius, Mom," Candy had said.

Candy's excitement over her boyfriend's scientific achievement may have been tempered slightly when Juanita said, "I don't know a lot about Dove's profession, but I doubt if he has many customers who like cocaine with body odor."

Juanita called it a tossup whether Candy was more of a worry than Grace.

Grace was Juanita's mother, a resident of the Trinity River Nursing Center. Grace claimed full credit for originating the migraine headache in 1946. Grace was also crazier than a Kraft Foods recipe.

On her way to work that Wednesday, Juanita had stopped by the nursing home to let Grace moan for her. It was something Juanita felt an obligation to do about three days a week.

A floor supervisor at the nursing home told Juanita that something would definitely have to be done about Grace's tape player. It was causing a problem for the staff. Grace was turning her music up too high in the middle of the night, one cassette in particular.

Grace's favorite tape was titled "Hymns to Get Straight With" as recorded by Rev. Buddy Jack Grady and Gospel Gus Emert, the reverend's God-lovin', psalm-strummin' sidekick parolee.

The music was resulting in late-night activities among many of the residents, activities which weren't altogether good for the nursing center as a whole. There had been spontaneous wheelchair races and raucous sing-songs.

The floor supervisor was a woman named Boteet, who, were it not for a vivid overbite, would have been fairly attractive.

Boteet said, "I ain't no atheist or nothin', Juanita, but I'm damned if old Buddy Jack Grady's "Love Lifted Me" don't sound like Armageddon going up against seventeen banjos."

Juanita went to Grace's private room and found her mother lying in bed with her eyes closed, a hand covering her forehead. The window in Grace's room looked out on a field overgrown with weeds and a distant power line.

Juanita asked her mother sweetly to keep her music turned down a little lower.

"Prop me up, Juanita. I'll try to drink some juice."

Juanita stacked the pillows behind Grace and handed her a cup of pineapple juice from the bedside table.

Grace opened her eyes, and said, "Juanita, feel my basilic vein and see what you think."

"Feel your what?"

"It's right here," Grace said, raising her arm.

Grace put Juanita's hand on the inner part of her upper arm, saying, "Oh, I'm so worried about arteriosclerosis I don't know what to do."

"Why, Momma?"

"There's so much of it going around."

"Momma, listen, we have to keep your music turned down in here. We really do."

Grace closed her eyes.

"Juanita, do you still eat pepperbelly food?"

Juanita stared at her mother for a moment.

"Some of it's real good, Momma."

Grace moaned and put her hand to her head again.

"Momma, I—"

"I've seen people stand in line to eat pepperbelly food," Grace said. "I don't know why in the world anybody would stand in line to eat pepperbelly food."

"Momma, did you hear me about the music?"

"Beans and cheese and cornmeal is all it is."

"Momma?"

16

"Pepperbellies eat pepperbelly food but they don't know any better."

"I have to go to work, Momma. Can I bring you anything Friday?"

"Don't bring me any pepperbelly food, for goodness' sake."

Juanita kissed her mother and left, thinking that she liked Mexican food almost as much as she liked Grace asleep.

A captivating young girl now entered Herb's wearing a grimy sweatshirt, a pair of see-up jogging shorts, knee socks, sneakers and dark glasses. Her matted blonde hair hung to her waist like a relic of the 60's.

The girl tapped Lonnie Slocum on the shoulder.

"Car's here," she said.

Lonnie slowly looked around.

"Who the fuck are you?"

"Toby said to tell you I been hired as a medic."

"You a roadie or a groupie?"

"What's the difference?"

"They both give blowjobs but a roadie has to carry an amp."

The girl laughed at that.

Lonnie used his nasal spray.

"Is that flake?" the girl said. "You ought to see what Toby's got. The car looks like an ice rink."

Lonnie hopped off the barstool.

"I'll catch you later, Juanita. We might play warm-up for Willie at the convention center in December. When we find out for sure, I'll let you know. I'll get you a stage pass."

"A backstage pass will do."

"Roadies sell backstage passes for $500 now."

The leader of Dog Track Gravy bent over the bar and gave Juanita a kiss.

"Happy trails," said the barmaid.

Lonnie left Slick puzzling over a cult handshake—the high five—and went out the door with the girl, whose see-up jogging shorts were gaining his attention.

17

Juanita gazed at the closed door. In reality, she was looking somewhere else.

When Juanita saw someone like the girl who came to fetch Lonnie, she was reminded of how fortunate she had been with Candy. Candy wasn't a troll. Candy was a good girl, her angel. Juanita only wished her daughter were more selective about roommates.

If Candy could fall in love with a nice computer analyst, she could get married, have babies, live in a home with a swimming pool, and invite Mam-maw over on Sundays to watch everybody play with the Labrador retriever and inflated toys.

But Candy had no sense of patriotism. None.

Down at the other end of the bar, Doris Steadman and Roy Simmons were entangled like a freeway interchange. In fact, Doris was gnawing on Roy's ear. But she was positioned so that she could observe the side door through which Lonnie departed; thus, minutes later, Doris happened to see Lee Steadman, her husband, as he stuck his head into Herb's through the same door.

Curiously, Lee Steadman's head vanished as quickly as it appeared. In and out. Like that.

"Was that Lee Steadman?" Juanita glanced at Slick.

"If it wasn't, the Pope don't have warm clothes."

"Christ!" An alarm was clanging for Juanita. "He's never in this neighborhood, never!"

Juanita spun toward Doris and her two furry friends to suggest they get unraveled, but Roy Simmons was already in the act of fleeing.

Roy Simmons had heard Doris whisper "uh oh" at the sight of Lee. Roy had wheeled around and caught a glimpse of a wet-head wearing granny glasses and a windbreaker. He presumed it was a husband.

Even a wet-head in granny glasses might carry a pistol. The experienced adulterer trusted nobody. Roy Simmons tore through the other entrance to Herb's bar, the door leading into the dining room by way of a foyer. From the dining room came the sound of crashing dishes and overturned chairs.

The dining room had a rear exit to an alley. Roy Simmons found it. There was every reason to believe his rig would be on I-35 within minutes. He might blaze through Hillsboro so fast he would create work for three roofing companies.

"Good-bye gun's up, hello finish judge," Slick Henderson said, his eyes twinkling.

Truckdrivers have this gift. Not only can they recognize a husband when they see one, they can sometimes sense the presence of a husband in a neighborhood, as if the husband's creeping Pontiac awkwardly sends out warning signals to the adventurously undressed in America's bedrooms.

It was the first time in this marriage that Doris had been caught in public by her husband. A confirmed kill.

Doris reacted to the incident with a distracting calm, however. As casually as she would file her nails, she wriggled out of the mink and laid it across the bar.

"This is yours, Juanita. Your Aunt Bernice left you this in her will. I was trying it on."

Juanita wasn't sure she heard that correctly.

"Don't you have an Aunt Bernice who died in Brownsville?"

"I did," Juanita said.

"Didn't she have a good florist business?"

"I suppose she had the Pinto paid for."

"I am *talking* about your aunt who toppled over from an angina while she was arranging centerpieces for a Jaycee banquet. *You* told me about it, Juanita!"

"Florists don't make enough money to buy mink coats, Doris."

"People die! People get married all the time! That takes flowers!"

"Do you know how hot it is in Brownsville, Texas?" Juanita's voice was calm.

"Rich women in Brownsville need mink coats the same as rich women in Fort Worth—because of the damn air-conditioning!" Doris barked. "You better back me up, Juanita. I'm going to tell Lee I came in here on my coffee break and tried on your coat "

That was only part of it.

Roy Simmons was Juanita's cousin from Louisiana, just passing through town. Why were they hugging? They weren't hugging. Doris had dropped her cigarette lighter as Lee looked in the door. Doris and Roy were trying to catch the gold Dunhill before it hit the floor and got damaged. They were grabbing for the lighter, not hugging. Lee knew how much the lighter meant to Doris. It was the engraved Dunhill the B & PW gave her when she was installed as treasurer.

"What are you going to do with the coat, Doris? You can't take it home."

"Hang it in your closet. I'll borrow it when *The Pajama Game* opens at Casa Mañana. Or is it *The King and I?*"

"Fine," Juanita said sarcastically. "I'll keep it in storage till your next car date."

Doris looked insulted. She smoothed a side of the oversized gold helmet, her hair, and said, "For your information, Juanita, I don't have *dates*. I'm a happily married woman. I may have a few friends. I don't know where it says a woman can't have men friends this day and time. Anyhow . . . nobody can say I don't make a good home for Lee Steadman."

The possibility did exist that Lee Steadman was a contented man. Doris almost never ran out of Skippy crunchy peanut butter at home. She never switched the TV channel when *Hawaii Five-O* came on. She stubbed all her checks.

Doris started for the door. She was going home to fix dinner for Lee, something delectable like her famous tamale pie. It would make it easier for her to explain things to Lee, tell him what he had actually seen in Herb's.

Josephine McClure said, "When H. B. was alive, I'd cook a nice brisket the day my Sanger Harris bill came in."

Vera Satterwhite hiccupped. "Ed Satterwhite wasn't alive . . . even . . . when he was alive."

Doris patted Juanita's hand.

"Don't you worry, Hon," Doris said. "Everything will be fine. It's only a matter of clearing up some of Lee's wrong impressions. Look after my coat."

Doris smiled cheerfully at Slick, waved to the B & PW's, and was gone.

Juanita plopped down in her tall chair and lit another Winston and looked through the casement window at the sun retiring behind the laundromat and the Exxon station. Slick Henderson's chin rested on one hand. His other hand toyed with a Budweiser. The B & PW's were silent, fanning their hot flashes.

Slick finally looked up at Juanita.

"I can't believe I was never married to Doris," he said.

Chapter Two

The B & PW's eventually went through their Wednesday ritual of trying to find their car keys, scarves and glasses—then their cars. Slick left for a while to close up the service station. It was early evening. By then, Juanita had begun to write another song.

Juanita's songs started out as poems because she had never learned to read music. Chinese looked easier than those mysterious hieroglyphics, the notes.

There was a vague melody in her head, but there always was. In her formative years as an unpublished songwriter, the melody would turn out to be so similar to a song Willie Nelson or Kris Kristofferson had written, Juanita would be moved to smite her forehead and make a noise like a fat man sitting down.

But in these more mature years of being an unpublished songwriter, the tunes were original, if memorable only to her.

Juanita would not be able to finish the song until she got off work and went home to her apartment. There, she could play around with the Martin and pick out something.

She was bolstered by the knowledge that many Country & Western entertainers did it this way, those who wrote their own material. They couldn't read music either. They picked.

Some were known to carry around pocket-size tape recorders in the event that whisky, dope, their brain cells—or all three—suddenly gave them a new tune.

There were many accomplished composers who hummed melodies into tape recorders on buses and planes, and anxiously scribbled hit lyrics on envelopes, table linen, motel stationery, and shirttails.

In a recurring fantasy, Juanita emerged as the first C & W star with four first names—Juanita Fay Matilda Gaylynn Hutchins—and she raced up and down the aisle of her custom-designed Eagle International bus trying out lyrics on her entourage, lyrics she had composed on her wig box, lyrics that would settle into the American consciousness.

Juanita Fay Matilda Gaylynn Hutchins would be eternally remembered for: "It don't take a dentist to pull a fast one on a fool" . . . "Be it ever so humble, there's no place like the Midtown Motor Inn" . . . "She passed the rash around until it wound up back on him" . . . "Penicillin don't cure headaches but it sure relieves my mind."

Now in Herb's, Juanita pitched her Pentel down on top of her yellow legal pad and confessed to Slick Henderson, "I need my guitar."

"What have you got so far?"

"The Rime of the Ancient Mariner," she said, smartly.

The title of Juanita's song was "God Don't Care About the Red Lights in Life." It was written from the point of view of a healthy American male, one whose sexual appetite was not so much unique as simply different from American males who wore caftans and spoke with lisps. Roy Simmons, in other words.

> You'd think that God would help a fool
> Instead of actin' kind of cruel
> To someone out here on the road,
> Being on his own.
>
> See, I been free, I been fine,
> But I'll get a woman on my mind
> And it seems she'll be somebody
> Else's wife.
>
> We'll have a drink, have some fun,
> Then a husband sees what all we've done,
> And there I am,
> Stuck at another red light!
>
> God don't care about the red lights in life!
> Dallas-Houston
> Turnarounds,
> Just me and
> 15 milligrams.
> Some woman's body
> Haunts me.
> Boostin' speed,
> Spillin' coffee,
> My lonely road
> Ain't ever
> Headed home.
>
> Creepin' down a double lane,
> Buckin' traffic like I'm lame,

23

Or slidin' through a drivin' rain,
I'll know a gal to see.

She'll be lonesome, wantin' to.
We'll have ourselves more
Than a few,
Then live out some old goofy
Fan-ta-sy.

It's the kind of deal I know so well.
I've even used the same motel.
Too bad she'll be somebody
Else's wife.

'Cause kickin' on my door of fate
Comes another husband full of hate,
And there I am,
Stuck at another red light!

God don't care about the red lights in life . . .

"You repeat the chorus and so forth," Juanita said, watching Slick study the yellow legal pad and peel off the label of his Budweiser. "Lonnie says it doesn't take long to write a song if you're stricken with a severe case of the Tennysons. He wasn't necessarily talking about a chart-climber."

In Slick's opinion, Juanita had been a little harsh on Lonnie Slocum about Nashville that afternoon.

"I know," she admitted. "But he plays such good Austin sound, I hate to see him go anywhere near that establishment twang."

The Nashville establishment had never really cared much for Western Swing.

The Country Music Hall of Fame had existed for seven years before Bob Wills was inducted.

Christ. *Roy Acuff* got in ahead of Bob Wills.

Willie Nelson had been driven out of Nashville by record producers who wanted more Bibles, mothers, American flags and soda pop in Willie's lyrics and plinking banjos in the background.

Juanita served two strays at a table in Herb's, strays being strangers in her terminology. She then continued with Slick.

"Lonnie's a great picker. Nobody would put him up there with Chet Atkins or Django Reinhardt, but he's better than Glen Campbell."

Slick pointed out that Glen Campbell was an actor.

"Hell on the guitar, is what he is."

"How come people don't know that?"

"Session people know it."

"I guess that's why I don't know it," Slick said.

Lonnie was beautiful on melodies, the trademarks of good pickers. But he could play jazz, too. He could "burn it" with the fury of a Joe Pass or Wes Montgomery. All around, he had the range of a Ry Cooder.

Lonnie insisted, however, that the greatest guitar players were probably pumping gas or sitting on porches on the back roads of Texas, Tennessee and Alabama.

Juanita took up the guitar as a hobby. She wanted something to do besides wait around for Grace's next illness or wonder where Candy was irrigating another marijuana field.

Learning the guitar wasn't easy for her. She had made the dreadful mistake of being born without calluses on the balls of her fingers. She had little tolerance for cramps in the palm of her hand.

Grace had been floating from one sanitarium to another at the time, scolding doctors for not finding anything wrong with her, for not sending her to the Houston Medical Center for shock treatments or a lobotomy.

Juanita had mentioned the guitar to her mother one day at Sanford's Sanitarium.

"Oh, my word," Grace said, collapsing in a chair.

"What is it, Momma?"

"Musicians," Grace moaned.

"What about them?"

Grace let out a long, painful and indecipherable cry.

"Are you all right, Momma?"

"Juanita, I just don't know what's going to happen to you."

"Because of the guitar?"

"Oh, if I only had my strength," said Grace.

"Momma, I don't really know what the problem is."

Grace said, "Musicians are always around cigarettes and alcohol. Land's sakes."

"It's only a guitar."

"Oh, dear God," Grace had said, mashing on her temples.

Lonnie Slocum had started Juanita out on "Hang Down Your Head, Tom Dooley," a good beginner's song. For many weeks, Juanita's version of it sounded like a baby beating a spoon on a plate. But she finally mastered a blues progression. She could strum a tune.

Once she humbled the 1—4—5 blues progression, Juanita had to overcome the discouragement of finding out no one could teach her how to pick. Picking was a long boring process of doing exercises to build up the strength of her fingers, then listening to tapes and records and practicing endlessly to imitate the licks.

Today her rendition of "Malagueña" wouldn't get her a lot of work in the supper clubs of Mexico City, but she wasn't a bad guitar player.

"I could teach you the one-four-five blues progression," she bragged to Slick in Herb's. "It's simple. There are six strings on a guitar, right? The one-four-five in the key of G would be the C, F and G strings."

Juanita held an imaginary guitar.

"First you learn to bar the twelve basic chords down the neck of the instrument with your index finger—like this. Then it's the middle finger, the ring finger and the pinkie that play the chords."

Slick nodded.

"If you learn just three chords you can play any country song ever written," she said. "If you ever learn four chords—well, you can play Beethoven. You know 'Good-Hearted Woman?' That's just D-one, G-four . . . D-one, G-four . . . D-one, G-four, A-five."

"Well," Slick said, massaging his right shoulder. "I bet Harvard can get to the bottom of it."

The first wave of regulars hit Herb's Cafe at twilight. Tommy Earl Bruner, who was in the used-car business, came in with Hank Rainey, the society carpenter.

Tommy Earl Bruner looked like the Marlboro Man's younger brother. He had been a football immortal at Paschal High and TCU. Although he was now thirty-five and those days were well behind him, he still thought of himself as a local celebrity. This gave him the right to be drunk in public.

Hank Rainey was near fifty, a quiet man, somewhat uncomfortable with his success as a building contractor.

"I wish one fuckin' time the United States government gave a shit about the small businessman," Tommy Earl babbled as he entered. "Juanita, gimme a double Junior. You got a syringe? I'll take it in the fuckin' vein."

Junior was Tommy Earl's brand of Scotch. J & B. Junior B. If there was no J & B in a bar, Tommy Earl drank Curtis. That was Cutty Sark. Curtis R. Sark.

Tommy Earl slapped Slick Henderson on the back of Slick's olive drab grease-repellent shirt.

"You ain't got any problems, do you, Slick? Americans are gonna buy gasoline, don't make a fuck what it costs, ain't that right? They'll buy gas for a fuckin' Toyota, sure! What am I supposed to do with all them Cadillacs I got?"

"You shouldn't have repossessed them," Juanita said.

Hank Rainey seized a barstool. Tommy Earl remained standing.

"Toyota's ass," Tommy Earl said, tasting his Junior B. "I'm proud to say there's only two Japanese words I ever learned. Hiroshima and Nagasaki."

Tommy Earl gestured to Juanita. Buy Slick a beer. Give Hank Rainey some Curtis.

"Arabs are worse," he went on. "We're at war and nobody knows it but the Jews. Right there we got a

problem, though. There's a lot more Arabs than there
is Jews. Am I lying to anybody?"

Very few people ever knew when Tommy Earl was
serious and when he wasn't. Juanita usually knew.

"The answer could be wheat, who can say? If I was
the President of the United States, I'd give it a try. I'd
charge them fuckin' Arabs twice as much for wheat—
four times as much—as they charge us for crude oil."

Tommy Earl's tone grew presidential.

"Well, lookie here, Mohammed. The price of
wheat's done gone up again today. You know what? If
you and old Abdul can't afford it, you better learn to
pan-fry all them fuckin' cobras you got crawlin' around
over there."

"What if that doesn't work?"

It was Slick's question.

"We take it back."

"The Nile?"

That was Juanita's.

"The fuckin' oil," Tommy Earl said. "It's ours. We
found that shit. It's our pipe, our drills, our pumps. Our
technology. If it hadn't been for us, them fuckers would
still be sittin' around in their burnooses trying to figure
out who let all them sphinxes out of the cage."

"Want to bomb 'em?" Slick asked.

"We don't have to bomb 'em," Tommy Earl winked
at Juanita. "All we got to do is go over there with a
bunch of underarm deodorant."

Hank Rainey's lip curled up.

Tommy Earl said, "Them fuckers'll faint if they ever
smell anything good. We go in there and bang! Hit 'em
with the Ban and Right Guard. They keel over. We
haul out the oil. Every time an Arab comes to—wham!
Right Guard. Ain't nothin' to it. Am I lying, Juanita?"

Slick Henderson suggested Tommy Earl stop reading
the papers or listening to the news on television because world events were so depressing.

"That's the damn truth," Tommy Earl said, going to
the cigarette machine. "Ain't nothin' in the paper but
Arabs jacking around, SALT talks, and recognition

deals. There's not a motherfucker in the world ever read a story about a SALT talk."

Tommy Earl gambled on the cigarette machine and won a pack of Kents.

He said, "Anybody know what the SALT talks are? Hank? Slick?"

"Got something to do with Russia, don't it?" said Hank Rainey, the society carpenter.

"SALT is an agreement Princeton wants to sign with the Communists. Princeton or Yale, I forget which." Tommy Earl directed Juanita's attention to his half-empty glass. "The agreement gives Russia the right to build the world's biggest H-bomb and shove it up our ass, and it gives the Democrats the right to scuttle all our nuclear submarines."

"Henry Wallace wouldn't even vote for that," Slick Henderson said.

"Liberals will," Tommy Earl predicted. "Liberals and environmentalists."

To Tommy Earl, a liberal was anyone who hadn't been trapped in a gas line in 105-degree heat. People became environmentalists when their view of existing scenery was threatened.

"Some son-of-a-bitch developer wants to block your view of the boat dock, that'll turn you into a fuckin' environmentalist overnight," he assured everyone.

"Who'd we recognize today?" Juanita asked Tommy Earl.

"Aw, fuck, I don't know," he said, wearily. "All I saw was the headline in the *Star-Telegram*. 'U. S. Recognizes Akka Bokka Boo.' Recognition deal. One of them countries that has earthquakes and tidal waves. Somebody we give wheat to—so they can kick our ass out . . . take over our embassy . . . charge us four billion dollars for them ivory billy goats they export."

"That all they do in Akka Bokka Boo? Make ivory billy goats?" Slick inquired.

"They'll sell you a coup," Tommy Earl said. "We can get a real good coup over there for a hundred billion dollars. A hundred billion good U. S. tax dollars will buy us a hell of a good deal. A fat nigger with a Gucci sword."

The cashier who sat on the dining room side of Herb's was Esther, whose orange makeup blended into her orange bouffant. She called Juanita to the phone.

"Your running mate sounds irritable," Esther said through the window that opened into the bar.

"Probably misplaced her saddle Oxfords."

Doris Steadman was locked out of her home.

"I can't find Lee anywhere," Doris said. "Has he called there?"

"No."

"I've been to Jack-in-the-Box, Pizza Hut, Taco Rio . . . Burger Shake. I've looked for the dumb-ass all over this side of town."

"You sound mad enough to eat a thousand calories."

"It's not funny, Juanita. I even went to Your Mom and Them's Fried Chicken. I knew there wasn't anybody in there but niggers, Mexicans and sorry folks."

"Doris, how can you be locked out of your own home?"

Lee did it. Doris never carried keys and Lee knew it. The Steadmans never locked their doors. What had been the point of buying a home at Mirage La Grande if the doors had to be locked? Mirage La Grande, a development inside a high brick wall, had a gate and a security guard. There hadn't been a hippie burglary at Mirage La Grande since the Steadmans moved in. Lee was punishing Doris for what he saw in Herb's—or what he *thought* he saw. He had locked her out before, the time she had mailed all the bills without stamps and the phone got cut off.

"I'll look a few more places and call back," Doris said. "I may have to spend the night at your apartment."

Juanita said, "Lee wouldn't do anything violent, would he?"

"He don't have the energy," said Doris. "He's

driving around town, screeching his tires, slamming on his brakes, honking at red lights. You'd have to go to Albania to find a bigger fool."

Shorty Eckwood limped into Herb's and went to sleep at a table by the Wurlitzer.

Shorty was a square little man in his faltering sixties who never removed his green plaid Eisenhower jacket. He never removed a soiled Stetson. Shorty's hat predated the governorships of Ma and Pa Ferguson. When he was awake, Shorty's cough brought to mind a cement mixer. He owned Shorty's Barbecue, three blocks from Herb's. Shorty's Barbecue specialized in grease.

Shorty drank Lone Star beer, starting at breakfast. By being among the living, Shorty offered a convincing argument that the best cure for a hangover was getting drunk again. He was Herb Macklin's dearest friend. Herb and Shorty hunted, fished and went to football games together. Shorty Eckwood held the record for taking the longest piss in the history of Herb's parking lot. On the late evening of August 13, 1973, Shorty pissed for eight minutes, fourteen seconds, according to Tommy Earl Bruner's Rolex.

Foster Barton arrived. He owned Barton's Funeral Home—and some said the bookmakers owned Foster Barton. He was a tall man with an ingratiating voice and his suits were a size too large. Lately, Foster had taken to drinking straight gin.

Foster moved up to the bar, saying, "Everybody better get down on Baylor Saturday and give Rice the six."

"I wouldn't give you dogshit for either one," Tommy Earl said.

"Think about it," Foster Barton reasoned. "Rice is tough on academics. How's a nigger at Rice gonna run fast with a football if he's worried about math and engineering? I love Baylor, give six."

Juanita asked Foster how Susan and the kids were. Happy as larks, he said. He had pleased Susan, his wife, by giving the Trinity Episcopal Church a $1,100 contribution. The church had only wanted $1,000, but Foster thought the church ought to get the juice just like the bookmaker.

Foster furnished insights into Alabama-Tennessee, Auburn-LSU, Tulsa-North Texas State, the Sunday pro games, the Monday night "get-even" game, his 6-point and 10-point teasers, his open-end parlays, his Overs and Unders. He said if anyone didn't like the Cowboys over the 49ers Sunday—not just to win but to cover— he had a fine mahogany casket he would be happy to show them over at Barton's Funeral Home.

"We're coming up on a big one, Paschal and Arlington Heights," Foster said. "That'll be for the city championship. A car wreck is what I call it."

Tommy Earl Bruner said, "Paschal ain't gonna do nothin' but kick ass and take names."

"We'll see," Foster said. "Right now, I like Heights."

"Why?"

"They're bigger."

"Their assholes are bigger."

"Well, when the time comes, my window's open."

"I'll be there with both hands. You silly fucker, you'd have had Germany in them two world wars."

Foster smiled at the barmaid. "What do you think, Juanita?"

"I have to go with Paschal, the old alma mater," she said. "We're undefeated, aren't we, Tommy Earl?"

"*Are* we? Can Jews do arithmetic?"

"So's Heights," Foster said.

"Yeah, but you ain't got Billy Boy Bobbit." Tommy Earl sloshed his Junior. "He's the greatest thing Paschal's had since me. Billy Boy Bobbit can run *and* throw. He ain't ever seen a fuckin' third down!"

Foster Barton said, "I'll leave it up to you, Slick. Would you rather have Billy Boy Bobbit or Rusty Woodruff?"

"Rusty Woodruff!" Tommy Earl said. "Rusty Woodruff's daddy sells Toyotas! He's a Goddamn foreign agent! That's another reason we're gonna stomp their ass."

"His kid ain't a bad fullback," Foster said. "Rusty Woodruff will be about all Paschal can handle till the Red Chinese come in to help out."

"I'm staying out of it," said Slick Henderson.

"I'll make you two bets, Foster," Tommy Earl said. "Paschal don't let Heights piss a drop. That's one bet. The other is, it takes Rusty Woodruff from November till Easter to get his pussy screwed back on."

Juanita resupplied Hank Rainey with Curtis. She said to him, with a touch of mischief, "How's Ernestine?"

Hank Rainey was remodeling a kitchen in the Westover Hills home of Ernestine McLaughlin, a wealthy, attractive widow, a zealous socialite. Like all cities, Fort Worth had a battleground for WASP-offs and dueling mansions. That was Westover Hills.

"Strange woman," Hank Rainey shook his head. "She calls me up to come over and rehang a painting."

"She wants to fuck," Tommy Earl said.

"I don't know," said Hank Rainey, the society carpenter. "There's always a lot of decorators around."

"You send them fags off to buy antiques and you fuck her, that's all."

Hank Rainey agreed to think about it.

Tommy Earl pressed on. "Them women are lonely. Their husbands are either dead or they been sentenced to golf without parole."

There was a drawback to fucking Ernestine McLaughlin, as Tommy Earl Bruner saw it. She was handmade.

"She went down to Rio and got her a butt-tuck," said Tommy Earl. "She went to Beverly Hills and had them tits put on. She went up to New York City and got her a face-lift. I hear she's had her appendicitis scar removed so she can wear a bikini. Know anything about that, Hank?"

Hank Rainey blushed. He had been the society carpenter for five years, ever since he had built a new wing on Mrs. Burvin Elliott's villa in order for Mrs. Burvin Elliott to have more room for her Remingtons and Russells.

No new homes were now constructed nor were any old homes refurbished on the West Side without Hank Rainey overseeing the job. Word-of-mouth had made Hank Rainey the society carpenter, although Juanita's personal theory was that it had less to do with his thoroughgoing handiwork than it did with his appearance. Hank's toupee rarely blew off in the wind and he was still trim.

"Hank'll fuck Ernestine, I'm not worried about it," Tommy Earl said to Slick.

Dr. Neil Forcheimer of the TCU English department arrived. He brought with him a student, a thin young man with chalk-white skin and a sweater flung around the shoulders. The student carried three massive hardcover novels.

Dr. Forcheimer, tweed suit, red vest, bow tie, led the young man to a table by the window. Juanita welcomed Dr. Forcheimer with a Gibson.

"Do you have any huakwa tea?" the student asked Juanita.

"You can put what you want to in it, but it'll be Lipton's when it starts out from over there."

"Juanita, it's a *trial*," Dr. Forcheimer said, banging a cigarette on his wrist. "An absolute trial! Have you ever tried to get anyone even remotely interested in the symbolism of wolves and lightning in eighteenth-century literature?"

The massive hardcover novels lay on the table. One of them was *The Brothers Karamazov*.

"Smerdyakov did it," Juanita said to the student. "That news was all over this room last week."

Juanita returned with a cup of hot water and a tea bag as Dr. Forcheimer's thin friend was saying, "Tell me about Avery."

Dr. Forcheimer said, "He's more than a foot taller than me. Unfortunately, he has a biochemical deficiency which tends to make him see life as largely suicidal.

Still, as houseboys go, he's quite attentive. We have a very tender relationship."

The professor sipped his Gibson. "But I want to talk about this book idea of yours, Ron. I would simply call it *Lenin in Poland*. I would open it with Lenin's wife in bed with Trotsky. Right away—I'm talking first page—I would have a door burst open. I would have a man shouting, 'Where is Lenin? Where is Lenin?' I would have the wife say, 'He's in Poland.' "

Dr. Forcheimer leaned back in his chair and shrugged.

"Cinemascopic, yes. But the book would be off and running, wouldn't it?"

An hour passed before Doris called back.

"I give up," she told Juanita. "Let the idiot drive around town if he wants to. I just hope he don't wind up in a ditch with his head sticking through the all-night news on the dashboard radio."

Doris was exhausted.

"I've been to Shirley's Topless Stampede," she said. "I've been to the Bottomless Baton Twirler. I even looked in at Teri Jean's Pressure Cooker. Saw every damn husband I ever knew in there but Lee."

"What's Shirley's like?"

"Teeth and hair. Louder than emphysema."

Doris was going to sleep over at Juanita's apartment. Juanita would have to leave work early and let her in.

"Do you think Lee is okay, or what?"

"Oh, hell, he'll be all right as soon as he finds out the truth."

"Lee doesn't need to find out the truth about anything."

"You know what I mean."

Doris was on her way. She would be at the apartment in forty-five minutes.

"Where are you now?"

"I'm back at Your Mom and Them's Fried Chicken. I can't believe the pay phone works in here."

When Herb Macklin was not around, Juanita had the authority to make executive decisions regarding the bar and dining room. She summoned a waitress named Nedra from the dining room and put her in charge of the bar.

Juanita got it together. The yellow legal pad, the pen, her cigarettes, Bic, shoulder bag, the khaki whipcord jacket. She lifted the mink off the coatrack by the jukebox. She draped the jacket over the white cotton turtleneck she was wearing with a pair of corduroy jeans. She lugged the mink toward the side door.

Slick Henderson delayed her from his command post on the barstool.

"When are you going to break down and let me take you out to dinner?" he said, his hand on her hip.

"Soon as I verify you're married," Juanita smiled. "I wouldn't know how to act if anybody single took me out."

Slick said, "Do you ever *not* make jokes?"

Juanita gave that question some thought as she drove home.

Chapter Three

Most Americans, Juanita maintained, had been living in homes they couldn't afford since the Japs called it quits. She was no different. As she often said to friends: "Give me your tired, your poor, your huddled masses. Meet me in the Personal Loan Department."

On the other hand, Juanita's apartment was well situated for her. It was near Herb's Cafe, downtown, TCU Stadium, a Junior League resale shop, a grocery store where the check-out line took less than thirty minutes, a dry cleaners that did not lose her belts and blouses. And it was near three excellent Tex-Mex restaurants, the kind where nobody had to ask a waiter to hold the chocolate on the chili relleno, or go easy on the duck sauce over the tamales, or whoever heard of putting seafood in an enchilada, you pretentious asshole?

All these things made it worth the suspense of waiting to find out every month whether she could pay the rent.

The apartment was reasonably new, modern. It was located in one of those complexes a male divorcee often searched out, hoping to find a tricky stewardess around the swimming pool who would wink at him and say, "Coffee? Tea? . . . Tie me up?"

Every unit in Juanita's complex—the Sans Su South —featured two bedrooms, two baths, central air-conditioning, and wall-to-wall carpet furnished by the builder, which meant the carpet was orange.

Her apartment was on the second floor, the top floor. It had a balcony. By leaning over the railing, Juanita could see hackberry trees, scrub oaks, mesquite. By looking straight ahead, she could see other balconies where young executives drank beer in deck chairs while their overnight guests stood around in fringed-suede bikinis, brushing their hair and pouting.

Juanita had taken the apartment three years before this, partly as a fortieth birthday present to herself, partly because her old place had become flanked by "the warehouse Riviera" and partly because Candy was coming home from the Oregon commune.

She had wanted to provide a better place for Candy to live. It might give Candy a higher opinion of herself, might be a force in redirecting her daughter's life.

Candy was barely out of high school when she went to Oregon. The daughter had gone to the same school as Juanita, Paschal High, but Candy had grown up in what was known to most bewildered parents as a period of dope-crazed hippie-scum revolution. This was in contrast to Juanita's wonderful era in which kids stalked the elusive V. O. and 7-Up and got angrier at the results of football games than they did at politics.

Candy's friends in high school dozed more often than they wrote book reports. Their arms and legs moved only when it seemed urgent for someone to change the movie on TV from *Dracula's Nephew* to *Revenge of the Slime People*.

Juanita used to wonder from what source the flower children generated enough energy to protest against anything. The ones she met could barely get to their feet at the mention of chocolate chip ice cream, and even then they looked in need of life-support systems as they dry-fucked the chrome on her G.E. refrigerator.

One afternoon Candy brought home a bleached-blonde girlfriend whose hair was longer than Cher's and whose blood had stopped circulating because of the tightness of her leather pants. Juanita talked to the girl for thirty minutes before she realized it was a boy.

Candy was lured to Oregon by the promise of a religious experience. There was a "religious person" at the commune growing topless vegetables and thinking "oceanic." Candy learned this from Skylab, the skeleton with braided hair. Juanita had pondered the incongruity of a religious experience being described by someone whose entire vocabulary consisted of "Wow," "Far-out," "Really," and "Kick-in."

Juanita made only three predictions about the "religious person" in Oregon who was enabling hundreds of young people to achieve a heightened consciousness: he would be a twenty-seven-year-old dropout with surfing scars, his sermons would be as deeply meaningful as the dialogue on "Star Trek," and he would, if he weren't watched closely, sneak a meatball into his tofu.

Juanita loved her daughter sinfully, had always tried to show it, had always tried to understand her. Juanita dealt with the things in life she thought wrong or incomprehensible with the only weapons with which she was familiar: love, kindness and humor.

The mother was intelligent enough to know that if she forced a hard-nosed confrontation over the commune business with Candy, and lost it, she might lose her daughter forever.

This was why she hadn't tried to stop Candy from going. She *did* insist on Candy being fitted for an IUD before leaving.

Juanita hauled Candy into the office of Doc Matson, a frequenter of Herb's, and instructed the general practitioner to give Candy the Rolls-Royce of IUD's.

"I want the Goddamn thing to trip the buzzer on the security gate in an airport," Juanita had said. "I want to put my head in her lap and hear the Cowboy game when they're playing in Green Bay."

Juanita wept steadily for a week after Candy left, and at odd times thereafter. Once in Herb's she had fallen completely apart, and Red, the black cook who wore dark glasses and a headband, presumed her tears had something to do with his black-eyed peas and meatloaf. Candy's parting gave Juanita a song. It was a song written by a person who had lost something of herself and whose life would never be quite so full again until that something returned.

> Come back home, little girl
> Before it's too late.
> Before you're down on the world
> And you've become second-rate.
>
> You've gone to find your friends
> But your friends aren't the same.
> They've been so high so often
> Their minds have burned away.
>
> They scuffle for a food stamp,
> Doctor on a rash,
> Sit through endless evenings,
> Fumbling for their stash.
>
> There's your girlfriend now,
> Sitting in the street,
> She's been stoned for hours,
> Not knowing how to speak.
>
> She's evidently gazing
> At nothing humans see.
> Her brain no longer functions,
> Her body's obsolete.
>
> Come back home, little girl,
> Before your eyelids turn to lead,
> Before your hair turns to straw,
> And you're living but you're dead.

Candy devoted a year in Oregon to the study of agriculture. When she did come home, she brought back a report that made Juanita want to swing from a trapeze.

Candy had said, "Momma, communes aren't nothin' but bullshit and body putty."

Candy Taylor was a gorgeous girl. She had long auburn hair, big welcoming eyes, and a body that could only be described as fierce.

Two things that went with her age had to be overlooked—her vacant expression upon hearing a reference to anything historical, philosophical or literary, and her genuine uninterest in any activity which did not involve pleasure or comfort.

But Candy had these things in common with most young girls who grew up observing material excesses and were taught by their peers that a spiritual enterprise was discovering a new rock group.

Juanita presently questioned whether it was possible for Candy to improve in these areas by living in Aspen with a coke dealer.

Juanita herself was slender and curvy. Her skin was creamy white with only microscopic evidence of adolescent freckles. She would receive an A+ on the high-cheekbone test. Juanita easily looked ten years younger than forty-three.

Her hair was the shade of brown which reddened when the sun hit it. Her eyes matched the blue of faded denim. Juanita's looks were enhanced by a quick grin. She laughed boisterously, smiled sweetly. In rooms lighted a certain way, her beauty seemed almost upper-crust.

Juanita had never "let herself go," that thing some women said of other women—friends, usually—who had grown too fat, too haggard, or too poor, the worst mistake of all.

Juanita had pride. That pride may have been instilled by the grandmother who raised her and for whom she was named, Juanita Fay Hutchins. Her grandparents, Juanita Fay and Jeff, had struggled to feed, clothe and give her plenty of love through all the years Grace squandered on self-indulgent anger and creative illnesses.

Grace had been left a thriving business, Hutchins Hardware, by Juanita's father, Burl Hutchins. The father left home when Juanita was only a child. The grandparents explained to Juanita that their son "just couldn't take it any longer."

What Burl Hutchins couldn't take any longer were the rooms in the house that Grace kept dark at all times because of her headaches, Grace's incessant criticism, and Grace's unrelenting belief that everyone in the family should drink goat's milk to combat the undulant fever she thought was periling Fort Worth.

Burl Hutchins moved to Bakersfield, California, married a manicurist named Maureen, sold furniture, and played golf every day until he died of a heart seizure on a short Par-3 with water behind the green. Burl had always overclubbed.

Juanita occasionally had received a postcard from her father. The postcard would be a picture of Smiley Burnette or a road hollowed through the trunk of a redwood tree. Her only letter from him came when she was in the seventh grade at E.M. Daggett Junior High. The letter had said:

Dear Pine Knot:

Well, you are a grown up little girl in the Kodak pictures and I hear you're not a bit of trouble. It was sure smart of me to leave you with your grandparents. They're full of love.

When I get a little ahead, I want you to come out here to California and see how nice it is. Everybody keeps their grass mowed and there are palm trees and ice cream flavors you never heard of.

You would like Maureen. She's hardly ever sick. I'm writing from Fresno. I got a little time before I tee off in the furniture salesmen's golf tournament.

You be sweet like your grandmother, and tell

your granddaddy I shot an 81 at Pebble Beach the first time I seen it.

I only have one regret, really. I wish Grace and Joe Louis could have fought one another when they were both in their prime. You take care now.

All my love,
Dad

Grace managed to donate all of the income from Hutchins Hardware to doctors, hospitals, clinics, sanitariums and shock treatments as rapidly as she got her hands on it. She even had herself confined to the state mental institution at Wichita Falls to see what that was like. She had been booted out when the medical staff couldn't find anything wrong with her but an impacted lower wisdom tooth.

Medicare and Medicaid were sustaining Grace at the Trinity River Nursing Center these days, but Juanita lived with the fear that the next form she sent in was going to cause every computer in Washington, D.C., to dance across the room like a Hot Point dryer.

Juanita's grandmother had been a delicate woman, a true lady, one who might have made herself more alluring if life had given her the opportunity, or if it had seemed more important to her than frying pies and selling them to WPA laborers during the Depression, then working at the quartermaster depot during World War II.

Her grandfather held down two jobs in the 30's. He janitored the Tarrant County Courthouse during the week and delivered prescriptions for a drugstore on weekends. When the war started, he went to work at the bomber plant. For recreation, Juanita's grandfather listened to football games on the radio and drank gin he kept hidden in a drawer with his BVD's.

Juanita learned to cook, sew, repair, adapt, create and imitate from her grandmother, thus developing a knack for originality and style. Style came from taste, not money. Taste came partly from being observant. Juanita's grandmother had been observant.

Juanita was among those women who could do anything with her hair, whatever a magazine ad, a movie, or a gossip column called for.

Keeping herself up improved her attitude about her daughter, mother, music, past, future, especially those days and nights of wearing Herb Macklin's permanent flea collar.

Juanita had worn her hair like curtains—the dead hippie look. She had worn it like Fonda, Barbra, Farrah, Cheryl. She had worn it long, layered, short, crinkly. Often, she would have to go to Neiman's to have the cut and coloring done properly by a Rinaldo or a Travis, and this would cost a week's tips, but the flirtation with elitism would be worth it to her.

Today Juanita's hair was styled in what she called a Lib frizz. She kept it herself. It was easier. The modern woman who worked and had artistic juices flowing no longer had the time to fritter away an afternoon on a hairdresser.

Fuck it. Hair styles were like jeans now. Jeans weren't going to disappear any time soon. Look at the TV commercials. Jean Wars.

Juanita was surprised at how easily she won this argument with herself.

Candy had wanted to become a waitress when she returned from Oregon.

Juanita rebelled. In a tone with an uncharacteristic bite, the mother said, "You know why I've been a waitress . . . tended bar all my life? So you wouldn't have to do it."

Juanita talked Candy out of the notion by explaining the simple fact that waitresses were foredoomed to go in and out of a hot steamy kitchen constantly, and it did not take long for a girl's body to exude the aroma of navy beans and ham bits.

Thus, Candy went to work in a record-tape-stereo center called Yo Daddy's. In Yo Daddy's, however, Candy met a number of musicians, therefore she met a number of dope dealers, one of whom turned out to be Dove Christian.

Juanita had smoked grass with her daughter, principally to determine in her own mind whether getting high was worth the risk of going to prison.

Juanita had been disappointed with her pot-smoking experiences. She had been forced to conclude that the effects of marijuana on a human being hardly differed at all from the effects of, say, mononucleosis.

Candy was naturally responsible for Juanita's education about cocaine.

First, Juanita learned where cocaine could be obtained if you were only a pretty young girl with an inquisitive nature instead of an heiress who could afford it.

Guys shared their cocaine with pretty young girls. At least guys shared it with them until the pretty young girls developed noses that could outperform an Electrolux.

"Musicians got the best flake in town," Candy had said.

Candy was now an impassioned defender of cocaine as a harmless social substance, not a drug. Her plea on behalf of cocaine went something like the following:

Coke made you smart and alert instead of dull and boring, which was the problem with strong grass. Coke was not habit-forming. It was too expensive. They used to put cocaine in Coca-Cola. If it hadn't been for cocaine, America wouldn't have had soda fountains.

All kinds of famous and wealthy people used coke. Kings and queens and earls and dukes and tycoons. You had to be pretty naive to think it was Garratt's Snuff the kings and queens were sniffing out of those jeweled rings they wore.

Rudyard Kipling used coke. That's what *If,* the poem, was all about. Edgar Allen Poe wrote his best horror tales when he thought he was running out of coke. Robert Louis Stevenson was a heavy user. That was the real point of *Dr. Jekyll and Mr. Hyde*. Winston Churchill's best speeches were delivered on coke. Churchill wanted to "fight them on the beaches" because that's where the coke dealers had summer homes.

Coke didn't make you horny. Quaaludes did that. Coke made you brilliant and you never lost control.

The only really bad thing about coke was the law. A long time ago some uninformed government nitwit lumped cocaine and heroin in the same category. The fools who run things haven't bothered to find out that cocaine and heroin are as different as coconut-cream pie and okra. Okra kills.

But one of these days the lawmakers would get enlightened. They would make coke safe for people who didn't have expensive attorneys. This would be a good deal for middle-income Americans. When the average people tried it, they would discover coke was nothing but a smartiner, a mellow speed. And people would get to use it freely and feel intelligent like the people did in the Old West when the peddlers drove their wagons into town and sold tonic—which had coke in it.

If coke was so destructive, how come everybody connected with Hollywood, Broadway, television, sports, politics, big business, science, education and the arts was using it like fresh air and doing plenty okay? Answer that.

This was the whole truth about cocaine. And every jerk in the Drug Enforcement Administration could sit on it till his balls turned into ripe olives.

So spoke Candy, who did agree that sprinkling cocaine on your breakfast cereal every morning would be going too far.

Candy's graduate study in cocaine had been supervised by that noted scientist, Dove Christian. But her attitude had been re-enforced by two years of continuous snorting with no evidence of harm, unless greed had become a personality trait.

Juanita had been surprised to be taken with Dove Christian's good looks, politeness and subtle wit.

When she first met him, Dove talked of having a number of professions. They ranged from trading oil leases to managing rock groups. But the black Lincoln he drove, Bulgari Quartz wrist watch, his $800 Charlie Dunn boots, and his lack of an address indicated to Juanita that he was a dealer, which practically anyone could have figured out, she felt, except a narc.

Dove was getting up there in years, pushing the old three-oh mark. But he still had the build of a lithe athlete. He once was, after all, Ronnie Lee Dickerson, Old 88, Longhorn flanker. His dark hair was groomed like that of a male model. His cool manner suggested he had studied all of Robert Redford's films. It may have been equally important to Candy that Dove had a seemingly limitless supply of "tooth powder."

A loving mother and swell apartment were no competition for Dove Christian.

Juanita liked Dove in many ways. She sensed he was a bright young man who could succeed at anything he tried. Perhaps one day Dove might try something legitimate, if first he didn't wind up making license plates on the farm.

Dove never gave Juanita any phony talk about searching for the new sensitivities, getting off on altitude, looking for hidden dimensions in the human spirit. He wasn't in quest of the cosmic nose.

Upon breaking the news to Juanita that he was taking Candy to Aspen, Dove had said, "I love your little girl here. I want to look after her."

He didn't plan to stay in the cocaine business forever. Aspen, as he sized it up, was where he could make a load and become a civilian again.

"Aspen's into blow," Dove said. There were sophisticates all over the Rockies who required multiple Baggies of tooth powder for numerous social occasions.

"Texas is no good now," he said. "It's getting overrun with scum dealers who majored in killer-pimp and the 440."

Dove made Juanita a promise: Candy would never have any "smart stuff" in her pocket. He would never let her "hold."

Dove rented a plush ranch house outside of Aspen proper. Candy and Dove were now sharing the residence with another couple, old friends and business associates of Dove's.

There was Keala, a darkly beautiful girl of Armenian-Japanese extraction who had been a stewardess for Pan Am before she got fired for smuggling, and there was Remillard, a Frenchman who had ranked among the top professional ski racers until he ruined his knee on a dance floor.

Candy had become a waitress, after all. But Juanita judged from Candy's letters that it was chic to be a waitress in Aspen, particularly in the place where both she and Keala were employed, Keala as a bartender. The place was The American Dental Association & Cocaine-Palmolive. It was Aspen's newest celebrity hangout.

Their social lives centered around The American Dental Association & Cocaine-Palmolive, a restaurant, bar, deli, and sidewalk café. They also frequented The American Dental Association & Cocaine-Palmolive's private disco, which was called Fluoride.

An excerpt from Candy's most recent letter revealed:

Keala's a fantastic bartender, Momma. She's as fast and neat as you are. Only I have to admit she cheats. She takes her vitamin compound out of an atomizer, if you know what I mean.

Dove bought me a yellow MGB. Wow! I can't believe I have a sports car! He bought himself a big TV screen and a thing where you can tape programs and show movies. He's having some kind of microwave disc put in the yard so he can pick up a hundred channels and porno flicks from Rome. Business has been real good.

This town is crawling with celebrities all the time. They're great at wearing disguises you can recognize them in.

Don't worry about us, Momma. Dove's real careful and smart at what he does. He says to tell you not to be concerned about the morals of it. He's only 'serving the people' like a Congressman.

I have to go fire out some ratatouille and Monte Cristos to the ladies of the New Orleans Ski Club. Sure do love you. Go Paschal, beat Heights!

Juanita was reading Candy's letter again when her apartment doorbell rang. The persistence of the ring told Juanita she would open her door to find a Jehovah Witness asking for a dollar, perhaps Burt Reynolds, or even Doris Steadman.

Doris marched to a closet and put on Juanita's old blue chenille robe. She went to the kitchen-breakfast room-den to slice radishes and green peppers into a helping of cottage cheese.

Doris collapsed on the beige velvet sofa from Sears. She propped her panty hose up on a trunk which had become a coffee table.

"This cottage cheese doesn't taste very fresh." Doris made a face.

"Do you want a drink?"

"Are you having one?"

"I will."

"Vodka, then. Splash of water."

"No Rusty Nail?"

"How long have you had this cottage cheese, Juanita?"

"Let's see. How long ago were they flying open cockpits?"

Juanita mixed herself a white-wine-and-soda. While she was up, Doris asked Juanita to rummage through her purse and find a pink pill. No use leaving sleep to chance.

Prowling around in the purse, Juanita said, "Here's a little black capsule, what's this?"

"Dear God, don't gimme that," Doris said. "I'll read the phone book to you and start on the dictionary."

Juanita found a pink pill, handed it to Doris, then sat in the oversized gray chair with the ottoman.

"Song?" Doris noticed the yellow legal pad on the coffee table.

"Part of it rhymes."

"I don't know why you write songs. Looks like you'd find a better hobby. It's like those scrapbooks of yours."

"My movie star collection? Don't knock my movie star collection, Doris."

"I've never understood why anybody cut pictures out of one thing to paste 'em in something else."

"At the time it seemed important to keep the Clark Gables together and the Linda Darnells together."

"We ought to take up tennis," Doris said. "I'd play if you would. We have eight courts at Mirage La Grande and all they do is sit there."

"I can't play tennis. I'm not left-handed and I've never slept with a hairdresser. I couldn't play tennis anyhow with somebody who knocked my movie star collection. It was the funniest thing I ever found in my grandmother's attic. Do you know what they used to let me do?"

"The movie stars?"

"My grandparents," Juanita smiled. "God, they were great. They used to let me cut pictures out of newspapers and magazines before they'd even read them."

Doris yawned. "Juanita, if Lee calls, tell him I'm too upset to talk. Try to mention your aunt's coat. Your cousin. And the cigarette lighter, if you can work it all in."

They were back to Doris' hobby.

"Lee saw you plain as day," Juanita said. "He was looking right at you."

"Lee doesn't notice details unless they've got something to do with carpet. He saw what I'll tell him he saw."

"Doris, have I told you before you've got more nerve than Del Monte's got hamburger dills?"

"I'm just a woman, is all. I don't do anything the majority of women wouldn't do if they thought they could get away with it. Anyhow . . . I do more than Lee Steadman to hold our marriage together."

Juanita couldn't avoid looking astonished.

"I do!" Doris said, squirming around. "How good a wife would I be if I never had any adventure in my life? I'd be dull. I wouldn't have any zest. You think about it from that angle."

Doris rattled the ice in her vodka.

"It's as simple as the difference in people's personalities. I don't get *involved* with other men, Juanita. I get laid. It's fun, damn it. Anybody who says it's not fun is a liar or scared of the Bible—and you can write that down right here on this paper right now tonight!"

"Do you love Lee? Did you love him when you married him?"

"Of course, I love him!" Doris was shocked by the question. "I wouldn't want to lose him. Lee Steadman is a good person. He's sweet, gentle. He's been better to me than any man I've ever known. He's generous. I couldn't ask for any more than I've got in the way of comfort and security. Lee is a fine, honest, thoughtful, considerate man."

Doris yawned again, covering her mouth. "But that don't make him no Tiffany diamond."

Juanita and Doris had been friends for ten years. They met in Herb's Cafe when Doris came in for the first time and drank six vodkas to celebrate her divorce from A. C. Tolbert.

That day, Doris had said to Juanita: "Well, here's to my Ex. If there wasn't anything in the world but A. C. Tolberts, I'd be a volunteer V. D. carrier."

Doris, give or take a bruise, was the same age as Juanita, but Doris saw herself as a "girl" in her late twenties, somewhere around the age when she moved to Fort Worth from Greenville, Texas, her hometown, a town once distinguished for a sign at the edge of the city which said: "Welcome to Greenville—Home of the Blackest Land and the Whitest People." Doris, in her own mind, was still the vixen whose thighs had not thickened, whose hips were not in danger of getting stabbed by the corner of every piece of furniture she circled, whose bosom was not beginning to require rigid support, and whose hair had not become a gold helmet.

In Doris' past, there were no doubt people who could testify she had once been a sultry young lady. She may have been the pioneering girl in her high school class who got nailed first. She would have been prettier in these downhill years if she were not the false-eyelash queen, and did not wear so much costume jewelry that parts of her looked like souvenirs for sale.

Doris had worked her way up to assistant manager of Wickley's Drug by screwing Ross Wickley every Thursday on his office couch while Rita Wickley went to her bridge club. Before that, Doris had been a receptionist for an orthopedist, which was where she had met A. C. Tolbert. A. C. Tolbert had come into the office with a broken wrist. He had caught his 2-iron in the roots of a fairway at Goat Hills muny after taking the club back past horizontal.

A. C. Tolbert's plaid sport coat and pink shirt with a roll collar had convinced Doris she had found something in a size $25,000-a-year, so she married him. In fact, the combined salaries of Doris and A. C. had left them with just enough money each week to splurge for a can of Underwood's Deviled Ham. They lived in a two-room garage apartment which didn't even have a second-hand window unit. In the summers, Doris and A. C. had not been able to scrape the heat off their bodies with a wire brush.

A. C. came up with an idea for an investment that

would turn things around. He sold one of their cars and two of his three sets of MacGregor golf clubs, and borrowed money from everyone he knew, and put everything into a flagpole business.

A. C. had a theory that America was ready to stand up to Communism. Americans needed bigger flagpoles to give the Russians something to think about as the Russians looked down at America from sputnik.

"Sputnik was 19-God-damn-57!" Doris had protested.

"You bet," A. C. had said. "They're still up there, too."

A. C. sold only one flagpole in two years. He sold it to Biff & Peggy's Auto Parts, but he didn't even get paid for it. Biff had bought the flagpole while Peggy was underneath a Dodge. When Peggy learned of it, she cancelled the order.

Peggy had said to A. C., "I'll reconsider the flagpole if I happen to see a Mig strafing Buddies Supermarket."

This had been the point at which Doris had taken A. C. Tolbert's name off the scoreboard.

Doris pounced on Lee Steadman the first time he came into Wickley's Drug. She astutely noticed Lee's shoes were shined, his fingernails were clean, and he bought Certs. Lee was a quiet duty-minded man who had never been married. He had devoted his life to caring for a mother who wrote lengthy letters to characters on soap operas. Lee Steadman was a push-over for Doris, a woman with a centerfold's chest going for her and hair the color of No. 2 yellow pine.

Their whirlwind courtship lasted a month. They honeymooned in Dallas where their hotel unfortunately was host to a world-wide convention of travel agents.

"Lee don't ever have to take me to Hawaii," Doris told Juanita, describing the honeymoon. "I've stepped over all the drunks and ukuleles I ever hope to see."

Juanita had acted enthusiastic about the wedding, but she knew as well as any of Doris' chums in the

53

South Side B & PW that it was going to be less of a marriage for Doris than an opportunity for her to get rid of her old towels and flatware.

After Doris surrendered to the pink pill, Juanita carried the Martin and the legal pad to her bedroom. She sat on the kingsize bed and tuned the outside strings, the E's, only two octaves apart. Then she worked on the tune to her song, picking the guitar and singing quietly for two hours, far into the night.

Around her, on the peach-colored bedroom wall, was Juanita's collection of the wisdom of other songwriters. She and Candy had started the collection a few years ago. The list grew to more than two hundred lines. Candy had once printed Juanita's favorites on a sheet of construction paper, had it framed, gift-wrapped, and had given the artwork to Juanita as a Mother's Day present. In the frame were:

I DON'T KNOW WHETHER TO KILL MYSELF OR GO BOWLING.

HOW CAN WHISKY ONLY SIX YEARS OLD WHIP A MAN OF 32?

MY WIFE RAN OFF WITH MY BEST FRIEND AND I SURE DO MISS HIM.

ALL HE EVER GETS IS OLDER, AND AROUND.

I MAY FALL AGAIN BUT I'LL NEVER GET UP THIS SLOW.

WALK OUT BACKWARDS SO I'LL THINK YOU'RE COMING IN.

YOU PRETEND I'M HIM AND I'LL PRETEND YOU'RE HER.

YOU WALKED ACROSS MY HEART LIKE IT WAS TEXAS.

IF FINGERPRINTS SHOWED UP ON SKIN, I WONDER WHOSE I'D FIND ON YOU?

I WANT TO BE A COWBOY'S SWEETHEART. I WANT TO LEARN TO ROPE AND TO RIDE.

TOO MANY TIMES MARRIED MEN THINK THEY'RE STILL SINGLE.

ALL THE GIRLS KEEP GETTING PRETTIER AT CLOSING TIME.

WALKING IS BETTER THAN RUNNING AWAY, AND
    CRAWLING AIN'T NO GOOD AT ALL.
HE LIKES THE NIGHTLIFE, THE BRIGHT LIGHTS, AND
    GOOD-TIMIN' FRIENDS.
IF THE PHONE DON'T RING, YOU'LL KNOW IT'S ME.

Lee Steadman never called.

Chapter Four

When the doorbell rang at sunrise, Juanita wrestled out
of bed and managed the old Hindu trick of slipping into
a white terrycloth robe while standing on her feet in a
coma.

She made it to the front door with the aid of only two
Anacin and one Winston.

Opening the door, she saw a dark blue tailored suit
and white blouse on a coat hanger. Her eyes moved
slowly upward from the hand holding the hanger to a
pair of granny glasses, hair shining like mopped linole-
um, and a fatuous grin.

"Nobody smiles this early, Lee. Nobody."

Juanita tromped to the kitchen-breakfast room-den
as Lee Steadman followed. She made two cups of
Taster's Choice and fell into a chrome-and-leather
bar-style chair at the butcher-block table.

Lee hooked the suit and blouse on a doorknob. He sat in the twin chair.

"Thought I'd save Doris the trouble of driving all the way back to the East Side to get dressed for work," he said, blowing on a spoonful of coffee.

Despite what anybody said, Mirage La Grande, where the Steadmans lived, was every bit as accessible to Fort Worth as Minneapolis. All anyone had to do to get to Mirage La Grande was drive east toward Dallas, turn left at the D/FW airport, stay faithful to a farm-to-market road through a maze of farms, markets and factories, circle three high school football stadiums, avoid the dead end at a lake, and stop at the last Tom Thumb grocery before the Oklahoma state line. The best thing was, Mirage La Grande had bargains in French provincial town houses.

Lee Steadman made a confession. He *had* been angry and confused the night before. He had indeed driven around town, screeching his tires, honking at red lights. "I must have ate four Bonus Jacks." But Lee had overcome his anger and confusion by convincing himself there had to be a logical explanation for his wife hugging a total stranger in a public place. Likely as not, Doris had been depicting a scene from a movie she'd seen.

"What were you doing on the South Side, Lee?"

"I'd measured Tucker's Hair Mill for some green shag. I was stopping in to grab a Pepsi and say hello. Who was that old boy in the fur coat, anyhow?"

Juanita looked at Lee in amazement.

But she went ahead with the story as planned. Aunt Bernice, the coat, her cousin, the lighter.

"Naturally, Doris didn't want her Dunhill to get broken," Juanita said, satisfied with how smoothly she recited the narrative.

"Yeah, I know how Doris feels about her lighter," Lee said. "That's why I brought it with me. She left it home yesterday."

Lee put the Dunhill on the table.

Juanita's coughing spell lasted a full minute.

"Good," she said, choking, swallowing, gradually recovering. "You found it. Doris will be thrilled. She was afraid she'd lost it. She borrowed Vera's lighter yesterday, the one the B & PW gave Vera when Vera was installed as vice-president. I blame the whole thing on timing, myself."

"Where did Doris see Vera?"

"Yesterday was the B & PW's luncheon."

"Hey, that's right, it was."

Lee mulled the story over, staring at things.

"I was glad to see my cousin," Juanita said. "He lives in Lafayette, Louisiana. He's probably the happiest married man I know."

Juanita went for overkill.

She said, "You ought to see his wife. She makes Jacqueline Bisset look like a throw-rug."

Lee said, "Well . . . boy, hidy. It just goes to show you. Your old eyes sure can deceive you, can't they?"

Juanita relaxed.

"Is Doris mad at me?"

"She didn't like being locked out of her own home. She was mainly worried about you having an accident."

"I did chip a tooth." Lee probed a bicuspid with his finger. "Bit down on something in a Bonus Jack."

Juanita went for more coffee. Coming back to the table, she said, "So . . . how's the carpet business, Lee?"

It was a question she wouldn't dare ask under normal circumstances.

"Oh, about as good as can be expected," Lee said. "Got the same old problem with delivery. Seems like I'm always calling the mill in Chattanooga to complain about delivery. Lost a job the other day because of delivery. Fellow named Todd in the advertising business wanted quick delivery on a maroon wool. I could get delivery on a red check in a synthetic fiber, but I couldn't get delivery on a maroon wool. Same thing with an old boy named Sweeney in the lumber business. He didn't know the name of what he wanted. All he said was, it looked like coffee-flavored Häagen-Dazs. I told him I could get delivery on something that looked like jamoca almond fudge at Baskin-Robbins, but I didn't know about . . ."

Lee's attention was diverted to the doorway behind Juanita. "Good morning!" he said.

Doris languished in the doorway in the mink coat, striking a pose for a fashion photographer.

Seeing her, Juanita sadly turned back to the table and shut her eyes and propped her head on her hand.

Lee said, "Where'd you get that coat, honey? It looks like Roy's."

"It looks like *whose?*" Doris squinted, abandoning the fashion pose.

"Juanita's cousin—that fellow in Herb's yesterday."

"Roy's a *man.*"

"I thought he looked funny in a coat like that."

"*I* was wearing the coat. This one! It's Juanita's. I was trying it on yesterday when you looked in the door and lost your stupid mind."

"I'm sorry about last night, honey."

"You damn well should be!"

Juanita intruded to say, "Doris, I explained to Lee how he happened to look in Herb's at the very instant you dropped *Vera's* lighter."

"That's right!" Doris said, keeping a cold stare on Lee. "Just as you opened Herb's door, I accidentally dropped . . . Vera's . . . lighter."

"I found yours," Lee said. "It was on the floor by the toilet underneath your *Cosmopolitan.*"

Lee held up the Dunhill.

"Thank God for small favors," Doris said, as Juanita looked at her with awe.

"I brought you some clothes," Lee said, going to his wife.

"Well, you did *something* right."

Lee tried to kiss Doris. "I haven't brushed my teeth." She looked away. Lee stroked the Blackglama mink on the shoulder.

He backed off and said to Juanita, "Hulen to 820 the best way to get to my showroom this time of morning?"

"Good as any," Juanita said.

"Guess I'd better get out there. What about Berry to 820 and 303 to 360? Or . . . I could take 81 to 30, then 360."

"Call me later," Doris said, opening a can of tomato juice.

Lee said, "If I take Berry past 287, I'll hit 820. I could hop on 121 and go to 3029. What would that do?"

"See you, Lee," Juanita waved.

In moments like this, Juanita yearned for the past. The old arteries leading out of, or into, Fort Worth had better names. Jacksboro Highway, Waco Highway, White Settlement, Cleburne Road, Old Mansfield Road, Dallas Pike.

"Tell you what I *could* do," Lee said. "Hulen to 820, hit 81. Get on 121. Stay with 121 to Pipeline, cut through to 183. I could be wrong, of course. But if I'm right, well . . . I'll have a pretty interesting story for everybody when I go to lunch at Luther's Cafeteria."

As the front door closed behind Lee, Juanita playfully got up from the table and pretended to measure the mink coat, saying, "It would make a good jacket for Roy, don't you think? Cut it off about right here? It'd be real warm."

Juanita and Doris began to laugh, snickering at first, then uncontrollably. Kleenex laughter.

Juanita then had an impulse to show Doris a song she had written. She decided to take advantage of Doris' good mood. There might never be another time to share "Only a Hobby" with the lady who inspired it.

Juanita went to her song file. Her song file consisted of a row of binders standing end-wise on a countertop between her cookbooks. She opened a black binder to the song and placed it in front of Doris, who was sitting at the table in the mink coat.

Doris read the song twice.

She's still collecting lovers.
Has herself a ball.

Can't even run an errand
Unless she gives someone a call.

She'll meet Roy at the laundry
With her husband's shirts and shorts.
While she's holding Roy
The laundry holds the starch.

She'll greet Bill in a store,
Politely shaking hands.
Then they hug and kiss
Behind the pots and pans.

She'll take Steve for a drive
But turnpikes have their woes.
Making love ain't easy
When you're always paying tolls.

She'll go to Jimmy's home
If his wife's out that day.
She'll walk right in the door
And model lingerie.

She'll meet Ed in a movie
If she's seen it in the past.
She needs to know the plot
In case her husband asks.

Today it's Bob for lunch,
Her Wednesday matinee.
They're dining at the Hilton
In Room 428.

Sure hope she don't discover
How her husband spends his time.
He's got a matinee
In Room 429!

"What's the tune?" Doris asked, solemnly.
"What's the *tune?*"
"Most songs have tunes," Doris said.

"Forgetting the fact it doesn't have a tune, what do you think of it?"

"I'm not offended, if that's what worries you," said Doris. "It's inaccurate, of course."

The coffee almost went down the wrong way, and Juanita said, "Doris, you can't look at me with a straight face and say it's inaccurate."

"Lee Steadman would never cheat on me," Doris said. "Lee Steadman? Go to a hotel with another woman? In case you don't know it, Juanita, Lee Steadman has too much character to do a sordid thing like that!"

Juanita crept back into bed after Doris left for work. She fully intended to stay there until "Mom's Movie" came on TV at one o'clock. She was expected to be at Herb's by around 2:30. But if Gestapo agents went barging into compartments on the Arlberg Express or intimidating people at sidewalk cafés while the dark clouds of war hovered over Europe, Juanita didn't go to Herb's until after 3 P.M., maybe even later—certainly not before Claudette Colbert escaped from Budapest.

Juanita barricaded herself with down pillows and slept for two whole minutes before the phone rang.

"What time is it, Juanita? My watch don't have a big hand."

Lonnie Slocum was calling from Houston.

Lonnie sounded as if he were trying to speak above a fire in his hotel suite while people fled through doors and leaped out of windows.

Juanita heard scuffling noises, shouting, groaning, screaming.

"We haven't quite made it to bed," Lonnie said. "Somebody drove us to an airport after the gig in Waco. They put us on a plane and here we are. What time did you say it was?"

Ten o'clock in the morning, Juanita answered. A Thursday. October. An OPEC year. America was at peace with all but one enemy, Washington, D.C. The TCU Horned Frogs were playing the SMU Mustangs Saturday in Dallas. It was a great time to be alive. Buy precious metals.

"How long since the Frogs won a game?"

"Wooden stadiums."

Juanita assumed Lonnie was not addressing her when he yelled, "Hey! Tell that bitch to get the fuck out of here!"

Juanita smoked. "Sounds like show biz hasn't gotten any easier."

"I'll tell you," Lonnie wheezed. "Show biz is so fuckin' hard I just want to get my album finished so I can lay down and die."

Things were pretty normal with the other members of Dog Track Gravy, according to Lonnie's update.

Toby Painter, rhythm, was on a divan catching herpes from the young girl in the see-up jogging shorts.

Jim Hensley, bass, was devouring two breakfast steaks under a mound of scrambled eggs on a room-service table.

Chet Woofter, steel, was organizing a dozen lines of cocaine on a mirror laying across his lap while fighting off three groupies and two roadies.

Wendall Dacus, keyboard, was looking for his pants.

Rob Stinson, drums, was on the floor performing a Ceasarean on an aspiring actress.

"Dr. Rob Stinson . . . O.B. . . . gyn," Juanita said.

Lonnie Slocum, lead guitar, was distracted again.

"Jim! Toby! Somebody kick Julie's ass out of here! She's gone through a fuckin' gram since I been on the phone!"

Juanita said, "You run into a lot of gluttony in your line of work, don't you?"

"You know what, Juanita? I fell in love on Braniff this morning. She was so good-looking it made me want to push her grocery cart. Friendly, too."

"Stewardess?"

"Naw, a real person. She fucked up, though."

"How?"

"Asked me not to smoke."

"Bitch."

Lonnie wrote her a song, anyhow. A romantic ballad. In the deep and abnormally weak voice of a man who had not slept in forty-eight hours, Lonnie sang:

"Lord, I hate to let you go . . . your body drives me wild. But I'm a smoking window . . . and you're a non-smoking aisle."

Juanita said she liked it. He ought to finish it.

"It ain't worth a shit," Lonnie said. "You know why? It's like one of your songs. It's too elite. Too oblique. Nobody could understand it but world travelers."

"I understand it. Who am I, Lowell Thomas?"

"That's why we ought to get married, Juanita. You and me. Our souls match up. I need a good woman. You're the only good woman I know."

"Thanks, Lonnie."

"Don't you want to marry me?"

Juanita said, "I think I've been about as entertained by marriage as I care to be."

"You think you're too old for me, don't you? You're not too old for me. How old are you?"

"Let me put it this way, Lonnie. Your mother and I could have taken a high school elective together."

Lonnie said he needed a good woman to save his life. Juanita would be the kind of woman he wouldn't have to beat the shit out of.

Juanita wondered, as a general rule, how often a man had to beat the shit out of a woman.

Lonnie explained it was something which had to be done on the morning after the wedding night. Done properly, it might not have to be repeated.

Whapping the shit out of a woman on the morning after the wedding night let the woman know how it was going to be.

"You know what'll happen if you don't whap the livin' shit out of 'em?"

Juanita did not, in all honesty, know.

Lonnie said, "If you go out at night, them fuckers'll

make you dance. They'll tell you not to drink too much. Make you eat molded salads. I've heard all kinds of horror stories."

Juanita asked Lonnie if he were too physically whipped to listen to her new song. She had performed over the phone for Lonnie on other occasions. She had become skilled at sitting on the edge of the bed and singing into a receiver draped over a lamp and hanging in front of her like a microphone.

"Yeah, just a second," he said. "Toby! Jim! Gimme a fuckin' break! Julie looks like a God-damn glacier! I paid seventeen hundred for that shit!"

Lonnie apologized to Juanita for the farm animals in his hotel suite.

Juanita got the Martin and the legal pad and rigged the receiver. She tuned the guitar.

"Tuning," she said into the receiver, "is one of the most important features of my act."

She strummed some chords.

"Right now," she said, nervously, "I'd like to do a medley of Welsh mining songs."

Juanita then sang "God Don't Care About the Red Lights in Life."

The lack of an immediate response from Lonnie Slocum suggested to Juanita that her song, by and large, wasn't going to make platinum.

"Well?" she said.

"I don't want to hurt your feelings," said Lonnie.

"You've always told me the truth. I'll never get out from behind a damn bar if I don't keep learning. What's wrong with it?"

"Sure you want to hear it?"

"No . . . but go ahead."

Lonnie said, "Why the fuck are you wasting your time on a truck-drivin' song, Juanita?"

Doris, Roy Simmons, the mink coat. They were the things that inspired it.

"If there's anything the world's got more of than truck drivers, it's truck-drivin' songs," Lonnie said.

"Why don't you write a song about you? Something *you* feel? How many songs you laid on me over the past four-five years? Thirty?"

Juanita said she had written fifty others but they were too oblique.

"You've never written a song about something you love. Something that hurts. Shit, man. Life hurts."

Juanita asked Lonnie to hold the line a second. She would knock off a quick ballad about hepatitis.

"You're pissed."

"Yes."

"I don't want you to be pissed."

"I'm not pissed at you, Lonnie. I'm pissed at me."

"I bet I got something to un-piss you. It's the reason I called as a matter of fact."

No reply.

Lonnie said, "You know this album we're doing? I've got a spot on there for a song by you. I been thinking about it since the last cassette you sent me. You're getting close to writing a good song. We're two months from finishing the album. You got plenty of time to come up with a good song."

More silence.

"Make it a song I can sing myself. My point of view. Understand?"

"Are you joking, Lonnie?"

He said, "I may have to fix it up *cosmetically,* as we say around Nashville. Doctor it a little. But I won't put a calico dress on it. It'll be your song. Maybe old Ralph Emery will play it on WSM and we'll both get famous. So how 'bout yourself? You got a chance to be a songwriter lady."

"For God's sake, Lonnie. What can I say?"

"Want to marry me now?"

"No," Juanita laughed, "but I'll go down on you."

Juanita plunged into her song file. She spent the rest of the morning examining her old material, wondering if there were any songs she could rework, recycle, draw

65

an idea from. She was also curious to see if the songs were as impersonal as Lonnie had said.

Most of them were, or so they seemed in the afterglow of his criticism. Impersonal, trite, trivial. A title for an album of her own: *Impersonal Triviality*.

One song presented itself as a possibility for Lonnie. The drinking song. "Fritos Never Let Me Down." Nothing impersonal about that one. The song had resulted from all the nights Juanita had spent watching alcohol take prisoners.

> *I say gin is quicker,*
> *Martinis always win.*
> *My vodka tongue gets thicker*
> *When Gibsons are the trend.*
> *Scotch makes me rich.*
> *Anybody need a loan?*
> *But I always eat a Frito.*
> *The Frito drives me home.*
>
> *Brandy makes me flip.*
> *It's Alexander's fault.*
> *Sure ain't ever whipped*
> *Margarita and her salt.*
> *Rum makes me dance*
> *Till I turn into a stone.*
> *But I always eat a Frito.*
> *The Frito drives me home.*
>
> *I can go from whisky sours*
> *Into stingers like a breeze.*
> *But then I spend those hours*
> *In the bathroom on my knees.*
> *Fine'ly drank up all the lovin'*
> *I ever had at home,*
> *But I still got my Fritos*
> *In this bar where I'm alone.*

Juanita heard a spectral voice as she looked at the lyrics. The voice of Lonnie Slocum. "Nice try, Juanita," the voice informed her, "but Loretta's already said it better in only one line. 'Don't come home a-drinkin' with lovin' on your mind.'"

"Well, fuck," Juanita said quietly to herself.

And she went to get dressed for work.

Chapter Five

Juanita wanted first to tell Candy about her opportunity to write a song and win a Grammy. She tried to reach her daughter by long distance through all of Thursday afternoon and evening, but nobody was home at the ranch house in Aspen. Juanita kept getting a recording of Dove Christian's voice, which said:

"Hi, this is Adolph Hitler. Me and Eva ain't in the bunker right now. We've gone out for a stroll to cheer up the troops. It's touch and go around here these days, but on the sound of the beep, go ahead and leave the name of the country you want invaded, and we'll try to get back to you on it."

Juanita couldn't resist sharing the news with someone. She whispered it to Slick Henderson at the bar in Herb's, making him promise not to spread it around. She didn't want the South Side B & PW or any of Herb's regulars pitching in to help out on the chorus.

Slick said the news demanded a celebration. This was

the perfect occasion for Juanita to let him take her out on a date. He proposed they go to the TCU-SMU football game in the Cotton Bowl Saturday afternoon, then treat themselves to a "gourmet experience" in a swank Dallas restaurant.

"A real date?" Juanita said.

"Yeah. With car doors opening and cigarettes being lit. Everything."

Slick said he knew for a fact that Dallas had a dozen expensive restaurants with cozy atmosphere where the veal didn't have to be cut with a power tool, where the pasta wasn't floating in more than a foot of water, and where the sauce was reliable because it came right out of a Ragu jar.

"Sounds romantic," Juanita said, accepting the invitation.

Juanita had not had a "date" in a while. She didn't have much luck with dates. Doris was always trying to fix her up with an eligible gentleman, but it never worked out to anyone's satisfaction.

Over the past six months, Juanita had gone out with only two men, Cecil Pulliam and Sonny Hawkins. She met both of them through Doris.

Cecil Pulliam, a stockbroker, had been considered a catch because he was nice-looking and getting divorced. Cecil Pulliam had explained to Juanita quite honestly—right up front—that he preferred to take her to dinner on a side of town where he wasn't likely to see his wife. His wife was being pretty contrary about the divorce settlement and he didn't want to give her any extra ammunition. Juanita went to dinner with Cecil Pulliam four times on the West Side, always to the Baboon Rocket Club. They sat in the outdoor garden under the trees where Cecil Pulliam was often distracted by the jeans and T-shirts of TCU coeds.

On their last evening together, they were sitting in the outdoor garden at the Baboon Rocket drinking a pitcher of beer and eating nachos when Cecil Pulliam suddenly ducked under the table. He did so in the exact instant that a woman and two little boys appeared at a gate to the outdoor garden.

The woman was wearing tennis togs, and the boys were covered with sweat in their Little League baseball uniforms.

When Cecil Pulliam raised up from the table, he had on a beret, dark glasses, and a false beard.

"What are you doing?" Juanita said in a slightly bewildered tone.

"That woman," said Cecil Pulliam in a low voice. "She's a client. I sold her some shares of Nitron and Quantrex over the counter. They haven't performed well. I don't want to have to talk to her about it."

The woman and the little boys came straight to their table.

Mrs. Cecil Pulliam glared at Juanita, and said, "You can have this silly son of a bitch with my compliments, honey. But you're gonna have to take these two little farts with him. I'm so sick of baseball, I could cry!"

Juanita left the Pulliams cussing each other while the Little Leaguers fought over the beard and beret.

Sonny Hawkins was next. Sonny Hawkins was a sporty dresser and free spender. He laughed at everything he heard, funny or not, and called everyone "sweet baby doll." He owned an office-supply business but he liked to say with a hearty chuckle that the name of his company was "Hawkins Against the Elements."

Juanita agreed to go out with Sonny Hawkins after Sonny Hawkins swore he was single. Doris confirmed it with an oath of her own.

Doris arranged an evening in which she and Juanita would "double-date." Juanita would be with Sonny Hawkins. Doris would be with Wayne Carlisle, a lawyer. Wayne Carlisle was married, naturally, but that wasn't a bulletin for the CBS Evening News.

Juanita and Doris were to meet Sonny Hawkins and Wayne Carlisle at Wayne Carlisle's secret apartment. They would charcoal steaks on the patio, then go dancing and listen to music afterward.

The evening began pleasantly enough. Everyone enjoyed a cocktail in the living room of Wayne Carlisle's secret apartment, which nobody knew existed except Sonny Hawkins, a few stewardesses, some topless dancers, and now Juanita and Doris.

But the door chimes interrupted Sonny Hawkins' third Aggie joke. Juanita innocently went to the door and opened it. A petite blonde with bangs brushed past her carrying a tray of food.

Sonny Hawkins jumped up from a chair in his white sport coat and jacaranda trousers. Sonny broke into a big smile, held out his arms to the petite blonde, and said:

"Sweet Baby Doll!"

The petite blonde snarled, "You rectangular asshole! You low-life scumbag! You can crawl up my butt so far I hope it takes you a month to get an outside line for long distance! Here! I didn't want your dinner to get cold!"

With those words, Mrs. Sonny Hawkins hurled the tray of homemade chicken-fried steak, French fries, pinto beans, green salad, and cream gravy on Sonny's white sport coat and jacaranda trousers.

"Sweet Baby Doll!" Sonny Hawkins stammered, going into a fox trot.

Two minutes later, Sonny Hawkins said it again as Juanita left.

Juanita told Slick Henderson she would consult *Texas Monthly*'s restaurant ratings and pick out an exquisite place in Dallas for Saturday evening.

On Friday before going to work, Juanita visited Grace at the Trinity River Nursing Center.

She found Grace in the community room, where the residents had a view of a cactus garden through a glass wall. Some of the residents were reading, some were having snacks, some were seated around a long table where a rotund nurse shouted out bingo numbers, and some looked at cactus.

Grace had pushed her wheelchair to a table where Mrs. Grimes was eating a bowl of fruit. Grace was wearing a housecoat and slippers. Mrs. Grimes wore a red pants suit.

Juanita asked Grace and Mrs. Grimes if they wanted anything from the cold-drink machine before she sat down to join them.

"I couldn't put anything on my stomach today," Grace said.

Juanita got a Sprite and sat down.

Mrs. Grimes said, "They stole Melba's glasses. I don't know why anybody would do that, do you, Juanita?"

"Who's Melba?"

"They do such strange things around here," Mrs. Grimes said. "Those jigsaw puzzles have two or three pieces missing."

Grace moaned.

"Oh, my stomach. Land's sakes, I'm too sick to die."

"Mrs. Bates died," said Mrs. Grimes.

"She did?" Juanita said.

"She's better off." Mrs. Grimes put her bowl of fruit on the floor. "I don't think cats will eat this. It's got poppyseed dressing on it. Juanita, is Mr. Wilcox still on I.V.?"

"Mr. who?"

"I bet he dies. Mrs. Bates died."

Juanita wheeled Grace back to her room. She helped her mother climb into bed. Grace closed her eyes.

"Juanita?"

"Uh-huh."

"You there?"

"I'm here, Momma."

"Juanita?"

"Yes."

"I saw a nigger yesterday."

"You did what, Momma?"

"There's a nigger man in a room across the hall."

"I'm sure he's sick, Momma. Like you are."

"I didn't know they let niggers in hospitals. I knew they worked in hospitals."

"Can I get you some juice, Momma?"

"Oh, I couldn't put anything on my stomach today."

"What about a glass of milk?"

Grace wailed.

Juanita drank her Sprite.

"Juanita?"

"Yes, Momma."

"I wish you wouldn't smoke."

"I'm not smoking, Momma."

"You're not supposed to smoke in here."

"Want me to brush your hair, Momma?"

"A nigger came in the store all the time. Had that old dog with him."

"What dog was that, Momma?"

"Just a filthy old dog. Came in the store with that nigger."

Juanita helped Grace turn over on her left side.

"Juanita?"

"I'm still here."

"You better go tell the nurses."

"Tell them what?"

"You better go tell the nurses about the nigger in the room over there."

Juanita ran cold water on a rag and Grace laid the rag on her forehead.

As Juanita was leaving the nursing home, she bumped into Boteet, the floor supervisor. She asked Boteet if there was a Mrs. Bates among the residents.

"Oh, sure. Viola Bates," Boteet said.

Juanita wondered how Mrs. Bates was getting along.

"She passed over. About three days ago." The floor supervisor put two sticks of Juicy Fruit in her mouth.

"Passed over?"

"Yep," Boteet said, genially. "Viola Bates has gone in for her last drivin' layup."

Late Friday afternoon, Beecher Perry came into Horb's Cafe and Juanita gave him a hug.

Beecher Perry was neither a regular nor a stray. Beecher Perry was an "occasional," a very rich occasional. He was Beecher Perry of Bookman-Perry Oil &

Gas with offices in Fort Worth, Houston, Midland, London, Aberdeen, Cairo, Peking and Tampico.

Beecher Perry could do his drinking at River Crest Country Club, "21" in New York, the White House, Saudi Arabia, anywhere he wished—and frequently did—but he was also fond of Herb's Cafe. It was a dependable hideout for him.

Herb's was regarded as somewhere in outer space by the wealthy people of Fort Worth. Herb's was in the heart of the old South Side, where the granddaddys lived when they made the fortunes for the heirs who now lived on the West Side.

It was monstrously improbable that Beecher Perry would run into any of his wife's social friends in Herb's, or, more important, that he would run into Edna Perry there. Which was why Beecher Perry brought his young ladies to Herb's.

Beecher Perry's female companions may have been known as young ladies to their pastors, but to Juanita they were steel-bellied airheads.

Juanita once defined a steel-bellied airhead for Tommy Earl Bruner. A steel-bellied airhead was a young woman with a butt like a baby robin, a frightening set of homegrown jugs, and a stomach flatter than the stainless-steel door to the safety deposit boxes.

"She looks best in her stretch-fabric, all-weather fuck suit," Juanita had said.

Tommy Earl's next question was, "How does that differ from somebody you'd like to have a date with?"

Beecher Perry was paunchy, gray-haired, well into his fifties, but he was tan, he dressed expensively casual, and drove antique automobiles.

As different as their interests, bank balances, and friends were, Juanita and Beecher Perry had something in common. Their daughters, Candy Taylor and Babs Perry, once ran together in the Fort Worth subculture.

The fact was not lost on Juanita that Candy and Babs were the same age today as Beecher Perry's steel-bellied airheads, but Juanita figured from everything she had heard about Edna Perry that Beecher deserved a little sporting fun now and then. Edna Perry could outspend the Pentagon, and evidently she only smiled approvingly when she entered homes of 45,000 square feet or more.

Beecher Perry managed to discover steel-bellied airheads the same way other men in other cities did. Word of a new entry traveled like electro-magnetic radiation through the country clubs and saloons where steel-bellied-airhead collectors congregated.

If, for example, Beecher Perry were having a cocktail at the stand-around bar of the Baboon Rocket, he would learn he had another scholarship to grant if he were to overhear one gentleman say to another:

"God damn, Larry, have you seen that good-lookin' little long-haired, big-titted, nasty-talkin', dope-smokin', home-wreckin' son-of-a-bitch down at Rankin Title Company? She just come in here from Cisco. Somebody better scoop her up before she moves to Dallas!"

Beecher Perry had scooped up one of those, and now Tina Busher was with him in Herb's.

"Juanita, this is my long-lost niece," Beecher Perry said. "She'd like a tequila sunrise, and I'd hold me a Chivas-and-soda in abeyance."

Tina Busher's homegrowns were luxurious. They were bursting out of a message T-shirt. Her jeans fit like body paint. Medical science was bound to determine eventually that jeans worn as snugly as Tina's rendered irreparable damage to the cervix.

The message on Tina's T-shirt was not original, but she *was* flaunting it in public:

IF GOD DIDN'T WANT A MAN TO EAT PUSSY, HE WOULDN'T HAVE MADE IT LOOK LIKE A TACO.

The message on the back was:

THEY'RE REAL. 335-2107.

Tina Busher was a diminutive girl. She would be even smaller when she stepped out of her clogs. She had frizzy blond hair brightened in streaks. Her finely carved features wavered more toward cute than beautiful. All this was overwhelmed by her shape, which was, to borrow from the language of the steel-bellied-airhead admirer, "just fuckin' lights-out."

Tina's expression was noticeably sour. Being in the company of a man like Beecher Perry, she may have been disappointed to find herself in Herb's Cafe instead of on a Lear jet making its cheery way to Cuernavaca. But Tina sat patiently at the bar and drank her tequila when she wasn't going to the pay phone or the powder room.

This gave Beecher Perry and Juanita a chance to speak of their daughters.

Juanita was told to be grateful Candy hadn't gone to the University of Texas like Babs Perry had. It wasn't the same university Beecher Perry had known as a Kappa Sig—except for football, of course.

There were sixty thousand students at the University of Texas now. Half of them wore turbans, the other half wore bedsheets. Encircling the campus were one hundred thousand dropouts selling needles and vials. Beecher Perry thought Austin, Texas, made Berkeley of the 60's look like swans and lily pads.

Babs should have graduated three years ago, but she had risen above traditional education.

"Schools are part of the establishment that's putting poison in our food plants," Beecher Perry said with scorn, quoting his daughter.

Beecher wasn't sure which influence had been the worst on Babs, the Communist professor who taught her the Constitution of the United States would have made more sense if it had been written by Donald Duck, or the freak who had lately convinced her not to eat anything but bananas, and fish you could catch with a net.

Babs had cautioned her father to take a close look at the next hurricane to strike Galveston or Port Isabel. It could be God's final warning about aerosol products.

"Babs is such a pretty girl," Juanita said. "I always thought she'd go to New York and be a model."

Beecher Perry said, "I'd settle for an urban guerrilla. They eat right."

Things had looked up for a while in Austin when Babs expressed an interest in real estate. To encourage that interest, Beecher Perry bought Babs an elegant old colonial house near the state capital building. Babs was supposed to remodel the house and put it on the market.

Instead, Babs donated the property to an eighteen-year-old guru. She met the guru at the Soap Creek Saloon one night when Jerry Jeff Walker was falling off the stage. The guru held a two-week series of meditations in the elegant old colonial house before *he* sold it, moved to Malibu, and opened a wind-surfing shop.

Babs now lived in a tree house near Lake Austin. The tree house was multileveled and had a large plastic roof through which the Heavens could be observed at night.

Babs shared the tree house with Heidi and Loraine, her good friends from an all-girl rock band called Family Clothes. Their relationship was so spiritual as to be indescribable. Babs was becoming a freer person by disposing of all her material possessions, although Heidi and Loraine had talked Babs into keeping the Alfa Romeo because Austin did not yet have a rapid transit system.

"I don't know what you're supposed to do about kids," Beecher Perry said.

"Love them," said Juanita. "Hope one day they love you back."

"How's Candy? What's she up to these days?" Beecher emptied his Chivas-and-soda.

"Oh, she's fine," Juanita said. "She's living in Aspen with a cocaine dealer."

Beecher Perry apologized for laughing. Then he said, "God damn, Juanita, I don't think kids have any idea how much Preparation-H they sell."

Tommy Earl Bruner clutched his heart and stumbled into the jukebox. He bumped into a table, knocking over a chair. He fell to the floor. He had seen the art objects in Tina Busher's T-shirt.

Tommy Earl got up, brushed off his denims, and walked toward Tina and Beecher like a man with a clubbed foot and a withered arm, saying, "I believe you're the best-lookin' motherfucker I ever saw."

He rubbed Beecher Perry's stomach.

"How you doin', big guy? Them fuckin' old wind sprints get you down, don't they?"

Grinning at Tina and reaching for his Junior B., Tommy Earl said, "It's a good thing I didn't see you when I had on my white Panama suit and there was a puddle of mud near me. Damn, Beecher. I hope you're gonna put this fucker up on your back and carry her around the world."

Tina Busher said she would settle for another tequila sunrise.

Tommy Earl snapped his fingers at Juanita. "I'll buy you any fuckin' thing you want. Why ain't you in Hollywood? You're stronger'n the Cowboys' Front Four, you know that?"

Tina gave Tommy Earl a subtle once-over.

He said, "What do you do, sell vibrators?"

"I'm a plastic curator," Tina said. "I check out credit cards to see if they belong in a museum."

"You check 'em out in town or on the road?"

"Whatever makes you feel good."

Juanita was putting the tequila sunrise in front of Tina when Tommy Earl said, "Just set it here on them tits, Juanita. It ain't gonna fall off."

Tina Busher turned to Beecher Perry. "Who am I talkin' to?"

Tommy Earl extended his hand. "I'm sorry. I should have introduced myself. I'm Frank Gifford."

Beecher Perry made the proper introductions.

Tommy Earl raised his Junior in a toast to Beecher's discovery of Tina and said, "Them rich folks got it all, don't they, Juanita?"

Tommy Earl once thought he was going to get rich himself—the easy way. When his football career was over at TCU and he proved to be too nonchalant for the NFL, he had gone to work for Loyce Evetts, Jr., TCU's wealthiest alumnus.

Loyce Evetts, Jr. was the heir to a West Texas oil, cattle, and land empire. He had been a TCU classmate and admirer of Tommy Earl's, and he was delighted to hire Tommy Earl, football star, as his personal joke-teller, door-opener and coffee-brewer.

Tommy Earl didn't mind the work at first. Like TCU itself, Tommy Earl expected to come into a vast amount of money from the Evetts family.

For years, TCU had been anticipating an Evetts endowment that would turn it into Stanford overnight. But the university had received only two gifts. One was a row of sycamore trees from Loyce Evetts, Jr.'s mother, now deceased, and the other was an outdoor fountain from Loyce Evetts, Sr., who was still alive but was forced to spend most of his time in a strait jacket while he stared at the sun.

Despite five years of loyalty to Loyce Evetts, Jr., Tommy Earl never received a promotion, raise, or even a stock tip. He resigned. But he did so in a style that made him more of a legend in the city than his two broken-field scampers which nearly beat Arkansas one season.

On a morning when Loyce Evetts, Jr. was in his office lecturing a group of local business leaders, Tommy Earl intruded. He walked over and put a jumbo-size jar of Vaseline on Loyce Evetts, Jr.'s desk.

With that, Tommy Earl pulled down his trousers and his jockey briefs. He bent over and pointed his bare ass at Loyce Evetts, Jr., and said to the other men in the room. "I'm tired of seeing this motherfucker have to work so hard to get anything done, ain't you?"

Two of the business leaders present that day bank-rolled Tommy Earl in the used-car venture. Tommy Earl had still escaped becoming rich, but he was comfortable, a good provider for his wife and children.

Sheila Bruner, Tommy Earl's wife, was a beguiling former Cotton Bowl Princess whose children, little

Tommy Earl and little Sheila, had recently been the cause of her gall bladder removal.

"You know anything about dope?" Tommy Earl now asked Tina Busher, as a joint materialized from his pocket.

"Somebody gimme me this the other day. I don't know what it is. They said if I ever met a lady in the home-entertainment business, she'd explain it to me."

Tina snatched the joint out of Tommy Earl's hand.

She lit it before anyone realized she might do something so brazen—in public, in front of strangers, in a state where hundreds of poor Mexicans and so-called hippies were serving prison sentences for having done nothing worse.

Tina drew on the joint. It burned down by a third. "Woo," she said. "Thank you, Jesus." A pleasant expression came over her for the first time.

"You crazy little shit!" Tommy Earl pryed the joint away from Tina. He squashed it out, stuck it in his mouth, chewed it up and swallowed it. "You snort in public, too?"

Tina said, "You know, I tried cocaine for the first time not long ago. I said if anybody ever offered it to me again, I wouldn't turn it down. Got a toot on you?"

"You're fuckin' perfect," Tommy Earl said. "I bet your armpits taste like apple juice."

Beecher Perry put a hundred-dollar bill in Juanita's hand, instructing her to keep most of it for herself.

"We better head on out," Beecher said to Tina.

Tina eased off the barstool. She reared back and took a deep breath and exaggerated a sigh, purely for the benefit of her male audience.

Tommy Earl was spellbound by Tina's chest and the message about the taco.

"I take it all back, God," he said, shaking his head. "You know what you're doing."

Tina Busher attached herself to Beecher Perry's Ultrasuede arm. As they left, she looked up at Beecher, and said, "Were you a lot of big talk earlier, or can we go light some incense?"

An instant after Tina and Beecher had gone, Tommy Earl grabbed his heart again. He staggered and gagged and plunked down on a stool next to Slick Henderson, who had been drinking in his corner all along.

"That little motherfucker's a hired assassin," Tommy Earl said. "She's wanted in six states for murder. Am I lying to anybody?"

"Yeah, she's a dandy," Slick said. "But a man always needs to remember one thing about a pretty girl. Somewhere, somebody's tired of her."

The regulars multiplied in Herb's Cafe Friday night. The evening brought out Judge Derrell Wishcamper, C. L. Corkins, the insurance man, and Bobby Jay Keeney, the police character, among others. Herb Macklin himself stopped by.

Herb and Shorty Eckwood had been down at Herb's farm near Jacksboro, shooting tin cans, remembering better days.

Nobody called it a farm but Herb Macklin. It was five acres of rocks, brush and ditches with a muddy stream running through it and a screened-in porch attached to two rooms of shotgun shells and baloney sandwiches.

The problem with the farm was, it had an overabundance of S's. Unmentionables. Juanita couldn't even say the word. She would not have the word spoken in her presence. S's were those evil things which slithered through weeds, hid under rocks, coiled up, uncoiled and struck.

Juanita could not even stand to see a picture of an S. If an S came onto the screen in a movie, Juanita stormed out of the theater and spent the next several hours hoping the director, producer, and writer of that movie wound up blind and legless.

Herb's farm featured R. S.'s. In supporting roles, the farm also had Water M's and Copper H's. Juanita almost stepped on a Copper H at Herb's last Fourth of July picnic for the staff. She had been going to the buffet line to see what Oscar Mayer had catered. Her scream may have disturbed people in the next area code.

For the rest of the picnic, Juanita sat cross-legged on the hood of her car, ever alert, praying to almighty God the little shit-ass didn't know how to climb things.

When Shorty Eckwood and Herb came in, Juanita asked Shorty if he had put up the sign yet. She had come up with a slogan to attract new customers to Shorty's Barbecue: IT'S NOT THE BEST—BUT IT'S THE CLOSEST TO WHERE YOU ARE RIGHT NOW.

"Close don't make up for fat," Shorty said, taking his Lone Star to a table.

Judge Derrell Wishcamper sat with C. L. Corkins, drank his Early Times, and detailed a trip he had made to the Odessa, Texas, Holidome for a West Texas Chamber of Commerce meeting. C. L. Corkins, having a club-soda-and-lime, tried to interest the judge in a new household insurance plan.

Bobby Jay Keeney looked debonair as usual in his dark suit, shades and smirk. He stood alone at the bar drinking Jack Daniels, looking through his address book. Bobby Jay was a husky man with waves of black hair.

Bobby Jay used the word "Vegas" to excess, and seemed to enjoy his reputation as an employee of the Fort Worth underworld. No one knew exactly how he earned a living, but Juanita's guess was as good as any: Bobby Jay was a pimp.

"Hi, Bobby," she said when he entered. "How's Al Capone?"

Dr. Neil Forcheimer of the TCU English department was accompanied by two students. One of them was a young man in a battered fatigue jacket. The other was a young woman in a sack dress with her hair in a bun. The students began editing a manuscript at the table.

Dr. Forcheimer said, "Juanita, I've been explaining to Richard and Diane about the vast space of life, the range of it. As we know, life stretches from the squatting East Indian untouchable, a feeder on carrion, to the mind of a Shakespeare, a Spinoza, a Dante. May *this* feeder on carrion have *two* Gibsons, please?"

The students wanted nothing to drink. The young woman did look up from the manuscript and say to Juanita, "Do you serve crème brulée here? I guess not."

A while later, Foster Barton approached Dr. Forcheimer at the literary table.

"What's the English department think about TCU and eight tomorrow? I say no way SMU covers the seven-and-a-half."

"What are SMU's colors?" the professor begged to know.

"Red and blue."

"Ah ha!" said Dr. Forcheimer. "Richer, more intense . . . in some respects even more variant than our purple and white. Well, let me simply say I am as fascinated by color as Goethe was."

"That mean you like SMU, give eight?"

"I will answer that with the crystal clearness and perfect imagery of a Katherine Anne Porter," Dr. Forcheimer said. "Yes."

Herb Macklin announced to the room that he and Shorty were having a tailgate party before the TCU-SMU game. Everyone was invited if they could find his Buick Skylark in the parking lot at the Cotton Bowl on the State Fair grounds.

"I'm supplying the beer," Herb said, standing behind the bar, cleaning his horn-rimmed glasses.

"That's a dish towel," Juanita said.

"What is?" said Herb.

"That dirty rag you're wiping off your glasses with."

"Shit," Herb Macklin said. "How you supposed to clean your glasses if you can't take 'em off?"

Juanita finally got in touch with Candy before the end of the evening. Her long-distance call disrupted a project in Aspen. Candy and Keala were helping Dove prepare a pizza he was going to deliver to a condominium where some movie stars were having a party.

"When did Dove get a pizza oven in the ranch house?"

"Don't be silly, Mom. It's not a real pizza. We're rockin'."

In a Dove Christian pizza, two sheets of wax paper separated the tomato paste and mozzarella from the crust. Between the sheets of wax paper was the quantity of flake which had been ordered, in this case $12,000 worth.

"Candy, I hope to God you don't deliver those things."

"I could," Candy boasted. "It's no big deal. All you do is ring the bell and hand the box to somebody you've seen on TV."

Candy was excited about her mother's chance to write a song for Lonnie Slocum's album. The mother and daughter would have jabbered about it a while longer if Candy hadn't passed along a tidbit of her own.

Narcs were infiltrating the Rockies. That was the rumor. Dove heard it in an Aspen tearoom called Snow White and the Seven Grams. A narc had been sighted in the Dallas Alps.

"Where?"

"Vail," said Candy.

There was no cause for panic. Vail was a long drive from Aspen.

"Don't narcs have cars?"

Candy said, "They're a cinch to spot, Mom. Dove says narcs in ski areas wear new quilted jackets, keep their goggles on top of their heads at night, and drink sherry. They say things like, 'Hey, man, know where I can score some whiff?' Nobody talks like that but a narc."

Juanita said, "Candy, if any narcs come to Aspen, I want you out of there, do you hear me?"

"It's cool, Momma."

"I mean it!"

"We'll be careful, honest. I love you. Write a good song."

"I love you, too, sweetheart, but I don't want you to get busted, damn it!"

Juanita hung up the phone and peered at Esther in the cashier's window.

"Kids," Juanita said. "Jesus."

"I know," Esther said. "I got two. I'd let a lizard run up my spine before I'd have another one."

Chapter Six

Saturday was normally a day when Juanita wallowed in her privacy.

She would put the Willies and Waylons back in their sleeves, categorize her albums, alphabetize the bookshelves. She would weed out her closets, sometimes discovering an old three-piece Kimberly knit suit she could give to the dishwasher's wife.

She would *not* pay bills. She would re-string the Martin, maybe work on a song. She would drink coffee, linger over the morning paper.

Saturday would find her watering the ficus tree, the ivy, the potted chrysanthemums she recognized as an extravagance. They died faster than her cartons of Winstons.

She would tear pages out of catalogues. She would look ahead in *TV Guide* to circle the old black-and-white movies coming up.

She would soak forever in the Vita Bath. Wash out the gray with Loving Care. Squeeze on her face. Do sit-ups. Read Herman Wouk.

Often she just lolled and smoked and daydreamed.

A football Saturday was different. This was a football Saturday and Juanita was engaged in a furious battle with her wardrobe. Slick Henderson, who had arrived to pick up his date, drank coffee and read the paper in the kitchen-breakfast room-den as the battle went on.

Weather was the cause of it. The day was cloudy with a menacing chill in the wind. It wasn't going to freeze and bring every acrylic beaver out of hibernation, but what the well-dressed woman should wear outdoors to the Cotton Bowl and indoors to a restaurant in Dallas was testing Juanita's ingenuity.

As she passed by Slick with an iron, she said, "It's easy to be warm and chic at the same time if you own a sable and don't have anything to do but fuss at decorators."

"Wear Doris' mink," Slick said.

"It's not that cold."

"What do you want with a sable, then?"

"Sables transcend hot or cold."

Juanita wanted to wear her high-heeled Western boots, but what to put with them? She had been wearing boots long before the broncobusters up East discovered them and sent word back to Texas that buckaroo garb was a victimless crime.

All she wanted to do was to put together an outfit that wouldn't imply to the big leaguers of Dallas that she had blown in from Mineral Wells with a U-Haul.

Juanita loved football. Most Texas women loved football or acted as if they loved it whether or not they understood the tactics. Most Texas women had

gone to a high school where football was more important than personal hygiene, a school prone to send
tank divisions and commando units into another
school's neighborhood to avenge a heartbreaking
loss.

Juanita's interest in football had begun before high
school. She was certain it went back to a childhood
when she used to watch the TCU homecoming parade.
Those were the days when the parade was lavish and
held on the streets of downtown Fort Worth.

Parades only happened on momentous occasions.
Football must have been as important as the rodeo, the
circus, Armistice Day. What was Veterans' Day?

In the more glamorous days of the TCU homecoming
parade an odd collection of traffic cops played musical
instruments. They wore white billed caps, white coats
and trousers, and Sam Brown belts that were purple,
not brown. That was the TCU band.

Beautiful girls waved at people from the seatbacks of
slow-moving convertibles. The beautiful girls had dark
red lips, bright pink cheeks, green eyes, and yellow
hair. They wore tailored suits like the ladies who
worked in ready-to-wear. They clung to Greta Garbo
hats.

Cowboys rode by on horses weighted down with
silver ornaments and purple leather saddles. The cowboys carried flags and many of them humorously
pumped their middle fingers at spectators on the side-
walks.

Strange animals turned up in the parade. A longhorn
steer named "Bevo," a pony named "Peruna," a
grizzly bear in a cage towed by a truck. "Here comes
Baylor," Juanita's grandmother had said on one occasion. Funny name for a grizzly bear, Juanita had
thought.

Once a whole army appeared. The soldiers chanted
in a foreign tongue. "Hull-a-ba-loo, ca-neck, ca-neck."
The soldiers' stern faces were fixed straight ahead of
them and they kept marching despite the water bombs,
rotten eggs and fruit that rained down on them from

the rooftops of buildings. The soldiers were Texas Aggies.

"What's an Aggie?" Juanita had asked her grandfather.

He had said, "Aw, it's just an old boy whose daddy made him go to A & M."

The TCU band always stopped in front of the old Texas Hotel, now a Hyatt Regency. The band would form a half-circle around a trumpet player who would imitate Harry James for a group of men in camel's-hair overcoats and white Stetsons who sat on a reviewing stand. This would stop the parade. It would allow a boy on a bicycle to catch up with the homecoming queen's convertible and return her Greta Garbo hat, which would have blown away—up and over the Flatiron Building and down to the T & P station. Downtown Fort Worth lay in the path of a wind that built up momentum in Oklahoma and didn't slow down until it bumped into the Andes.

Juanita had not seen a TCU football game until she was grown, but she had often gaped inquisitively at the big concrete stadium on the campus.

One afternoon, as Juanita's grandparents were taking her on the scenic route from their home on Seminary Hill to Montgomery Ward, a roar had burst out of TCU's stadium. The roar was immense. It grew louder and seemed to hang there, somehow suspended in the air—a gigantic cloud of madness and joy. Then the roar evaporated above the purple, red, green, orange, blue and maroon pennants fluttering on the rim of the stadium.

Juanita was thrilled, mystified. Her granddaddy had said, "Them cheerleaders must have took off their clothes. TCU ain't scored a touchdown since Davy O'Brien throwed a pass."

An autumn Saturday never failed to arouse Juanita. If the game were filled with grave moments and her team won, fine. But that was subordinate to the day itself. There was just something about the gladiators crashing into each other for sporting purposes, the stadiums, crowds, roars, cheerleaders and bands. Juanita even liked halftimes.

Juanita settled on a wool crewneck sweater, a soft-pleated skirt, and Neiman's sincerest copy of a Paris policeman's cape for the excursion to Dallas.

She examined herself in a full-length mirror one last time as Slick held the front door open. She concluded that she was not even remotely in need of an eye job yet.

If nobody in vibrant, burgeoning, big-time Dallas knew how smart she looked, she hoped all of their baby Porsches grew up to have leaking valves together.

Juanita and Slick did not talk much during the drive to Dallas. Slick listened to the radio for a while until Notre Dame built a 72 to 0 lead over Northwestern. Juanita smoked and gave some thought to her "date."

Slick didn't have much hair in front or on top of his head but it was hard to imagine he had ever looked any differently. There was a cheerfulness, a kindness, in his face. He was six feet tall, not overly muscular, in pretty good condition for a man in his early fifties. Age, Juanita believed, was only a chronology.

Merely to look at Slick was to know that he was a patient, logical man. There were people who could fix things and people who could buy new ones. Slick could fix things.

Juanita had liked Slick from the moment she had met him in Herb's three years earlier. He had come in after the gala opening of the Exxon station on the corner where Obena Taggert's Dance Studio had burned to the ground.

She had never had any romantic thoughts about him. He had never acted that interested himself. They had been out together in a group of people, regulars from Herb's, to a TCU game, a Ranger baseball game, Angelo's for barbecue, Joe Garcia's for Mexican food, the White Elephant for Western music, but they weren't *with* each other.

Slick was a friend, a secret-sharer, a confidant,

someone who seemed as interested in preventive loneliness as Juanita, someone who might be just as reluctant as herself to let a relationship get out of control.

To anyone who asked her about him, Juanita would say, "Slick Henderson is one of the good human beings, the kind God didn't make enough of when he came to Texas, and forgot about altogether in Germany."

One evening in Herb's she had said to him, "What did you ever want to be, Slick? You're intelligent. You're aware of everything going on. You don't mind hard work. What did you ever want to amount to?"

He had grinned slyly, and said, "Aw, nothin' big."

Slick was originally from Tulsa, Oklahoma. He had two ex-wives in his past. No children. He had fought in what he cross-referenced as "the Jap-Hitler war." He hadn't finished college at the University of Oklahoma because his education was interrupted by those four years in the army and after the war he had lost his interest in lectures.

He had returned from the war to OU, where a football scholarship awaited him. But he had soon relinquished his job as a second-string defensive end to a more dedicated employee.

One morning an assistant coach had found Slick smoking a Chesterfield in a drugstore near the campus. It had happened during a week in which the Sooners were trying to muster a gallant effort against Bobby Layne and the Texas Longhorns.

The coach had gone into a blind fuming public rage at the sight of Slick smoking a cigarette. Slick was told he had no character, that a man who would break training like that obviously couldn't be trusted to cope with the pressure of a big football game.

"You know, you're right," Slick had said to the assistant coach. "I don't know how college kids handle the pressure. I used to worry about it all the time when I was layin' on my belly waitin' for them fuckin' 88's to start up again."

Slick had been a certified war hero. DSC, Silver Star,

Bronze Star, Combat Infantry Badge, all that. The fact came out on an evening in Herb's Cafe when Slick and Herb Macklin, amply loaded with Budweiser, had started taking bridges the Germans hadn't even built.

It began when Herb complained about his wife, Nadine, cleaning out the attic for a garage sale and getting rid of Herb's war treasures, his old uniforms, German uniforms, swastika armbands, helmets, flags, small weapons.

"She even sold my damn Nazi sword," Herb whimpered.

It happened that Slick Henderson and Herb Macklin had each been in Gen. George Patton's Third Army.

"You're shittin' me," Herb said. "Armored or infantry?"

"Red Diamonds."

"Fifth Division?"

"Pass in review. Eleventh Infantry Regiment, Third Battalion, I Company."

"Hell, I thought the Fifth was a bunch of old boys from New York or somewhere," said Herb.

"I forgot to ask the dead ones where they came from," Slick said. "I was a replacement, but I got there in time for a spelling bee. We did have a second lieutenant from New Jersey. Brendle. Goofy son of a bitch. He didn't want to shoot nothin' but Germans and dice. I think he had a bet he'd be the first asshole across the Rhine."

"I was Second Armored," Herb said.

"You got shot at."

"Some. But we made the end run. We missed Metz, thank the Lord."

Juanita had heard of Bastogne and Aachen. Van Johnson and William Holden and a lot of people had fought there. What was Metz?

Herb Macklin said, "They never made no movies about it, I don't think. Maybe it's because it was one of the shittiest deals we ever got into. Way I heard it, Metz was this siege town in France, about three miles up a cliff. The Germans were up there with ammunition and supplies out their ass. We were down at the bottom. Our tanks ran out of fuel. Goddamn Montgomery had taken it all. For three months our boys fought their way up them three miles with the Germans pouring everything they had at 'em."

"It was straight up, this steep," Slick said. "It rained the whole time. Rain and mud and German shells is all it was. I'll tell you one thing. When them tanks are out of gas, they ain't too easy to push."

Herb looked at Slick with admiration.

"Damn, Slick. Were you at Metz?"

Slick said, "I fuckin' took Metz."

Juanita's war was a bit different. To those who said she had no right to remember it, she was too young, Juanita said that if she could remember chasing balls of lint under a bed on a hardwood floor, she could certainly remember Dec. 7, 1941.

That Sunday had begun for Juanita in a church where a Baptist minister had sent everyone to hell again in a voice that would have made the Pearl Harbor attack sound like woodwinds.

Later on, an older girl on the block, Betty Jean Anderson, had taken Juanita to a double-feature at the Parkway Theater. In one film, a fearless range-rider on a white stallion chased gangsters speeding in automobiles and miraculously caught them. In the other feature, a mere handful of officers in the French Foreign Legion killed a sultan and a thousand caliphs and nawabs while singing an operetta.

Juanita had already seen both movies the day before, along with a Green Hornet serial and a live talent contest for preteen tap dancers whose mothers were coaching them to become Fort Worth's next Ginger Rogers.

When Juanita and Betty Jean Anderson came out of the theater, they ran into two teenage boys from their neighborhood, E. J. Simms and Freckle Belly Scroggins. They were pretending to be riddled by machine-gun bullets.

E. J. Simms raked his hand diagonally across his chest with a sound effect: "Ta-ta-ta-ta-ta." E. J. Simms then sank to the pavement, crying out, "Ah so, kai, yo, kine, aaaaiii!"

"What are yawl doin'?" Betty Jean Anderson had asked.

"We're joinin' the navy tomorrow," E. J. Simms said. "Gonna kill us some Japs."

"Why yawl want to kill Japs? Kato's a Jap."

Freckle Belly Scroggins said, "Him and his kind done bombed Pearl Harbor and we at war."

Juanita distinctly remembered Betty Jean Anderson asking where Pearl Harbor was.

"Los Angeles," said E. J. Simms. "But you don't need to worry. We're joinin' the navy tomorrow and them fuckers won't get no closer than Dumas or Monahans."

Freckle Belly Scroggins was 4-F and became a pool shark. But E. J. Simms became a gunner on a torpedo plane. His plane flew missions off an aircraft carrier. He was gone less than a year before his parents hung a gold star in a front window of their home. E. J. Simms was killed when the pilot of his plane dived into a Japanese destroyer during a battle in the Pacific.

Juanita saw the ribbons and medals in a frame on a piano in the Simms home, and she saw the portrait beside it, the portrait of E. J. Simms in his sailor suit, looking no more than sixteen years old.

Wars weren't fought by John Wayne. They were fought by E. J. Simms and Slick Henderson.

In a deteriorating area east of downtown Dallas, the State Fair's exhibits, amusements, and visitors formed a moat, a redoubt, a Great Wall of China, around the Cotton Bowl.

When Slick had the State Fair in sight, looming beyond the traffic, he said to Juanita, "Hang on."

He then sped, swerved, cornered and braked his LTD into the front yard of an old frame house. A parking place. Pure gold.

The window zipped down and Slick handed a Mexican boy a ten-dollar bill.

"Eight hundred left-hand turns and a bottle of milk," Slick said, pleased with himself.

"What's that?"

"The Indianapolis 500."

They had no time before the game to look for the tailgate party Herb Macklin and Shorty Eckwood were having, but they did walk briskly through the State Fair automobile exhibit where models in swimsuits acted as if the Winnebagos made them tingly.

The TCU Horned Frogs stayed in the thick of the football game right up to, and almost all the way through, the opening kickoff. But the SMU Mustangs recovered the kickoff in the end zone for a touchdown after a TCU lateral escaped the attention of every Horned Frog on the field.

Thereafter, Juanita and Slick amused themselves by counting the fumbles of TCU's star runner, B. E. (Belch 'em Up) Bodiford, and soaked up the splash and color of an autumn Saturday which so enthralled Juanita.

If Foster Barton took the 7½ points and TCU, he did not get to enjoy much pain. SMU won the game by the score of 56 to 3.

It was not a clash to compare with a TCU-SMU game out of the glorious past, a game which had come to be regarded less as an athletic contest than as a treasured interlude in Texas history. The TCU-SMU game of 1935 had become an integral part of Texas folklore. It deserved rank with the Battle of San Jacinto.

On a Saturday in the late November of '35, the two universities from intensely rivaling cities—"Dallas for culture, Fort Worth for fun"—collided with dazzling, powerful, undefeated teams after an entire season of bragging, counter-bragging and suspenseful waiting among their followers.

Two prizes of unbearable importance were at stake in the game. One was the national collegiate championship, or the right to shout, "We're No. 1!" The other was a bid to the Rose Bowl, which meant debauchery at the Brown Derby, taking the glass-bottom boat to Catalina, and hobnobbing with movie stars. Neither prize had ever before been awarded to a Texas team.

The big game was played in Fort Worth. Hollywood and Broadway celebrities came to town in slouch hats, along with newsreel crews, famed broadcasters, syndicated authors, legendary coaches. Tickets were scalped for a hundred dollars each—at the height of the Depression.

TCU's stadium at the time accommodated only twenty-four thousand, but more than forty thousand managed to see the game. They rammed their cars through fences, trampled policemen, and spilled onto the playing field. Three teenage boys named Herb Macklin, Shorty Eckwood and Derrell Wishcamper were among the fans in the stadium that day who whooped and sobbed themselves into fevers over the war that was waged on the tundra by TCU's Slingin' Sammy Baugh and SMU's Bobby (Will-o'-the-Wisp) Wilson along with six other bona fide All-Americans and associates.

In junior high school, Juanita had once been required to memorize the most significant events in the growth of Fort Worth. Her teacher, old lady Dawson, had seriously listed these historic occasions in the order of their importance. They were:

1. The TCU-SMU football game of 1935.

2. The day Vernon Castle, a famous dancer, died in the crash of his training plane during World War I in 1918.

3. The day the Texas and Pacific railroad came to town in 1876.

4. The day in 1902 when the Swift and Armour meatpacking plant opened.

5. The day Maj. Ripley Arnold started an army post called "Fort Worth" to protect settlers from the Indians in 1849.

As Slick drove north on a Dallas expressway toward the three-star restaurant Juanita had chosen for dinner, he said, "The Frogs could have used old Sam Baugh today. Of course, he didn't beat 'em either."

Slick referred to a tragedy unequaled in Fort Worth before or since. TCU lost that big game in 1935. The score had been tied at 14–14 after a whole afternoon of swirling action. But the SMU Mustangs broke the tie in the final three minutes with a daring, fourth-down, 50-yard pass and miraculous touchdown catch by their will-o'-the-wisp, Bobby Wilson, and they were the victors by the score of 20 to 14.

It was a stunning play from which men like Herb Macklin, Shorty Eckwood and Judge Derrell Wishcamper had never completely recovered. Only football could do that in Texas. To this day, Judge Derrell Wishcamper acknowledged TCU's loss as "God's will." Herb Macklin still recalled, "That's the sickest I ever been in my life, including illness." Shorty Eckwood everlastingly referred to the SMU Mustangs as "them lucky turds."

Shorty still wore a large souvenir button pinned to his green plaid Eisenhower jacket when he went to a TCU football game. The button was three inches in diameter, purple and white, and in the center was the photo of a wiry bareheaded man throwing a forward pass. The button proclaimed:

I AM FOR SLINGIN' SAM BAUGH AND THE FIGHTIN' FROGS OF '35—WE'RE NO. 1!

Slick Henderson said in the car, "Doesn't seem right for TCU not to have good football teams any more. Growing up, it was something you expected, like hominy wagons coming down the street."

"They're sort of quaint now, aren't they?" Juanita said, using the rearview mirror for some touching up.

"Well, the Frogs are the only team that ever changed the color of a Texas license plate."

"What do you mean?"

Slick said, "Aw, when TCU came back and won a national championship in '38 with Davey O'Brien and them folks, the Texas license plates a year later were purple and white in honor of it."

"Are you kidding me?"

"Nope. King Football did it . . . with the help of some rich oil men."

"I'll be damned," Juanita mused. "TCU had the first boutique license plate!"

They went to a restaurant called The Wandering Squid.

That was the translation. The name on the canopy was *Le Strange Voyage du Grand Foule Poisson*.

The Wandering Squid was near the lagoon, waterfall, ice rink, driving range, bridle path, safari land, and condominium development of Dallas' newest, biggest and fully enclosed shopping mall, L'Atrium Plaza Northtown Inlet Estuaria.

The restaurant's canopy was pressed between two other lease tenants, Thad's Unisex Face Works and Leetha's Sticky Buns, a pastry shop. Juanita and Slick twice walked past *Le Strange Voyage du Grand Foule Poisson* believing it to be an art cinema.

They stood for ten minutes at the reservations desk and watched the maître d' visit with three young men seated at a table in the main dining room.

The young men all looked alike. They were blonde, glistening with suntans, slender as riding crops. They wore black velvet jackets and their floral shirts were open to their belt buckles. Medallions and trinkets lay against their caramel chests.

"I thought Doris Steadman was the only person with a necklace made out of Marriott room keys," Juanita said.

The maître d' finally welcomed them.

"Oh, hello," he said. "I'm sorry to keep you waiting, but it was so funny. I was telling Barry and Dennis and their friend Raymond about this incredible thing they missed on television while they were in Acapulco."

Juanita and Slick were led through the main dining room's chandeliers and oil paintings to a room with Leroi Neiman prints on the wall and a ceiling fixture from Woolworth's.

The maître d' said, "Do you watch football? Of course you do. Did you see the penalty last Sunday when our Cowboys were playing the Chicago Bears? *Trying* to play them, I should say. Remember the time one of our Cowboys wiggled the ball in the face of that Chicago player? It was after we scored to keep from looking decomposed. I was telling Barry and Dennis and Raymond about it. It seems there's a rule against wiggling the football in someone's face. One of those Jack Whitakers explained it on TV. Did you hear it? The rule is called taunting. I mean, stop it! *Taunting?* We were howling about it just now, Barry and Dennis and I. Raymond doesn't watch football."

"Can we get food in this room?" Slick interrupted.

Ignoring the question, the maître d' said, "I was saying to Barry and Dennis, well, can't you just hear those referees with the microphones hooked up to them in the stadiums and on TV? 'Hey, ho, Eighty-Six. I've caught you taunting again, you silly taunter, you.' Isn't it wild? 'Hi, there, Forty-Four, you vulgar bitch! You're a naughty taunter, that's all you are! I've had my eye on you all day with your touching and feeling and taunting! Well, *I* have the football now, and *I'm* going fifteen yards *this* way!'"

Juanita and Slick were directed to a dark corner by the kitchen door.

"Your waiter will be Evan," said the maître d'. "We're completely out of fish tonight. Also, the soufflé must be ordered in advance. Everything else on the menu is just as marvelous as you've probably heard."

The Wandering Squid's leather-bound menu was much easier to lift than a workbench. It was printed in Chaucer.

Fifteen minutes went by before Evan brought their first drinks, a white-wine spritzer for Juanita and an imported beer for Slick, the only beer served in the restaurant. The beer came in a cologne bottle with three umlauts, two slashes, and a backward letter in the name.

"I don't think fifteen minutes is a slow-play record

for a greyhound joint," Slick said, having clocked Evan.

A greyhound, Slick explained, was someone who looked like he might spend too many hours hanging around the men's rooms of bus stations. Evan was only a latent greyhound now, but one of these days a body-builder in a tank top and a pompadour would come into a men's room at a bus station where Evan happened to be. The sight of the body-builder would be too much for Evan. Evan's eyes would blur, he would begin to whine. Suddenly, Evan would sink to his knees and do a zipper caper on the body-builder.

And just like that, old Evan would go from a latent greyhound to a greyhound.

The third white-wine spritzer led Juanita into her past.

She brought up Weldon Taylor after first passing along the judgment that "discos suck." In discos, people hopped around like turpentined cats. The music in discos sounded like a gang of demented Puerto Ricans had decided to improve on rhythm-and-blues.

"What about the Hustle?" she said. "Do you know what the Hustle is? The Hustle is the old Dallas Push after a Spanish guy fucked with it. If it don't have blues, I can't feel it."

Juanita had been a good dancer in high school. That was how she had met Weldon Taylor.

She had known who Weldon was. Weldon Taylor was a high school celebrity, a football stud, track star, street fighter, and choreographer from Poly High. Juanita and Weldon had gone to different high schools together.

Weldon's school, Poly High, traditionally turned out the city's best dancers. The Poly Rhythm Girls had been famous for years. Getting to be a Poly Rhythm Girl was like getting to be a Kilgore Rangerette. Poly girls taught the Poly boys how to dance. Paschal girls were either Juanita Hutchins, cheerleaders, cadet sponsors or sorority sisters who knew how to get abortions.

In Juanita's high school days the most popular hangout in town was a place called Jack's. It was nothing more than a beer joint on a two-lane road south of town, but Jack's had a large dance floor and the only jukebox in North Central Texas that featured rhythm-and-blues over the songs America was singing about wild geese and doggies in the window.

Juanita would go to Jack's with or without a date. It was acceptable to be without, to go there with other girlfriends. And she was always awed by the sight of Weldon Taylor's smooth, subtle, inventive moves as he pushed, slung, spun and "nigger shuffled" his partners around the floor.

Weldon had an array of partners, each of whom was an arch-backed, tight-skirted, ankle-strapped, spike-heeled sweater girl with a blasé expression.

Juanita had been half-paralyzed the night Weldon asked her to dance the first time. He had come over to a booth where Juanita was drinking a Coke with Priscilla Hunter.

As Weldon talked, he grooved to the beat of *Good Lawdy, Miss Clawdy*.

He had said, "Let's get some R. B. You push?"

"I ain't learned no Dallas yet."

"Poly drag?"

"Slow ones."

"Riverside shag?"

"Little bit."

"You must go to Paschal."

She said, "Yeah, but I'm a senior, so most of the swelling's gone down."

Juanita was tugged onto the dance floor. To her surprise, and Weldon's, she held her own. And she became a minor legend as Weldon Taylor's regular and most imperturbable dancing partner. She also became pregnant.

Juanita and Weldon had driven to Weatherford, a little town west of Fort Worth which once catered to couples in need of hasty marriages or annulments, and Juanita became Mrs. Weldon Taylor before she received her high school diploma.

When he graduated, Weldon's fame as a Poly half-back, broad jumper, street fighter and dancer enabled him to get a job driving a delivery truck. He dropped off bundles of comic books, magazines and out-of-town newspapers to grocery markets and drugstores.

Marriage had a peculiar effect on Weldon, and quickly. He suffered memory lapses. He couldn't remember where he lived, what time it was, or ultimately, that he was even married.

One evening, with Juanita in her seventh month of pregnancy, Weldon did not come home as usual. Home was three rooms in an asbestos-sided duplex near a Santa Fe railroad crossing. Juanita went to the movies that night with Patsy Wage, a charitable woman who lived next door and kept the gravel yard mowed.

They went to the Cowtown Drive-In, which was miles from home but the theater was running *All About Eve* and Juanita had only seen it five times.

Juanita waddled to the concession stand at the Cowtown Drive-In while the cartoons were showing. Returning to Patsy Wage's Plymouth, she was surprised to see Weldon's truck. She walked to the truck carrying a box of buttered popcorn, Milk Duds, and a root beer.

She saw no one in the truck through the window. But as she moved closer, she heard the unmistakable gasps of two people dying. Which was why she yanked open the door.

Juanita then watched in frozen shock as Weldon and a girl clumsily unhinged themselves. The girl may not have been a drum majorette, but there was the evidence of pancake makeup, penciled eyebrows, and a mouthful of chewing gum.

The girl made no effort to put on her clothes. She sat naked in the seat of the truck and looked at the cartoons and popped her gum.

Weldon slowly straightened up behind the steering wheel and lit a cigarette.

"Well, Juanita," he sighed. "You gonna believe me or your own eyes?"

Three hours later that night, Weldon came home and stuffed some things into a duffel bag. He took a six-pack of Pearl out of the refrigerator and went out the door without uttering a word about where he was going, when he was coming back, *if* he was coming back, or what he would like the baby to be named.

Juanita hobbled after him, trembling, tears cascading down her cheeks. Patsy Wage came outdoors to steady her. They stood in the gravel yard and watched Weldon Taylor get into his delivery truck.

Juanita would never see Weldon again, or even hear from him. But before he drove away, she stiffened and hollered out a question:

"If I don't know where to reach you, Weldon, what the *fuck* am I supposed to tell your stockbroker when he calls?"

Chapter Seven

Slick caught Evan in the middle of a death spiral and ordered four more umlauts for himself and a bottle of white wine for Juanita. It would save Slick the trouble of having to use semaphores between drinks. Any wine would be satisfactory, Slick said to the waiter, as long as it weren't a Chateau-le-$44.50.

"Pinot Chardonnay is a nice wine," said Evan.

"So is Gallo."

"I rather imagined you'd say that," Evan simpered, reaching for an overburdened ashtray.

Juanita rescued her cigarette.

Slick then settled back and confessed to Juanita that both of his ex-wives, like Weldon Taylor, had been crackerjack comedians.

The wife to whom Slick had returned from the army was Janet, his old high school sweetheart. Rather curiously, Slick had said good-bye to a Senior Class Favorite but had come home to find a metal-shop teacher.

Janet had done a darn funny thing back in their neighborhood in Tulsa. Almost single-handedly, she had popularized fat arms and screaming over the dinner table.

Slick's parting words to his first wife had been: "Damned if you haven't got me interested in loud voices, Janet. I'm goin' to the opera."

Nothing Janet ever did, however, was as hilarious as the stunt Bonnie pulled, which consequently made Bonnie, Slick's second wife, the wittier of the two women. In only twelve years of marriage, Bonnie fancifully transformed herself from Rita Hayworth into Joseph Stalin.

Bonnie deserved all the credit for driving Slick to a unique psychological discovery, the unearthing of Mankind's Ten Stages of Drunkenness, which were:

- Witty and Charming.
- Rich and Powerful.
- Benevolent.
- Clairvoyant.
- Fuck Dinner.
- Patriotic.
- Crank Up the Enola Gay.
- Witty and Charming, Part II.
- Invisible.
- Bulletproof.

The last stage was almost certain to end a marriage.

Slick had missed Bonnie's roll call one night in Tulsa because he drank himself Bulletproof and became involved with a persuasive home-wrecker who vowed he would not have to remove his socks.

Slick limped home about seven o'clock the next morning. His plan was to sneak into the house through the back door before anyone awakened and curl up on a couch and pretend to have slept there.

But Bonnie was already in the kitchen cracking eggs for her sister and mother, both of whom lived there—another of Bonnie's jokes.

"Where in the holy hell have you been all night?" Bonnie had bellowed.

Slick gingerly solved the riddle. He had worked past midnight on the transmission of a Chevrolet. He hadn't wanted to disturb anybody when he came home. That's why he had slept in the hammock in the backyard.

"I'll have mine over easy," he said.

"You lyin' bastard!" Bonnie exploded. "I took that hammock *down* three weeks ago!"

"Well," Slick had murmured sleepily, wandering off. "That's my story and I'm stickin' to it."

Juanita's second husband was Vern Sandifer.

Vern, as a figure in her past, was almost as distant as Weldon Taylor now, which was why Juanita could entertain thoughts of Vern without a return of the old combat fatigue.

In the five years between Weldon and Vern, Juanita lost the grandparents who raised her. Her grandfather died of a coronary as he sat in the swing on the front porch. He had been sitting there resting, smelling cotton seed from the elevators towering over the freight cars in the distance, and listening to the plaintive sound of beams falling at North Texas Steel up the road. Juanita's grandmother had died a year later because she missed him.

It was during these years that Juanita became adept at tracking down new clinics and sanitariums to keep

Grace occupied. She nursed Candy through everything from mumps to anthrax. And she launched her career in Herb's Cafe as a waitress.

Vern Sandifer sold mud.

Juanita did not understand his line of work immediately, but she was nonetheless attracted to him. Vern was polite, well-groomed, very tan, and had tassels on his loafers. A hundred-dollar bill covered the one-dollar bills in his money-clip.

They met in Herb's when Juanita served him a BLD, the breakfast, lunch and dinner. The BLD was a hamburger steak with melted cheese, scrambled eggs and ketchup on top.

The mud Vern sold was something nobody could drill an oil well without. Mud was pumped into the hole to cut down on the friction as the drilling bit churned away at the rocks and roots to get at the dinosaurs.

Vern's job kept him outdoors in an enchanted land where longhorns rumbled across the purple sage, and lovable old ranch hands sat around campfires telling stories about Wyatt Earp and the Clanton brothers. Vern insisted he worked closely with the independent oil operators themselves, his good friends H. L., Clint, Sid, R. E., Monty, Arch and Hugh Roy.

Juanita envisioned herself lounging in the leather chair of a Petroleum Club watching Candy bouncing around on the knee of Uncle H. L. Hunt.

Herb Macklin gave Juanita fifty dollars for a wedding present. The other waitresses chipped in on a shortie satin nightgown that revived her memory of the Vargas Girl.

And Juanita moved to Wander, Texas, as Mrs. Vern Sandifer.

One thing Vern left out was the trailer.

The Sandifers had to fold up something before they could sit down on something. Candy slept on their backs.

In Wander, Texas, Juanita quickly volunteered a scheme that would make Vern rich: sell shade trees instead of mud. She met no wives or other women around the prefab drilling compounds who had bathed since the Apaches staked them to the ground. Juanita yearned for a paved road, a newspaper, or a valid passport to San Angelo.

The Sandifers got a big break in the second year of their marriage. Vern was transferred to another part of the state, to an encampment somewhere between the Gulf Coast and the Big Thicket. It was, in any case, the humidity core of the universe. Days were described as sunny if the sky looked like cardboard.

But the Sandifers were near a real town with houses for rent. Their own home at last. Juanita planted a groundcover which conquered most of the oil slick in the yard. Candy had numerous insects to play with. For two years, it was the happiest Juanita had been as a married lady.

Juanita went to work in a diner, not realizing it would be her training ground for a return to Herb's. In the diner, she amused herself by asking the customers if they wanted French, Thousand Island, oil and vinegar or petrochemicals on their salad.

Vern started drinking heavily in the swamp. He got depressed about his job. His associates were being promoted and moving to Houston, but he was standing still. The drinking led Vern into escapades with women.

Juanita forgave him the phone call she received at home, the one from a girl who left the message for Vern to meet her at the same motel after she got off work at the roller rink.

Juanita forgave him the lipstick smudges she discovered on his boxer shorts as she sorted through things to put in the wash.

But she didn't forgive him the poetry.

One morning Juanita was on her way to work at the diner. She was going to pick up the cleaning that day so she went to the dresser to take some money out of Vern's wallet. Vern was sleeping off another hangover. Candy was feeding her dead goldfish.

The wallet lay on a cocktail napkin, a momento from Vern's previous evening. There was handwriting, undeniably Vern's, on the cocktail napkin. A ball-point pen.

Vern's poem began, "How do I love thee, Donna Jean? Let me count the ways, you little sportfucker . . ."

That was all Juanita read.

After the suitcases were packed, Juanita went to the bed, put her foot in Vern's back, and pushed him onto the floor.

Glowering down at him, she said. "I believe if me and my little girl try real hard, we can think up something better to do than watch your liver get to be the size of a moving van. I'm narrowing all my problems down to one, buddy. Arithmetic! I'm gonna see how many freeway off-ramps I can count between here and Fort Worth! It hasn't been all bad with you, and I mean that. You've got some good qualities. I'm grateful for the things you've done for Candy. But all in all, Vern, you could fuck up a nigger rent house!"

Juanita went back to Herb's Cafe. She returned to a hometown that was growing and changing. Suburbs were springing from suburbs. New bars were opening in cellars, on rooftops, with pianos, with dart games, with red velvet walls and aquariums.

Which was why Herb Macklin made Juanita a barmaid.

"I need me a pretty lady behind my bar," Herb had said. "Pretty ladies attract men and sell lots of beer and setups if they don't look at theyselves in the mirror too much."

There were no big secrets to tending a bar, Herb had promised. "Keep your limes close to your tonics," he said. "You'll learn soon enough how to grab the mix with one hand and a beer with the other. You'll learn how to open them lower supply doors with your toe and close 'em with the back of your foot. Bend down from the knees. Don't stoop. If you stoop over a lot, your back'll go on you quicker than a sick dog. Measuring whisky in a hurry ain't nothin' but a feeling you acquire. Smile at folks. Learn everybody's name. That's how you get them tips. I say in no time at all you'll be an out-and-out mercenary."

Juanita had consented to take the job if it wasn't mandatory she wear a low-cut peasant blouse.

Herb had added, "I got me something better than a pretty bartender. You done got worldly, Juanita, if you don't mind me saying so. I can tell by looking in your eyes. I bet you can smell a load of bullshit a hundred miles this side of the state legislature."

Juanita had not been all that interested in the further adventures of Vern Sandifer, but she was kept up to date by Vern's sister in Sulphur Springs. Twice a year, Vern's sister called to tell Juanita about Vern making peace with God and becoming a new man.

Vern remarried. A good woman named Irene. Vern had met Irene in a Bible-study group. Vern had left the mud business and had taken up God's work on behalf of a Christian radio station in Laredo. Irene owned the radio station.

One night in Nuevo Laredo, however, God made the mistake of leaving Vern on his own for a few hours. Vern had been killed when his Mercury Cougar plowed into the front of a combination tamale factory and costume rental company.

Vern was found in the car wearing only a sport coat and socks. An empty bottle of tequila was locked in his hand. There was a cocktail napkin stuffed in his coat pocket on which Vern had apparently begun to write a poem. Scribbled on the napkin was:

"How do I love thee, Dolores and Consuelo? Get thee over here and sit down on my face, you little bandits . . ."

The check at The Wandering Squid was $147.39.

Juanita laughed out loud when she saw it. Slick said it was a bargain. Now he knew, once and for all, he never had to eat anything in Texas again but Mexican food, barbecue, chicken-fried steak and country sausage.

"You didn't like your rubber bands?" Juanita couldn't hide a smile. "You should have ordered the little sponges."

"I tried your little sponges. They tasted like my rubber bands."

"No, they didn't. Your rubber bands were dipped in Almaden and chicken broth. My little sponges were dipped in Campbell's Hot Dog Bean before they stuck them back in my seashell."

"What do you suppose it was they splattered on my square spaghetti?"

"I'm not sure. It had basil in it."

"Basil served it."

"Basil leaves," Juanita said, rising, pulling on her Paris policeman's cape.

"I imagine if we look around in here we can find us a greyhound named Basil."

Juanita stopped to speak to the maître d' as they were leaving *Le Strange Voyage du Grand Foule Poisson*.

"Excuse me," she said. "We want to come back again real soon. But do me a favor. I've written my Fort Worth address on this matchbook. Would you be kind enough to drop me a postcard whenever you think your catch-of-the-day might be a can of Bumble Bee tuna?"

Slick took the road home that was still known as the turnpike although there were no longer any toll booths on it. The turnpike was a thirty-five-mile laser beam connecting a cluster of downtown Dallas banks holding mortgages on the entire South to a reduced Fort Worth skyline, which, when the buildings were outlined in Christmas lights, looked as if it ought to be sitting on top of a cake.

Between the two skylines were a thousand Dairy Queens and Self Serv islands calling themselves the Metroplex.

Juanita woke up from her nap when Slick stopped at a full-service Exxon in Fort Worth to get gas. He handed a twenty-dollar bill to a plump girl servicing the windshield.

"You got the real time of night?" Slick asked the girl.

"Sir, I don't," she said. "We was all down at Lake Granbury the other day when it was warm. An old boy shoved me off the dock. He knew I couldn't swim, too. Friend of mine fished me out before I drowned. My watch came off in that dirty water. Nobody ever did find it. I could have killed Olin Milford. He's the reason I can't tell you what time it is. I'm sorry. Here's your change."

Juanita lit a cigarette as Slick drove away.

"I love Texas, Goddamn it," she laughed. "It's the only place in the world where you can ask somebody a question and get back a plot."

"You love all of Texas?"

"Everything but the S's."

"You don't love the Panhandle."

"Sure I do. Old Amarillo High nicknamed its football team the Golden Sandstorm—on purpose. You have to love *that*."

"Isn't Wander in the Panhandle?"

"South Plains. I say Abilene's pure West Texas. Lubbock's the South Plains. Amarillo's the Panhandle. Are the High Plains the same as the South Plains?"

"You're the Texan."

Juanita dwelled on how many varied regions there were in Texas, of how abruptly the land could change, of the sprawling scrubby flatlands where it never seemed to change.

The person who had never seen Texas had been educated to think of it as a land where every home was designed in the conventional architecture of Hoss Cartright's hat and rhinestone oil derricks passed for shrubbery. That was Hollywood's lie. But Texas was simply a place where God had conducted a broad geographical experiment and merely forgot to paint half of it.

"Let's see," Juanita said. "There's West Texas . . . South Plains. Panhandle. Gulf Coast. Houston . . . which is its own place."

"King Ranch," Slick said.

"Austin and the Hill Country."

They were playing a game. Regions of Texas.

"Padre Island," said Slick.

"Big Bend."

"East Texas. Or Piney Woods. Whatever you call it."

"The Big Thicket."

"Cotton Belt."

"The Border."

"Edwards Plateau."

"The Valley."

"Mexiplex," said Slick.

"What?"

"San Antonio."

Letting that pass without a laugh, Juanita said, "It's amazing. You can go from a desert to a mountain . . . to rolling hills . . . a forest . . . wind up in an ocean. And never leave Texas."

"Yeah, I guess so," Slick said. "Of course, if you start out on the other side of that old Red River where I come from, you ain't goin' nowhere but Baja Oklahoma."

"Is that a fact?" Juanita bristled, blowing cigarette smoke at the driver. "Listen, friend. I've spent my whole life in Texas. Most of the time, I couldn't go to Baker's Shoe Store without matching funds from H.E.W. *That's* when you're living in Baja Oklahoma!"

Slick invited himself into Juanita's apartment and wondered aloud if he was going to get laid for the $147.39 dinner he bought.

Juanita thought not.

She had no moral hangups about it, and it wasn't as though she had to answer to a big sister in Pi Phi. In fact, Juanita said, under other circumstances perhaps, assuming Slick was not acting interested just to make her feel feminine, she might have to show him one of

110

these nights that she could still go three miles over brush and timber. But right now, quite frankly, she had a song on her mind.

Juanita tossed her Paris policeman's cape on the sofa and went to the bedroom to get her Martin.

The maplewood flat-finished Martin had represented the most outrageous luxury of her life when she bought it in 1971 for four hundred dollars. But Lonnie Slocum assured her the Martin was a good investment, even if she never learned to play it better than an acid head who was into heavy metal.

The Martin was worth maybe $1,000 now. There were other good guitars, Gibsons, Ovations, Guilds, Yamahas, but an old steel-string acoustical Martin was like picking air compared to the others. And the clincher was that Willie Nelson's guitar was a Martin.

Juanita went to the sofa with her guitar. The yellow legal pad and Pentel were on the coffee table.

Slick reclined in the chair with the ottoman. He was asleep before he turned two pages in a current issue of *Sports Illustrated* with a family of Nigerian joggers on the cover.

About an hour and a half later, Slick was jolted out of his sleep by Juanita shaking him, saying, "Sit up."

Juanita arranged herself on the ottoman in her sweater, skirt and boots. She strummed the Martin.

"What's going on?" Slick stammered.

"Be quiet."

Juanita then picked an original melody and sang "Baja Oklahoma" for him in a voice that was one third Loretta Lynn, one third Tammy Wynette, and one third ragweed allergy.

> *It's in the schoolyards on the faces*
> *Of the children playing games.*
> *It's a pasture looking greener*
> *In the spring and summer rains.*
> *It's a highway going nowhere*
> *As far as you can see.*
> *It's a cowboy singing songs*

About his craving to be free.
It's a river flowing gently
Through an older part of town.
It's a sky that's all around you
Touching every patch of ground.
It's a prairie where the wind
Can't ever tell which way to blow.
It's our heroes getting taller
In that tiny Alamo.
It's the laughter you can carry
Through the years that turn you old.
It's "Baja Oklahoma,"
But it's Texas in your soul!

Juanita was radiant. This was a performance.

It's a skyline swiftly rising
And poking at a star.
It's a thicket's tangled branches
Turning daylight into dark.
It's the breeze along the beaches
Where the gulf is at your feet.
It's a lonely town imprisoned
By the dust and the mesquite.
It's a drive across the border
To the music and the sin.
It's the blue that's in a norther,
It's football games to win.
It's a roundup stirring mem'ries
Of the rough-and-tumble days.
It's a detour off the freeway
To see where you were raised.
It's the laughter you can carry
Through the years that turn you old.
It's "Baja Oklahoma,"
But it's Texas in your soul!

Slick got out of his chair. "That almost makes me like Texas." He began to walk around the room. "Seriously, that's not half bad. Can I have a cup of instant?"

"I knew you'd like it," Juanita said, glowing.

"I didn't say I liked it."

"Yes you did. You just didn't say it out loud."

Slick looked at her, then started for the kitchen-breakfast room-den. "I *did* say I wanted a cup of coffee. I remember that part."

Juanita followed him, saying, "This is the song for Lonnie's album, Slick. I can feel it. If I get a song published, will you carry me off the field on your shoulders? Tear down the goal posts? Do some American thing like that?"

She turned on the fire under the kettle.

Slick was reaching for a cigarette when he said, "Well, I know one thing. Lonnie Slocum never said anything he couldn't take back."

"What do you mean?"

"Nothing."

"Yes you do."

"Aw, I don't know," he said. "I just wouldn't count on Lonnie too much, that's all."

"Lonnie's my friend, Slick. He wouldn't get my hopes up about something like his album if he weren't serious. He knows how much it means to me."

Slick said he was sure Lonnie wouldn't. Provided Lonnie remembered the definition of serious. A good part of the time Lonnie's brain was darker than the inside of a wolf's mouth.

Juanita struck a kitchen match to a Winston.

Slick said, "There's something else you ought to consider. Even if Lonnie likes your song—this one, or another one—he's got all those Nashville folks to deal with. Music executives and producers. What if they don't like your song? I doubt if that'll keep Lonnie from going ahead with the album."

"You really know how to make a lady feel good, you know that?"

"I've got another idea. It's been on my mind."

"What? Be happy tending bar?"

"I think you ought to take your songs over to Old Jeemy at KOXX. He knows everybody in the industry.

If your songs are any good, he'll know it. He'll know what to do with them. If Old Jeemy likes your songs, he can get 'em published while Lonnie's sniffing up dust on furniture."

"You must be joking."

Slick wasn't joking.

"I can't tell you what a dumb idea that is."

Slick didn't think it was a dumb idea.

"It's not even insane. It's just dumb."

Slick said, "All I know is, Old Jeemy's got influence in the business, and Lonnie Slocum can't remember what yesterday was like."

Juanita flicked ashes on her floor and kicked at the dark red vinyl tile.

"What the hell would I do if I went to see Old Jeemy?" she said. "I've never met him. I've never even *seen* him. Do you know how many stupid people do that kind of thing? Do you really? Twice a day somebody goes up to Old Jeemy and says, 'You don't know me but my name's Juanita Hutchins and I've written this song. Everybody says it's real good. It's a song about my husband's hemorrhoid operation when he was in prison and my Momma was dying in the rain. I think Tanya Tucker could make a hit record out of it.' Old Jeemy says, 'Happy to meet you, little lady. Who have you been writing songs for up to now?' The stupid idiot—that's me—says, 'Oh, I've written songs for Slick Henderson . . . Doris Steadman . . . Herb Macklin . . . almost anybody you can name.' Old Jeemy smiles and says, 'I'll sure take a hard look at your material.' The stupid idiot thanks him and leaves, and Old Jeemy throws the songs in the wastebasket."

Juanita drenched two coffee mugs with boiling water. A river ran across her countertop. She handed a mug to Slick and ripped a wad of paper towels off a roller attached to the wall. Slick retreated to the butcher-block table.

"How do you know that's what happens?" Slick said, putting the mug down. "You've never tried it. Might be one reason you're still working in a bar."

Juanita's eyes flashed, and she said, "I work in a bar because Prince Charles broke the engagement!"

Slick said, "Okay. Take it easy."

"And by the way," she added, "I don't need to be reminded about what I've done with my life by the king of the unleaded gas pump!"

"Whoa," Slick said. "Hold on! I didn't mean to make you hot. I think more highly of a good bartender than I do a good songwriter."

He went to her and put his hands at her waist. He drew her close to him. He kissed her on the forehead politely, a brotherly kiss. Then on the cheek.

"I was only trying to be helpful, babe," he said with unrestrained affection. "I was thinking it couldn't hurt to go see Old Jeemy. Give yourself more than one chance. If Lonnie doesn't come through in Nashville, well . . . maybe Old Jeemy could do something. That's all I had in mind. I'm rooting for you, don't you know that?"

"I'm not really mad," she said, truthfully.

Slick kissed her on the cheek again, not so brotherly. He gathered her up more firmly.

"You okay?"

"Yes," Juanita said softly. "I know you care about me."

She hugged him and put her head on his shoulder and he kissed her on the neck, the ear.

"I can think of a couple of things we can do right now . . . this time of night," Slick said, his tone more honeyed, his hand caressing her back. "You could let me hear that old song of yours again . . . if you want to. Or . . . we could stroll on in there to your bedroom. Maybe get to know each other a little better. That, uh . . . that would sort of get my vote."

Juanita voted for the song.

She eagerly led Slick into the living room and cuddled up with her guitar on the sofa and sang "Baja Oklahoma" three more times before he went home.

PART TWO

*They Hadn't Ought to Have Gone Ahead
and Did It Like They Went On and
Done It Because They Knowed They'd
Did Them Kind of Things Before*

Chapter Eight

A cold gray windy mist arrived in the city. It was called November. Juanita drove past Wuthering Heights on her way to work each day and went home in the evenings through the nicer sections of Smolensk.

She made side trips to the nursing center. Grace and the tapioca pudding were maintaining a status quo. There were phone calls to Aspen. The narcs were still a rumor and the tooth powder business was flourishing. Dove was talking twin Cessna.

Juanita settled on a tempo for "Baja Oklahoma." It landed somewhere between Bob Wills' "Faded Love" and Willie Nelson's "On the Road Again." After another rehearsal or two, she would put the song on a blank cassette and send it to Lonnie Slocum in Nashville.

Juanita went on another date with Slick Henderson, to dinner and a movie. They dined at Shorty's Barbecue where the ribs were still fatter than Janet's arms. They saw a foreign film in which a man and women either sulked in subtitles or skipped through fields of wildflowers. Juanita felt cheated. "How can they make a foreign movie without any rain in it?" she complained.

The big news of early November was Doris Steadman's decision to go totally pink. "I'm creating an aura around myself," Doris confided to Juanita as the two women sat alone in Herb's on a day when the wind was trying to warp the casement window.

"Pink is my favorite color," Doris was saying. She had dressed for work that Thursday in a pink summerweight suit and a pink wool coat. "Pink gives me pleasure. Pleasure attracts pleasure. My color will attract good things. If you eliminate the colors you don't like from your life, you eliminate aggression. My spirit will be unleashed. I will become the person I was meant to be."

Doris had been reading a self-help book titled *Tricky Woman* by an author named Florabelle Payne. Doris may have misinterpreted something in the book, or, on the other hand, Florabelle Payne may have been a loon.

It was too late in the year for Doris to have the exterior of her French provincial town house painted pink. Same for the Granada. Those projects would be held off until the house and car survived the winter.

But Doris' bedroom walls were going pink. All of her gowns, robes and lingerie. Most of her wardrobe. The towels, sheets, spreads and linens. Not everything in the house; only the things directly affecting her life.

Doris had begun to write with pink pens on pink stationery. Pink telephones had been installed.

The pink carpet throughout the house was almost in. Lee was in the business. The carpet was shag but it was pink. Doris' bathroom had been pink to begin with, everything but the scales. That was corrected. She had never used anything but pink Sofpac double-layer tissues.

All of the curtains and drapes had pink in them, anyway. They stayed. All of her figurines that weren't pink—out.

"Have you noticed any change in yourself?" Juanita was drinking coffee as if it were going off the market in a matter of hours.

"You can't expect it to work real good until you get completely pink," Doris said.

"Is it supposed to improve your relationship with Lee?"

Doris wrinkled her nose. "Why the hell would I do it for Lee?"

Juanita turned the dial on her radio to KOXX and picked up Music for Mourners. The voice of Old Jeemy oozed into the bar.

". . . so you just tell them folks at Bad Bob's Office Furniture that I sent you. If Old Jeemy didn't send you, you didn't go! Friends, here's a public-service announcement from the Texas Highway Safety Department. When you're shovelin' in the coal on them freeways, think about somebody shovelin' in the dirt on your casket. Thankee."

Juanita lowered the volume on Tanya Tucker's "Texas When I Die."

Doris continued, "If I surround myself with *my* color, there's more of *me* to attract the good things in life *to* me. Florabelle Payne makes it real interesting."

Juanita wondered how many pages it took for Florabelle Payne to tell her readers to pay more attention to the good things in life than the bad things in life.

"There's no bad," said Doris. "We are *all* good. That's what makes the book so different. We are all good but we desire to be better. Florabelle Payne tells you how. You have to look yourself up among all the good personalities, then you turn to the Improvement section and she tells you ways to get better."

Disdain would be an apt word for the look on Juanita's face.

"Don't take my word for it, Juanita. The book's a damn best-seller!"

Spinach pasta removed all limitations on the use of color, if one were to believe Florabelle Payne in *Tricky Woman*. The first sighting of green noodles in avantgarde American restaurants—and their acceptance without widespread rioting—had broken every color barrier.

"So I did my hair," Doris said, coyly.

"Your hair is the same."

"I mean the other."

"What other?"

Doris glanced at her lap.

Juanita's mind rejected that for a moment.

"Doris, are you talking about . . . what you're talking about? You did your deal?"

"It's pink."

"It's *pink?*"

"Well, it's as close as I could get it," Doris said.

Ordinarily, Juanita would have wanted more time to adjust to that revelation, but she was eager to hear the details of how, exactly, Doris had managed it.

"Common sense," said Doris. "I bleached it with peroxide and then I dyed it."

"I don't know why this occurs to me, but can you buy pink hair coloring?"

"Not that I could find. I could have used red, but I was afraid it would come out too red."

"Red's not your color."

"I mixed Clairol Light Auburn with more peroxide."

"What did you put it on with?"

"Lee's toothbrush."

Juanita was inhaling a Winston just then. Momentarily, her lungs acted like the game was up.

"Did you expect me to use my *own?*" Doris said, sullenly. "I'm not a damn pervert, Juanita!"

A final question from the barmaid. What could Doris do with it now—with her deal—that she couldn't do before?

"Florabelle Payne makes a big point out of creating happy surprises for your lovers."

Doris went back to work—to give Ross Wickley a happy surprise on his office couch. Juanita's mind was briefly occupied with soap operas. The Edge of Pink. As the Pink Turns. Can Doris Steadman go in for her sterility test, after all? Who would be cruel enough to blow air up the Fallopian tubes of anything dressed so daintily? Will Fred, the gynecologist, ask for the name of Doris' decorator? Will Lee Steadman get a matching geranium?

Juanita decided to withhold any strong opinions on the project until she heard a report on what the early tests proved. It was conceivable that Doris had hit upon something unique in the use of visual stimuli.

On Friday in that first week of November, Juanita went to the Trinity River Nursing Center and caught up with Grace in Mrs. Grimes's room. Juanita overheard Grace and Mrs. Grimes laughing and talking as she turned a corner of the hallway, but when Juanita walked into the room, Grace had a sinking spell.

"Oh, I would just give anything not to be sick," Grace moaned.

Grace and Mrs. Grimes were having lunch together. Mrs. Grimes was sitting up in bed with a tray and Grace had wheeled herself to a table.

"What is it, Momma?"

Grace was unable to reply. She closed her eyes and held her side.

"Is it the food, Momma?"

"Oh, Lord," Grace said, weakly.

"Do you have a headache?"

"Oh, no," said Grace. "If I had a headache, I wouldn't be able to stand it."

Mrs. Grimes said, "It's the smothered steak or the green beans."

Juanita suggested they go to Grace's room, where her mother could lie down.

"I couldn't move right now," Grace said. "I didn't sleep all night. I'd give anything to be well. Nobody knows what it's like to be this sick."

Grace held out a hand, her eyes still closed. "Juanita?"

Juanita took Grace's hand.

Grace said, "I worry so much about you in that old bar. In there with all those nasty men."

"I'm fine, Momma."

"I should have given you a pony."

"What?"

"You wanted a pony when you were a little girl, but there were so many medical bills."

"I remember wanting a bicycle."

"Oh, my word. Cars run into bicycles all the time."

Grace opened her eyes and released Juanita's hand. She took a bite of smothered steak and sipped some coffee.

"I shouldn't eat this," Grace said. "Lord only knows what it's going to do to me."

"I wouldn't let her touch those green beans," Mrs. Grimes cautioned.

Boteet, the floor supervisor, looked in the room with a cheerful smile. Juanita let Boteet in on the secret that Grace wasn't having a very good day.

"That right, Jack?" Boteet said to Grace, spinning Grace's wheelchair around. "Let's get you back in the box, then."

Juanita and Slick had the third date in their current series on Saturday night. They explored the old stockyards area north of downtown to see how Exchange Avenue was coming along in the throes of a much-talked-about renaissance.

Exchange Avenue was where the Fort Worth Live Stock Exchange was located, along with the meat-packing plants, the indoor rodeo arena, and the cattle pens, barns, saloons, cafés, saddle shops, boot stores, corrals, hotels and whorehouses where hundreds of cattle drives had ended.

For more than a century, Exchange Avenue had been notorious. Its fame had spread after a day in 1887 when Luke Short, a gambler, gunned down Long Hair Jim Courtright, a private detective, in front of the White Elephant Saloon.

In the old days, Exchange Avenue was not even a safe place for your big tough legendary Texas Ranger.

North Siders liked to reminisce about the time Ranger J. G. Hightower went looking for a bar-wrecking bad-ass named Buttermilk Collier in the Fandangle Lounge.

Ranger J. G. Hightower swaggered into the Fandangle Lounge wearing his neatly pressed khaki uniform with badges and patches stuck all over it, his Stetson at a mean eyebrow level.

"I'm J. G. Hightower and this riot's over," said the Ranger.

That was when Buttermilk Collier started laughing at the "sissy-dressed queer" in the room and took J. G. Hightower's pearl-handled popgun away from him and made him drop his pants and hop around like a kangaroo.

"One riot, one Ranger," Buttermilk Collier had said.

Those days were gone now. The packing plants had been closed for years, and the rodeo had long since moved to a larger coliseum in a better part of town, taking with it the annual Southwestern Exposition & Fat Stock Show.

All that remained were memories and some of the creaking buildings, which were being remodeled and preserved by groups of heritage-minded citizens.

Juanita and Slick ate dinner on Exchange Avenue at The Longhorn Chili Episode.

It was a quaint little remodeled storefront restaurant bordered by two other quaint little remodeled storefront restaurants, Le Boutique du Calf Fry and Mommy's Trust Fund. Across the street were Missouri Matt's disco, Clifford and Rodney's Manly Footwear, and the Right Hotel, which was becoming a Duck and Ale.

Juanita and Slick took a table by the window where they could look out on the spot where Luke Short outdrew Long Hair Jim Courtright. Now they could see men in Italian loafers strolling with women wearing necklaces made out of shellacked squashes.

Juanita drank Margaritas, bowing to the myth that Margaritas went well with chili and Mexican food. But she would have only three. People who drank more than three Margaritas did not eat anything but bathroom porcelain or bed pillows. Slick was loyal to Budweiser.

On her second Margarita, Juanita launched an attack on both women and marriage. Something she had heard on a TV talk show that day brought it up.

"The cliché is, women spend all the money," Juanita said. "Maybe we do spend most of it on things that are necessary, but I've never known a man to deprive himself of a Tina Busher if he wanted one."

"That doesn't come out of his salary," Slick said. "That comes out of his expense account."

Juanita said, "Do you know what the three lowest-paying jobs in America are? Cooking, cleaning and raising children."

Juanita put forth the theory that a wife's salary level and bonuses were directly related to how well a wife maintained her looks and ran the household. Even if a wife sensed the presence of a Tina Busher in her husband's life, her tendency was to ignore the mistress as long as her close friends didn't find out about her, and the wife didn't have to take a cut in pay.

This was called "working at a marriage."

"Women have the last word," Slick said. "We die and you don't."

It was only fair, said Juanita. The wife deserved a reward for being the Designated Shit-Taker in the marriage.

The husband enjoyed the fun of introducing his Tina Bushers to veal piccata and first-class air travel, and the wife got the new linen drapes and took the shit.

A Margarita pause.

"Then he dies and it's old Slim's turn," Juanita said. "Slim?"

"The wife."

Old Slim wound up with the window-and-door frame

business, the house on Autumn Lane, the cabin down at the lake, the savings books, the C.D.s, and eighty acres of vacant land where oil would be discovered, now that the husband was dead.

But most of old Slim's fun would come from getting to designate the new shit-takers.

"Her kids are the first," Juanita said. "Old Slim's grownup son wants a Mercedes like everybody else has, and her grownup daughter wants a marble foyer and a sectional divan the eighth grade can do a tumbling act on. Old Slim's got the money. But the kids have to eat all the shit between Corsicana and Waxahachie before Slim turns loose of it."

"That's it, huh? Man works and dies. Wife lives and stays pissed off."

"Yep. Amazing thing, too. Old Slim never smiles."

Juanita had always been puzzled by the fact that women had trouble laughing—like Doris, for instance. And rich women, as a species, rarely even smiled. What had been responsible for this human condition? Parents? Husbands? Kids? Operations? Churches? Teachers? Sororities?

Juanita didn't have the answer. She only knew that if she were a rich woman herself, she would wake up every morning and grab her sides with laughter. She would laugh so convulsively, she would bounce off furniture and regularly break every piece of Baccarat and Steuben she owned. Then she would laugh even harder as she went to the stores to replace it.

Now there was another problem. The Lib movement was drastically cutting down on what little laughter existed among women in the first place.

It seemed to Juanita that Libs ran in clusters, like motorcycle gangs, and the ones who shouted at her on television seemed bitterly opposed to laughter.

That was an obvious mistake, if you were into the ERA and things, and it had something to do with the fact that Lib infections were spreading very slowly in Texas.

The Libs needed a PR Lib. Somebody to make sure the Libs who went on television looked more like Miss Universe entries and less like ironworkers.

Juanita said to Slick, "You probably never got married again because of the Great Female Laughter Gap."

"No, that wasn't it," said Slick. "I think I never got married again for the same reason I became a mechanic."

"Oh?"

"You can't get a good night's sleep when you're married, even if you're happy. Somebody's always bothering you in bed. But it's cool and shady underneath a car."

Slick Henderson didn't get laid again Saturday night, but not because of that remark alone.

Juanita was at work by noon the next day. She worked in the daytime on Sundays to make extra money. She didn't mind working on Sundays during football season. The big color TV set up in a corner of the bar usually turned Herb's into a festive place.

Her first customers were Slick, Shorty Eckwood and Tommy Earl Bruner.

Tommy Earl was wretchedly hung over. He gulped three Bloody Marys and munched two stalks of celery in each drink, which prompted Shorty to ask for a stalk of celery to go with his Lone Star. Tommy Earl ordered six eggs over-easy and sat at the bar and slashed the eggs into over-easy soup and ate them in a way that sounded like a plunger unstopping a toilet.

"Sheila visiting her mother?" Juanita asked Tommy Earl, knowing the answer.

"Yeah," Tommy Earl said, sighing heavily. "That Goddamn city ordinance is about to kill me, too."

"Which one's that?" said Slick, having coffee.

Tommy Earl said, "The city ordinance that says when your wife's out of town you got to drink all the Junior you can get your hands on and fuck them homewreckers all night."

128

Tommy Earl held his head.

Foster Barton came in through the side door with his wife Susan and their three children, all under the age of ten. The Bartons were in for Sunday brunch, as was their custom.

"I had a surprise guest at the funeral home this morning," Foster said to Juanita. "My old friend Mrs. Scott. I've known Paula Scott for thirty years. She looks awfully pretty in the blue dress her niece picked out for her."

"She looks lovely," Susan Barton said.

"I know she would be very pleased with the roses, too," Foster assured everyone with a smile.

"How'd old Paula get in the end zone?" Juanita asked.

"Just age," Foster Barton said, leading Susan and the children into the dining room for brunch.

A table was soon taken by Dr. Neil Forcheimer of the TCU English department and three students, two young men and one young woman. The students each wore a trenchcoat with the collar turned up. They all carried spiral notebooks and chain-smoked.

The students were enrolled in an advanced English course of Dr. Forcheimer's, *Peasant Taste in Creative Writing*. The class met two nights a week in the professor's home where Dr. Forcheimer served chicken-skin sandwiches, avocado dip and Chianti.

This was apparently a field trip.

Dr. Forcheimer said, "Juanita, I have explained to Mark, Jason, and Suzanne here that it was precisely in places like Herb's that Dreiser learned to capture the essence of brakemen's daughters and laundry girls."

"Eating or drinking?" Juanita said, standing at their table.

"Suisse Mocha," said the young woman.

The other trenchcoats ordered.

"Cappuccino," said one.

"Espresso," said the other.

"Three coffees," Juanita surmised, turning to the professor.

"A Gibson, please."

"At *noon?*"

The professor raised an eyebrow and reached for a cigarette. "Juanita, the four great novelists, Tolstoy, Dostoyevsky, Dickens and Balzac, were lousy craftsmen. But they saw deeply into people, and they often found the scum of the earth to be quite decent. Were you of their mind, you would know that despite the time of day, this scum *does* want a Gibson."

"I couldn't agree more about craftsmanship," the young woman quickly said to the professor. "The Victorians would certainly have written briefer had they possessed Eudora Welty's gift for knowing where to put the kernel, the nut, in their stories."

"Oh, God!" said one of the young men. "Here she goes again, working up to that old recognition-breeds-decadence argument of hers. We *all* know it was responsible for Fitzgerald's formlessness and Thomas Wolfe's metaphorical enslavement."

Dr. Forcheimer said to the table, "But they were, like Marquand, happier for their ignorance, weren't they?"

"I'm sure it doesn't matter in the least to Suzanne," one of the trenchcoats said. "She'll insist that only Thomas Mann was capable of exploring the inner life."

"Do you *deny* it?" said the young woman.

The students began taking off their trenchcoats.

Juanita delivered the Gibson and three cups of coffee to the professor and the students. She then climbed on a chair and turned on the TV. The Houston-Oakland game was already in progress.

About ten minutes later, Foster Barton came into the bar from the dining room.

"Score?" he said, looking up at the TV.

"No score," Juanita said from behind the bar.

"Turnovers?"

"Not yet," Slick Henderson said.

"Zebras?"

"Two holding calls on Houston," said Tommy Earl. "Killed a drive."

"Figures," Foster Barton said, shaking his head sadly and returning to Sunday brunch with the family.

Only moments later, however, Foster was back in the bar, his fork in one hand, his knife in the other. Gravy trickled down his chin and his mouth was full.

"Uhrrrrrrrgggghhh?" Foster's eyes blazed at everyone with inquisitiveness.

Slick and Tommy Earl had anguished loudly at the sight of a Houston Oiler dropping an easy touchdown pass, and their groan had been heard in the dining room.

"Here's the replay," Tommy Earl said. "Hit him right in the hands."

Foster swallowed and wiped his chin on his sleeve as the Houston Oiler dropped the pass in slow motion.

"The points were out of line," Foster said. "That was my signal. I blew it. I bet the Oilers but the Oilers bet Oakland. Perfect."

Foster's eyes stayed on the TV. Through the cashier's window, Juanita saw Susan Barton glaring at the bar.

"It's the Zurich game," said Foster. "Here's where they lay it all into the numbered accounts."

Foster visited with the people on the TV, the pro football players and the officials, the zebras, as he looked up at them on the screen.

"The old Zurich flight, is that it, guys? Stuff it in the old Swiss banks . . . Take the wives . . . Take the zebras' wives . . . Hell, get Swissair to put on a second section, take everybody! Take Rozelle! . . . That's right, Stabler. Incomplete, you *cocksucker!*"

Susan Barton came flying into the bar.

"Foster, you are . . . the most despicable . . . the most disgusting . . . without a doubt the most obscene . . . obnoxious . . . selfish . . ."

"Flag!" Foster hollered, still watching the TV.

"You are a disgraceful idiot," Susan sobbed. "You are irredeemable . . . a human waste . . . a humiliation to *me* . . . to the chil . . ."

"No flag," Foster said more calmly.

"I am leaving you!" said Susan. "The children and I

131

are *leaving*. We will *not* be home when you get there! I am sick . . . I am *ill* . . . from living with a degenerate!"

Susan bolted to the dining room and brusquely dragged the children out of Herb Macklin's Bar & Cafe Restaurant.

Foster's interest had never left the TV, but now he turned to Tommy Earl Bruner, and said, "You know why that was a great call then? It was only second down. If the linebacker had dropped the interception, Stabler could have thrown it to him again on third down. Great call."

Foster braced himself on the bar and drank gin and spent the next two hours admiring the Houston Oilers for the style and cunning with which they lost his money.

"People don't understand," he said to Juanita late in the day. "Betting is a mental exercise. It's a game—like bridge. You hear this talk about how the bettor has a compulsion to lose. Crap. The bettor wants to win. It's an intellectual contest, your mind against the bookmaker's. I've tried to explain it to Susan. She won't listen. She says it's a sickness."

"Maybe Susan will call a doctor instead of a lawyer," Juanita said.

"Is there any sport you don't bet on, Foster?" Slick was curious.

"Yeah, soccer," the undertaker said earnestly. "You can't bet a sport where nobody falls on a loose ball."

Foster Barton had once made the largest bet of his life on a softball game. One spring Herb Macklin and Foster, for advertising purposes, had each fielded teams in one of those amateur industrial leagues.

Herb's Chicken Friends and the Crypts 'n Vaults of Barton's Funeral Home competed in a league with Obena Taggert's Dance Studio, Biff & Peggy's Auto Parts, Sparky Thurgood's Beautician School and O. R. Boynton's Poultry & Meats.

The Chicken Friends had only one player who could

hit, run, throw or bend over. That was Tommy Earl
Bruner. He pitched and batted cleanup. Shorty Eckwood played catcher wearing one of Herb's German
helmets. Herb was at first base in a straw hat, cigar and
hunting boots. Judge Derrell Wishcamper was at second in knickers and two-toned golf shoes. Hank
Rainey, the society carpenter, secured his toupee with
a knit cap and roamed third. Doc Matson handled
shortstop in Bermuda shorts and black socks. The
outfield was patroled by Dr. Neil Forcheimer and
intervening TCU English majors. The English majors
had lobbied for the team to be called the Novel
Russians with a fighting motto—"Suck It Up, Fyodor!"
—stitched on the softball shirts. The shirts were brown
and white, honoring Herb's chicken-fried steak and
cream gravy.

Juanita got pressed into service as the rover on the
nights when Bobby Jay Keeney was under arrest, and
she took some rather sharp criticism for her lack of
team spirit and popsicle overdose.

Going into the final game against the Crypts 'n
Vaults, the Chicken Frieds had scored only three runs
all season. Those runs came in a 27 to 3 loss to Obena
Taggert's Freds and Gingers. With two runners on
base, Tommy Earl had pounded a home run over a
Mexican family having a picnic in short left field at
Forest Park Diamond No. 2.

The runners who scored ahead of Tommy Earl had
been hit by pitched balls. Shorty Eckwood had taken
his base when a high changeup had come down on top
of his German helmet. He had advanced to second base
when a TCU English major strolled to the plate and
took a hard curve in his copy of *Buddenbrooks*.

Foster had certainly known how dreadful the Chick-
en Frieds were, but he had nonetheless bet fifteen
hundred dollars on them over his own Crypts 'n Vaults
when Puny the Stroller, his bookmaker, offered him
Herb's team plus 20 runs.

"It was the smart move," Foster still insisted. "I'd
broken the Japanese code."

This was his way of saying he had been armed with inside information. He alone had been aware of how handicapped the Crypts 'n Vaults would be that night. Two things had happened earlier in the day to encourage Foster to "step in" on the game.

First, Foster's star player, L. N. Varner, a hearse driver and fill-in pallbearer, had injured his leg. Foster had conducted a burial service at Rose Hill cemetery that morning, a day when the wind had been strong enough to wake up the deceased. In the midst of the service, a carnation wreath blew away. Lurching to grab it, L. N. Varner had tripped over a shopping bag belonging to a woman grieving on the first row of folding chairs. The shopping bag had contained a toaster-oven.

Hopping around on one foot, and clutching his shin with considerable distress, L. N. Varner had cried out, "Goddamn son of a cunt-eatin' piss-ass baby-rapin' dead motherfucker prick!" He had then lost his balance and fallen down backwards and rolled into the gravesite where the casket had yet to be lowered.

Not only would L. N. Varner be playing on a bad leg that night, but Foster himself would be out of the lineup because of a severely broken nose. Foster was no slugger, but he could get on base better than most gay activists.

Foster's mishap had occurred later that afternoon back at the funeral home.

He had been assisting the family of another Dearly Departed in the selection of a casket. He had led the family through the serene room where caskets were on display along with racks of shimmering gowns and men's suits for sale. He had lingered over an old metal casket which had been sitting in his showroom for a year.

"This one's marked down to eight hundred and sixty-five dollars," he had said. "Kind of reminds me of a speedboat. Didn't I hear somebody say Mrs. Thornton used to spend some time up at Possum Kingdom Lake?"

A bereaved man had asked Foster if the casket came in any other color.

Foster had replied, "Naw, that's it. The brochure calls it 'rose-bronze.' They got these high-brow names. Looks like a red-wine-and-soda, don't it? Maroon, maybe. But I'd say it's a lighter shade of maroon than them dip-shit Aggies wear when they're home at Kyle Field."

I ven though L. N. Varner had to limp around the basepath, he had turned four fly balls into home runs, all with the bases loaded, because of some confusion on the part of the TCU English majors in relaying the throws. Barton's stalwarts had won the sporting classic by 29 to 0.

Foster's fifteen-hundred-dollar bet on the game had begun to sprout wings that night when L. N. Varner hit his first fly ball. As L. N. hobbled slowly around third, Juanita had left her post as rover and walked over to Foster at the popsicle wagon, and said: "We can stick a fork in you, I guess. You're done."

On the Sunday of the Houston-Oakland football game, Foster had clung to some hope of winning his bet on the Under, but Ken Stabler's sixth interception had dashed those hopes.

"Zurich . . . Geneva . . . Lake Lucerne," Foster said to his glass of gin. "A chalet in Zermatt . . . St. Moritz . . . beef fondue."

Before Juanita got off work that day, Dr. Neil Forcheimer prevailed upon her to explain the Over-and-Under wager to himself and his students, Suzanne, Mark and Jason, who had been cramming their spiral notebooks with the dialogue they were overhearing in Herb's Cafe.

Smiling agreeably at the professor and students, Juanita said, "A bookmaker establishes a number on how many total points he thinks will be scored in a particular football game. Every week, he sets a number on each major game, college or pro. You can bet whether you think the point total in a specific game will be Over or Under his number. Say the bookmaker thinks the Cowboys will beat the Rams 24 to 14. That makes the number 38. You bet the final point total will be Over . . . or Under . . . 38."

Dr. Forcheimer said, "What if the total is precisely 38?"

"If you're Foster Barton, you lose," Juanita said.

"Oh, come on!" said the professor. "Henry James isn't *that* strict!"

Juanita concluded, "Foster's bookie, Puny the Stroller, runs a candy store. Puny will set a number on *anything,* not just football. For instance, he puts out a number every week on the highway death toll, statewide. If I was a bettor, I'd take the Over. One school bus could win it for you."

Chapter Nine

The weather worsened. It stopped kidding around and a hard freeze hit the city. Walls of sleet intermittently moved past the casement window of Herb's Cafe and motor vehicles did compulsory figures on the streets.

Juanita saw it as a time to be creative. She sat by the warm glow of the Wurlitzer with a feather and scroll and wrote two songs, each reflecting a mood of cynicism.

She was first moved to write "You Dropped Out of the Game." Maybe Foster Barton had something to do with it but so did her own past.

> *Well, when I'd try*
> *Starting over,*
> *I'd light the old flame,*
> *But you always*
> *Dropped out*
> *Of the game.*
>
> *Because when I*
> *Couldn't change*
> *As fast as you stayed the same,*
> *You always*
> *Dropped out*
> *Of the game.*
>
> *Do you still take this world*
> *   All that seriously?*
> *I've found a new love*
> *   Who'll laugh at it with me.*
>
> *And oh, my,*
> *How I laugh*
> *At how I took all the blame*
> *For those times*
> *You dropped out*
> *Of the game.*

In the other song, Juanita tried to come up with something befitting Lonnie Slocum's personality and mode of living. "Too Many Midnight Songs" was the result.

> *Too many nights.*
> *Too many dawns.*
> *Too many midnight songs.*

Too many pancakes,
Too much chili,
After too much Waylon,
Not enough Willie.

Too many rights
Turn into wrongs
After too many midnight songs.

Too many parties
Tryin' to kill me
After too much Waylon,
Not enough Willie.

Too many nights
Turn into dawns.
Too many rights
Turn into wrongs . . .
And there's too many
*   midnight songs.*

In the seclusion of her bedroom, Juanita recorded that song and "Baja Oklahoma." She sang them on a Maxell UD XL C-46 cassette tape, accompanying herself with the Martin.

She mailed the cassette to Lonnie's apartment in Nashville. Lonnie had a fighting chance to receive the packet at home, depending on how many dopers were staying with him.

Juanita never mailed any material to Lonnie at Mad Dog Music, the publishing company to which Lonnie was under contract. She had heard too many tales from Lonnie about the number of secretaries on Music Row in Nashville who had become Country & Western songwriters by tampering with the U. S. mail.

Before sending off the cassette, Juanita called Lonnie's brother, Horace, who worked at Yo Daddy's, the record-tape-stereo emporium. She asked Horace if he had talked with Lonnie recently. Had Lonnie and the band made it home from the road? For all Juanita knew, they could be in a methadone center.

"Yeah, they made it," Horace Slocum said. "Monsanto and Dow Chemical got 'em back to Nashville. They went to Baton Rouge after Conroe. Then Meridian . . . Selma. They played a week at Wanda's Vomitorium in Gulf Shores. I talked to Toby Painter the other day. He called up pretty frantic. He'd lost Dove Christian's phone number in Aspen."

Horace reported that Lonnie and Dog Track Gravy were working around the clock on the album. They weren't taking any calls and they were keeping the doors locked at Gip Hoover's Anti-Static Recording Studio.

"What if there's an emergency?"

"Dove Christian's already handled the emergency by Federal Express."

It was all set for Lonnie and the band to play warmup for Willie Nelson's concert at the Tarrant County Convention Center in December.

Horace said, "Willie's real good about giving a local boy a break like that. It'll be some night, Juanita. The damn place will be packed. It holds around fourteen thousand. You won't be able to walk down the aisle without getting raped or stoned or both."

Juanita included a note to Lonnie in the packet with the cassette.

The note said:

Hidy, Buckaroo:

Here are two songs guaranteed to take your album into platinum quicker than you can drink a bottle of Junior B. or Curtis R. Sark.

Don't let the singer distract you from the lyrics. She's a crazy woman who has been put back in private custody.

Please let me know what you think about these songs as soon as possible. I'm not hard to find. I have lunch every day at River Crest Country Club,

or you can have me paged at Neiman's where I go
for the style show and my pedicure.

> Burn it,
> Juanita Fay

The packet was mailed Nov. 2. A week had now
passed and Juanita had not heard from Lonnie. She was
trying not to be impatient, consoling herself with the
thought that it was better not to hear from Lonnie than
to find out the songs were unworthy of a sixth-grade
poetry recital.

At five o'clock in the evening on the worst day of
November, Herb's Cafe was unpredictably invaded by
regulars. It was as if they had all somehow agreed to
meet there and arm themselves with whisky and stand
firm against the dark sky and choral winds.

Upon entering, each regular had a comment about
the weather.

Tommy Earl Bruner hung up his sheepskin jacket,
and said, "No offense, Juanita, but it's colder outside
than a snowman's cock."

Herb Macklin shook his head, and said, "Dinner at
home ain't ever been this cold."

Shorty Eckwood came in with Herb. "I wish you'd
look at me," he said. "I'm shakin' like a dog shittin'
peach seeds."

Doris Steadman, resplendent in her pink cashmere
sweater, pink suit and pink wool coat, said, "In case
you haven't noticed, Juanita, that wind's blowing like
perfume through a high school dance."

Foster Barton, taking off a pair of mittens, said,
"That wind's blowing like Heights going through Paschal next week."

"Like rice through China," said Hank Rainey, the
society carpenter, straightening his hairpiece.

Bobby Jay Keeney said, "String of whores goin'
through Vegas couldn't make this much wind."

Slick Henderson turned down the collar on his

grease-repellent shirt, and said, "The roads are slicker than oil cloth."

Beecher Perry and Tina Busher entered and did nothing but nod pleasantly at everyone until Tommy Earl asked Tina if she thought the roads were slicker than Beecher's credit cards.

"Slicker than cum on your front teeth," said Tina.

Tommy Earl dropped to the floor. Then he got up grinning and started working the room.

He put his arm around Foster Barton's shoulder. "What's up, Foster? Still ahead for the year? Hope you've saved something to bet on them Heights fags."

Tommy Earl reached for his glass of Junior and gave Doris Steadman a squeeze at the same time. "Doris, them tits don't droop, do they? Tell the truth."

Clinking his glass against Hank Rainey's, Tommy Earl said, "Here's to Ernestine McLaughlin. You got yourself a hell of a woman, Hank."

"What are you talking about?" Hank blushed.

"Ain't the two of you gettin' married? I heard she proposed after you played wheelbarrow with her."

Tommy Earl moved on to Bobby Jay Keeney, saying, "Damn, I thought you got shot and killed. Didn't I read about it in the *Star-Telegram?*"

With a look at Juanita, Tommy Earl said, "If he ain't dead, what'd we have that victory dinner in here for?"

Bobby Jay Keeney didn't laugh.

"You ain't gonna start no fight, are you, Bobby? Juanita wants to buy you a drink."

"Finish fights is what I do," Bobby Jay Keeney said. "That wouldn't take long with you. What do you weigh now, hotshot?"

"Fuck, I don't know." Tommy Earl turned away with a grin. "I never weighed my knife."

Beecher Perry and Tina Busher were huddled at a table. In a serious suit and striped tie, Beecher looked as if he had come from a meeting with bankers. Tina looked as if she had come from a meeting with Yves St. Laurent. She had on a pair of fashionable boots, a mushroom wool suit with padded shoulders and a skirt slit up the thigh.

Tommy Earl approached them. "Thought you were in New York or Washington, Beecher. Didn't you go up there to tell them folks you were sick and tired of all this solar energy shit?"

"We got back from New York this afternoon," Beecher said.

"You go, too?" Tommy Earl looked at Tina.

"Certainly did," Tina Busher said, taking Beecher's hand.

"Hell, Beecher," said Tommy Earl. "I didn't know Tina made over 700 on her S.A.T.'s. What'd you all do up there? Look around at some boarding schools?"

An hour later a light snow mingled with the sleet and wind.

Until city workers sprinkled kitty litter on the streets, driving would only be safe for bobsledders. Few of the regulars dared to undertake a journey.

Hank Rainey, the society carpenter, was forced to leave, nevertheless. He got a call from Ernestine McLaughlin demanding that he come to Westover Hills and rehang an oil painting for her.

"High right on the clit," Tommy Earl advised Hank.

Bobby Jay Keeney excused himself to attend an occult and sinister meeting he did not care to discuss with anyone. Juanita announced to the room that Bobby Jay had gone to Reba's Lounge to have a drink and split open a bag of Doritos with John Dillinger.

Foster Barton and Shorty Eckwood shared a table. Foster quietly leafed through his stack of football tout sheets. Shorty peacefully went to sleep in a bowl of chili, no beans.

Herb Macklin retired to his office behind the kitchen to work on the details of a club he was organizing, a breakfast club for South Side businessmen. Herb's plan was for the men to meet in his restaurant once a week, same as the B & PW. It would be good advertisement for the place, plus the exchange of ideas and business tips would be a healthy thing for the community.

Doris Steadman called Lee to tell him the roads were too dangerous for her to drive to Mirage La Grande. Lee could heat up a tuna casserole for dinner. She was going to stay overnight with Juanita.

Tommy Earl Bruner used the phone at the cashier's window and informed his wife, Sheila, that he had a mound of paper work to catch up on and he would be late.

Juanita overheard the conversation. Hanging up, Tommy Earl looked at the barmaid and said, "Them kids don't need me to blow out the candles on their cake, do they?"

By now, Beecher Perry had held enough Chivas-and-soda in abeyance to address himself to the nation's energy problems.

"I'd like to ask everybody this," Beecher said. "Who gives a damn if people up East are freezing to death because they can't get enough fuel oil? I don't. Why am *I* supposed to go out and find oil so a bunch of assholes in the federal government can tell me how much I can sell it for to heat up rooms for people on welfare who can't even speak English?"

"There ain't enough Mentholatum to get me up East," Tommy Earl said.

Beecher said, "The biggest problem in this country is socialism in the federal agencies. We're up to our ass in pencil-headed federal regulators who sit around in Washington on their piss-ant salaries and tell *me* what to do!"

Beecher Perry lit a Sherman and elaborated. "I go out there and dig me a hole big enough to put all of Princeton and half of Harvard in. I'm trying to find oil and gas for this country. I make me a discovery. Then you know what happens? The federal regulators tell me I shouldn't have dug my hole there. The ecologists don't like it. *Now* they tell me! Here I think I've done hit a drive down the fairway, but the federal regulators have moved the white stakes on me!"

Beecher looked at everyone. "All of a sudden, I'm out of bounds! I'm not in the Goddamn fairway, I'm out of fucking bounds!"

"How can they do that?" Tina Busher said with a troubled expression.

"How can they do it?" Beecher rumbled. "I'll tell you how they can do it. They can do it because they're federal regulators. You can't fire 'em. You couldn't fire one if he pulled down his pants and crapped on a Russian's shoes at the U.N. Not that any American would go to the U.N. You can't go near the Goddamn U.N. without a sun helmet and a bayonet!"

"You're my man, Beecher," said Tommy Earl. "If we don't get the federal government off our ass, we're gonna have to change the name of this country. Fuck, just call it Italy. The United States of Italy."

"If I don't quit talking about it, I'm gonna have to get me a pacemaker," Beecher said. "I'll just say one more thing. For years, they wanted me to drill offshore down here in Texas and Louisiana. Find oil down *here* so I could send it up *there*—to keep New York City from freezing to death in the winter. Nobody could drill offshore up there, oh no! We had to drill offshore down here. Stick the rigs in *our* water. Well, I'll tell you when I'll give a shit about people freezing to death up East. I'll give a shit about *that* when I see a Goddamn offshore drillin' rig where the Goddamn Statue of Liberty used to be!"

Tina Busher was getting restless. She urged Beecher to take her home, home being the fourteen-room two-story house on Lake Arlington where Beecher had set her up. Beecher asked Tina if there was anything to eat at the house.

"Me," she said.

But there were other inducements. Tina let it be known that she had an ounce of flake, some terrific grass, a couple of dozen poppers, a box of ludes, a slide projector, a mirror ceiling, a jumbo vibrator, *Swedish Sluts* on Betamax, and a Water-Pik.

Beecher Perry called his wife "long distance" from

144

the cashier's window. He told Edna that his flight out of La Guardia had been cancelled because of the weather and he would have to stay another night in New York.

"What's the Water-Pik for?" Tina was asked as Beecher hurried her out the door.

"Hell, there's got to be something in it for *me*," she said.

Now at the bar, Doris Steadman was plainly getting drunk. There could be no other explanation for the fact that she brought up the pink business to Tommy Earl Bruner.

"I got to see it, Doris, no shit," Tommy Earl insisted. "I don't want to do nothin'. I just want to look at it."

Doris gave Tommy Earl a squint. "Maybe that's a good reason not to show it to you. As long as we've known each other, you've never acted very interested. That could give a girl a complex."

"Girl?" Juanita said quietly, looking at Slick.

Tommy Earl said, "I'm a deeply religious man, Doris, and totally dedicated to my family. You know Sheila. My little boy and my little girl. I talk big, but I don't fool around none."

"I'll squat on that line till it grows a fungus," Doris said, killing off another vodka.

Tommy Earl explained to Doris that the reason the two of them had been good friends for so long was because they had always kept their distance. They had not risked a relationship which might hurt both of them. Surely, Tommy Earl said, a good friend would let another good friend take a harmless look at Old Pink.

"Garbage," said Doris.

Tommy Earl motioned to Juanita for more drinks.

"Doris, I just can't believe what you're doing," he said. "I can't believe I ain't gonna get to see Old Pink unless I use up one of my hard-ons."

Tommy Earl had a theory that the average man could anticipate 14,965 hard-ons in a lifetime. Tommy Earl arrived at the total with a special formula based on a man's years between the ages of fourteen and fifty-five.

The formula had something to do with the number of times a man was married, with the fluctuation of his financial situation, with travel, alcohol consumption, smoking habits, dope usage, leisure time, workload, recreation, religious upbringing, early sexual education, and intimate exposure to Tina Bushers.

"Doris, I've only got 5,453 left," Tommy Earl said. "I'm way below where I ought to be for a man my age. And you want me to use up one just to see Old Pink? That's *greed,* is all that is."

"I'm sorry to hear about your condition," Juanita said.

"I need to drink and smoke more," Tommy Earl said. "That's how you conserve. If you drink and smoke a lot, you don't get no frivolous hard-ons. It gives you a chance to find out who the serious ladies are. Keeps you from getting trapped with them selfish bitches who don't use no imagination. You won't waste any of your 14,965 on 'em."

Doris said, "Tell me this, lover. What if word gets around you might be more trouble than you're worth?"

"Best thing that can happen," Tommy Earl said. "You get to be known as a challenge—like I am right now. They're talkin' about it everywhere. The Baboon Rocket . . . White Elephant . . . Teri Jean's Pressure Cooker. I got every fast-draw debutante in town lookin' for me."

Tommy Earl slid his arm around Doris' fleshy waist.

"I sure would like to see Old Pink," he said. "But you may be right, Doris. It's probably best if you and me don't fuck around with napalm."

Doris removed Tommy Earl's hand from her rib cage and put it back on the bar next to his Junior.

"You know what else?" Tommy Earl said, looking into Doris' eyes. "I ain't ever brought it up before, but I could sure hold them tits in abeyance."

He twisted on the barstool toward Juanita and Slick.

"You all ever stopped to think about the misuse of the English language? If you say you want to see some titties, here's what you get."

Tommy Earl pretended to hold a tablet between his thumb and forefinger.

He said, "That's why you got to say you want to see some *tits*. When you say, 'Come here, bitch, show me your tits,' here's what you're talkin' about."

Tommy Earl weighed imaginary basketballs in his upturned palms.

"Now these are *tits* right here," he said. "These ain't titties. Am I lyin' to anybody?"

The lecture on semantics was interrupted when the side door of Herb's swung open. A stray followed a gust of freezing wind into the room. The stray was a tall man, middle-aged, in a tapered white topcoat with epaulets and Tom Mix's ten-gallon hat. The stray's neatly trimmed beard was speckled with gray and he wore gold-rimmed tinted glasses.

"Lordy, lordy," the stray said, stamping his feet and unbuttoning his coat. "The temperature's droppin' like the needle on a Cadillac's gas gauge. It's colder outside than my third ex-wife. Them roads are slicker than cellophane on a record album."

Old Jeemy Williams of KOXX stacked his topcoat and Tom Mix hat on the red-checkered cloth of an empty table. Now he was wearing a Western-cut Ultra-suede aqua suit with epaulets, a blue polka-dot shirt and a silver thunderbird neckpiece.

"Have epaulets, will travel," Juanita observed.

"Where's my buddy?" Old Jeemy said. "Whoa, there he is! Hold it! Let me take off my ring and my watch so I can shake hands with him!"

Old Jeemy did an away-we-go in the direction of Slick Henderson. "My podna!" he said, grabbing Slick's hand, mashing Slick's upper arm.

"What are you drinking?" Slick said, remaining on the stool in his corner.

"Oh, I reckon I'd hold me a little cognac in abeyance."

Smiling at Juanita, Old Jeemy said, "There she is. It's Juanita Hutchins her own self. Darlin', I could have picked you out of a box of chocolate eclairs."

Old Jeemy extended his hand. Juanita shook it.

"I'm so pleased to meet you," Old Jeemy said. "I'm Old Jeemy Williams."

"Hi, Jeemy," Juanita said, putting a cognac on the bar. "I'm sorry we haven't gotten our stemmed glasses back from the party we catered for the prime minister."

"Oh, hell, you can drink whisky out of a bedpan if you're thirsty enough."

Doris Steadman backhanded Old Jeemy on the arm, and said, "Are you really Old Jeemy—from the radio?"

"Old Jeemy Williams, Ma'am. Eight-One-Seven in your area code. Number One in your heart."

Doris said, "You're a corny shit-ass, you know that?"

Tommy Earl helped Doris off her barstool.

"Don't pay no attention to my wife, mister," Tommy Earl said to Old Jeemy. "She's feelin' kind of down. I got laid off today at Bell Helicopter."

Tommy Earl helped Doris to the table where Shorty was asleep and Foster was studying his tout sheets. He placed Doris in a chair and pulled a chair up close and put his hand on her thigh.

"I been tryin' to get over here all week," Old Jeemy said to Juanita as he made himself comfortable at the bar. "Wouldn't you know I'd pick a night when you can't see nothin' through your windshield but an x-ray? Been busy, though. Real busy. Narrated another in-flight tape for Braniff. Emceed three supermarket openings. Wrote the jacket copy for Virgil and Betsy's *Songs for Unwed Mothers*. Spent one whole day gettin' a telephone interview with Charley Pride. He was a lot less trouble before he was white. Heh, heh."

A toast was in order.

"Here's to 'Baja Oklahoma,' Juanita," said Old Jeemy, "and all them other songs I hear you got."

With a subtle but deeply personal expression for Slick Henderson, Juanita said to Old Jeemy, "When did you and your old podna here become such big pals?"

"Oh, a week or so ago," Old Jeemy said. "Slick threw a side-body block on me when I was stealin' half of my secretary's egg salad sandwich. Handed me a copy of your song. He said the lady who wrote it played the guitar and sang about half-wonderful. He said she was good-lookin' enough to tie up traffic in the Ridglea Shopping Center."

Slick looked at Juanita, and said, "All I asked him was if he knew how to get songs published."

Old Jeemy's laughter rattled the clean glasses on a shelf near Juanita. "That's what he asked me. Did I know how to get songs published. Hot damn, I said, ho, podna! Whoo! God-a-mighty! Do I know how to get *songs* published? Damn! Does Dolly Parton sleep on her *back?*"

The laughter broke off suddenly and Old Jeemy grew serious. He acknowledged that one of his sidelines was representing artists in the Country & Western field. He was not just an agent. He was also a business manager if a client needed advice on investments, setting up trusts, tax shelters.

He did not have many clients. That was intentional. There were too many other demands on his time. And he kept the sideline confidential, of course. Too often, the owners and managers of radio stations confused free private enterprise with conflict of interest.

"Sure, there's glamour in my job at the station," Old Jeemy said. "It's fun being a celebrity around town. But the biggest kick I get is helping a new talent emerge. To track a star going across the sky and know I was the launching pad, well . . . that's pretty dadgum rewarding."

It all started with the songwriter, he said. A hit song could get an entertainer out of the box quicker than a cockroach. Willie Nelson's songs had freed more slaves than Raymond Massey.

"Here's to Willie," Old Jeemy said. Another toast.

"I'll drink to anybody who survived the Jacksboro Highway," said Juanita.

"What say, Darlin'?"

Juanita had no idea where Old Jeemy came from originally, but if he wasn't familiar with the lore of the Jacksboro Highway, he could not have been from within a two hundred-mile radius of where he now sat.

Nobody ever called it I-99. It was the "Jacksboro Highway," the road leading to Jacksboro, Texas—and many of the old boom towns of the wildcatting oil days. But the name was synonymous with something else: a five-mile stretch of that same road which linked downtown Fort Worth to the general area of the Crystal Springs pavilion, a stretch of road that was once the rowdiest, raunchiest, illegalest, toughest and most sinful honky-tonk strip in all of Texas.

That was what the Jacksboro Highway had meant from the late 1920's through the 1960's, and that was what it would always mean to people of a certain age, even if the roisterous days were over and the "sin strip" were nothing more today than dilapidated motels, shattered neon signs, and weeds advancing up the walls of deserted shacks.

Willie Nelson, like Bob Wills, Hank Williams and many others before him, had paid his dues on the Jacksboro Highway. Willie had picked and sung on stages protected by chicken wire so he and his musicians would not be struck by the bottles, chairs—and people—who might go flying through the air before an evening was over in such elegant establishments as M's Cafe, The Nite Owl, Tubby's Plantation, Pug's Beer & Dancing Nitely, Lurleen's Curb and Gutter, The Fifth Deuce, K's Melody Lounge, Fran's Do Drop Inn, and Connie's Tip Top Tavern & Full Body Massage.

Over a period of four decades, the city's plainclothes detectives needed only to drift through the beer joints and illegal gambling parlors of the Jacksboro Highway to find the thug they wanted to pistol-whip the most, and twice a year a noted underworld figure from Fort Worth or Dallas would be the victim of a "gangland slaying" on the strip.

As it happened, an exceptionally colorful murder of that type had once enabled Foster Barton to win an award.

When Howard (Pine Box) Watson was found in the

gaming room of Lurleen's Curb and Gutter with five bullet holes in his head, a *Star-Telegram* police reporter compared the sight of Howard (Pine Box) Watson's brain to the merchant's lunch at Herb's Cafe.

But the incredibly artistic job that Foster Barton did with wax and plastic on Howard (Pine Box) Watson's head was judged to be so innovative by the publisher of an undertaker's trade journal, Foster was honored as the magazine's Embalmer of the Month.

The spicy days of the Jacksboro Highway came to an end in 1971 when Texas legalized liquor by the drink. Brawling beer joints still existed in rural pockets of Texas, but around the cities they were greatly outnumbered now by bars named for days of the week and integral parts of sailing vessels.

In some ways, Juanita missed the old days. She had poured as many drinks then as she did now, whether anyone brought a paper sack—a "brown bag," a bottle —into Herb's or not. Herb kept whisky on hand for the thirsty. And Juanita used to relish the game of trying to spot the upstanding employees of the T.S.B.F.L.A., the Texas Shitheel Baptist Fucking Liquor Authority.

"They would have loved your little blue suit at M's Cafe," Juanita said to Old Jeemy. "What do you think of Lonnie Slocum, by the way?"

"Fine Texas boy and good picker. I'm trying my dangdest to get him a hit. If Old Jeemy didn't play it, you didn't hear it."

"Lonnie's a good friend of mine."

Ignoring that, Old Jeemy leaned forward, looking as serious as Lyndon Johnson.

"Now, Darlin', I'm not one of them fast talkers from Nashville. If I was, I'd come in here with a certified check for $500 and say I wanted to buy your song. I'd say Crystal or Tanya was gonna record it and it was gonna be a crossover hit that'd make you richer than six feet up a bull's ass. But that'd be the last dollar you'd ever see. If the song ever *did* get recorded, you might look on the label and find out you didn't even write it, depending on what kind of document you signed. But

I'm Old Jeemy. I'm not only a honest person, I think big. I want to hear the rest of your material. I want to see what we got here."

Slick said, "What do you want her to do?"

"Juanita," said Old Jeemy. "I want you to round up your songs and your guitar and come on down to the radio station. No hurry. Whenever it's convenient. You and me, we'll go in a soundproof room. You can sing your songs for me personally. I got an ear. I got intuition. I like 'Baja' on paper. Now I got to hear the tune. If you've got any songs I think we can sell, I'll know it like you know drunk from sober."

Old Jeemy put on his topcoat and Tom Mix hat.

"Well," Juanita said, hesitantly. "I appreciate your interest, but . . ."

"Don't worry about your voice," Old Jeemy said. "They got equipment today that can make a fart sound like a Renaissance choir."

"I've never sung for a stranger before."

"Darlin'!" Old Jeemy took Juanita's hand. "Don't think of me as a stranger. Think of me as a partner!"

Chapter Ten

Herb Macklin chewed on his cigar and surveyed the wreckage of Doris Steadman. Doris had passed out at the table. Herb offered Juanita a deal. He would close up the establishment if Juanita would stuff Doris in a dirty clothes hamper.

"We'll take care of her," Slick Henderson said. "She's just waiting for parts."

Juanita, Slick and Tommy Earl teamed up to get Doris on her feet, transported through the side door and outside, across the North Slope of Alaska and into the rear of Juanita's car, a used Camaro she had bought from Tommy Earl.

That accomplished, the three of them stood shivering in the parking lot, sounding as if they had run up several flights of stairs.

"Good luck on gettin' her out of there," Tommy Earl said. "I'd go with you to help, but I got to get home in time to play tooth fairy."

"Sheila Bruner is a saint," Juanita said.

As Tommy Earl trudged into the night, he said, "Yeah, she's a good one, but the secret's to keep 'em guessing. A woman don't give you any shit until she finds out you love her!"

Slick drove Juanita's car. As the Camaro moved

153

carefully over the chunks of unflavored snowcones falling on the city, the highway surgeon and the barmaid talked about the music business.

"You've got the first step behind you," Slick said.

"Which step is that? All I've done is meet a man in a funny suit who looks like he'd steal my butterfly collection."

"Old Jeemy can make something happen."

"What?"

"Whatever's suppose to happen next. He likes 'Baja.' You heard him."

"He hasn't heard the melody."

"I described it to him."

"How did you do that?"

"I said it was sort of a Willie Nelson, hold the onions."

Lighting a cigarette, Juanita said, "What happens next is, if he *does* like any of my songs, he'll hand me a contract written in Arabic. The contract will say Old Jeemy owns fifty percent of my life."

"I'd split fifty-fifty with somebody who could get my song on a jukebox if I couldn't. How much does a songwriter make on a record?"

"A little under three cents. Something like that."

"Who makes all the money?"

"Crooks."

Slick negotiated an icy turn, and said, "With a big hit, though, it don't matter, does it? There's plenty for everybody. Didn't you tell me once about some songwriter who gets a check for six thousand dollars every three months for a song he wrote fifteen years ago?"

"There are lots of those—and they aren't even 'White Christmas.' If it's a pop hit, it's an annuity."

"I wouldn't mind giving Old Jeemy half of $6,000 every three months. Right now, all he owns is half of what you've got, and all you've got is what's in the back seat."

Presently, Doris wasn't worth much.

Juanita said, "Can I ask you a question? I've been

writing songs as long as you've known me. Why are you just now getting around to trying to be helpful?"

"Didn't I mention it?" Slick kept his eyes on the road. "I've taken up the mandolin so we'll have something in common."

Unloading the steamer trunk from the Camaro took twenty minutes. Juanita and Slick lugged Doris up the stairs to the apartment, dragged her to the spare bedroom—Candy's room—and deposited her on the bed.

Slick left the room when Juanita began making Doris comfortable, unhooking certain things, unzipping others.

Slick went to the kitchen-breakfast room-den and made a cold meatloaf sandwich with lettuce and mayonnaise and a record-setting amount of salt and pepper for the Sans Su South. He poured himself a glass of milk.

Slick was having the snack when Juanita joined him, unable to conceal a look of embarrassment and guilt.

"I couldn't resist," she said. "The son-of-a-bitch *is* pink!"

Juanita drank a white-wine spritzer at the butcher-block table while Slick finished the sandwich. She then startled him by saying:

"Okay, sport. You're up."

"I'm what?"

"Tonight's the night."

"It is?"

Juanita walked around the table and smiled warmly at him. She took his arm and guided him to her bedroom. In there, the subject of music never came up.

The weather changed three days later and it did so with the suddenness for which North Central Texas was renowned. One afternoon the sun broke through the gloom. Ice turned to slush in an hour. And in another hour the slush magically turned the city's streets into the world's largest overflowing commode.

An improvement in the weather meant Juanita would have to get back on schedule with her trips to the Trinity River Nursing Center. She missed two visits with Grace because of hazardous driving; at least that was the excuse she used.

Grace had suffered over the telephone, but telephone suffering wasn't very satisfactory for people who were really dedicated to suffering.

Juanita had spoken to Old Jeemy on the phone and promised that when the Ice Age was over she would make the pilgrimage to the radio station and try to sing her songs for him.

Old Jeemy had invited Juanita out to dinner.

"Are you married?" she probed.

"Kathy passed away two years ago, God rest her."

"I'm sorry."

"Thank you, Darlin'. She was a wonderful person. I'll never meet another woman like her, but . . . life goes on, don't it?"

Juanita considered having dinner with Old Jeemy somewhere down the line.

"Don't take this the wrong way," Old Jeemy had said. "I'm just talkin' about a little *coq au vin* and Mouton-Cadet between friends. I know you and Slick are an item in the gossip columns."

Juanita had said, "Slick and I *do* have a relationship, but we manage to keep it wrapped in a lot of foil paper."

"I'll be in touch, Darlin'."

For Doris Steadman, prettier days ahead meant she would be forced to get out of her pink bed and stop eating Vitamin B like pistachio nuts. Since her drunken night in Herb's, Doris had confined herself to Mirage La Grande.

There was another reason for Doris to perk up. Lee Steadman was leaving town, going to Colorado for a carpet salesmen's convention. Lee wanted Doris to go along, but she wiggled out of it by having Ross Wickley tell Lee the drugstore was taking inventory.

In Herb's on the afternoon of the instant slush, Slick wondered where Doris would start out on her search-and-destroy missions after Lee left town.

"The yellow pages," Juanita predicted.

A break in the weather meant only one thing to Foster Barton. Firm footing. Arlington Heights was a slight favorite over Paschal in the big high school football game coming up, and the Yellow Jackets would have a better chance to cover the 3½ points on a dry field.

Foster said to Tommy Earl that day, "I'm down for six hundred with Puny the Stroller. How much you want?"

"I'll just take Paschal for a sentimental hundred," Tommy Earl said. "I don't really want to bet."

"What happened to all the big talk?"

"That was before Billy Boy Bobbit got hurt."

Foster looked at Tommy Earl distrustfully. "Billy Boy Bobbit ain't hurt. If Billy Boy Bobbit was hurt, it would be a headline in the newspaper."

"He's limping."

"Who says?"

"Somebody."

"Who?"

"Somebody I know."

"Somebody smart?"

"A girl."

"What girl?"

"A girl I met at the Baboon Rocket," said Tommy Earl.

"What's she know about it?"

"She's good-lookin' and goes to Paschal."

"That don't mean anything."

"It means she fucks Billy Boy Bobbit. She says he's limping."

"This is vital information, Tommy Earl. You swear you're telling the truth? If you are, I'm shovin' it all in on Heights."

"I believe her," Tommy Earl said with sincerity.

"Why?"

" 'Cause I fucked her, too. She'd give King Kong a limp!"

Foster lunged at the cashier's window and snatched the telephone out of Esther's hand. He dialed a number, his eyes roving impatiently.

"Puny?" Foster said into the phone. "Listen, you know those rolls of *dimes* I wanted delivered to Arlington Heights? I need fifteen more. You heard me. I want *fifteen more dimes* sent to Arlington Heights. Apartment three. What? Oh, yeah, I forgot. Apartment three and a half. So . . . what's the weather like? Is it overcast? Thirty degrees, huh? Seems low. I say it'll rise. I predict it'll be *over* thirty by . . . six o'clock. Right. Six. Like in *six dimes*. Got all that? Fifteen dimes, apartment three and a half. Six dimes, over thirty. Anything else going on? . . . Do I what? Ice hockey? What do I know about ice hockey? I'll talk to you later."

Foster made notations in a pocket diary. He then announced he had better go back to his funeral home.

"We're sure staying busy this month," he said. "Knock wood."

Herb Macklin wandered out of his office. He requested a favor from Juanita. Would she mind coming in early tomorrow morning for the inaugural meeting of the South Side Breakfast Tip Club? There would be important businessmen present and Herb wanted things to run smoothly. No burned sausage, no eggs coming out of the kitchen like Titlists, no biscuits resembling desk weights.

"It's only the South Side Breakfast Tip Club now," said Herb, "but this thing could grow into something bigger than we can imagine."

Juanita imagined the Greater Southwest Metroplex Breakfast Tip Club with meetings held once a week in a maintenance hangar at the D/FW airport.

Juanita would of course be there the following morning. She was Herb's second-in-command. Actually, she was more than that. She was his tape-burner, top skimmer, cigar-box custodian, and IRS trickster. All of which amounted to one thing only: friend.

It was Juanita's obstinate belief that Herb Macklin had worked too long and too hard over the years for the purpose of allowing the federal government to declare itself, rather whimsically, an equal partner in his restaurant.

As a matter of fact, it made Juanita livid every time she wrote out her own check to the IRS for income taxes. She was convinced the tax money went for only three things: to build public roads to private resorts owned by friends of Congressmen, to buy jet fighters for countries that didn't even have pilots, and to provide welfare for skiers and surfers who were too tired to get a job but had the energy to harvest a valley of buds and try to fuck her daughter.

It took a little creative bookkeeping, but Juanita gave the government what *she* thought it had coming. The bureaucratic swine could steal from somebody else, from the naive or idealistic. To Juanita, all bureaucrats and politicians were pickpockets who could only be told apart by the cut of their double knits and the magnitude of their scandals.

Herb Macklin had seen something in the paper that day which infuriated him almost as much as the IRS, and now he brought it up in the bar.

He said, "Juanita, did you see that ad in the *Star-Telegram* this morning? Damndest thing I ever heard of. There's this business course you can take to learn how to *shake hands*."

Juanita began brewing fresh coffee in both the Bunn-o-matic and Mr. Coffee machines.

"They teach this course where you learn how to use flattering words," said Herb. "Words you're suppose to use at the right time to impress somebody. You know what they're doing? They're teaching people how to be somebody they ain't. I'm a son-of-a-bitch. If a man has to *study* that, he's only got one thing in mind."

"He wants to poison your dog," Juanita said.

"He wants to sell you something that ain't worth a shit," Herb said.

Juanita had listened often to the discourses of both Herb Macklin and Tommy Earl Bruner on the trends in American business which angered them. Seminars, resumés and position papers were particular irritants to Herb. Juanita once prepared her own position paper on these irritants and posted it on Herb's bulletin board in the kitchen.

It read as follows:

DEALING WITH
BUSINESS PESTILENCE

RESUMÉS

Never take a resumé seriously. Resumés only make money for the people who write the resumés. No resumé ever tells an employer how many times a job applicant has had the clap.

Why, indeed, would anyone hire a person based on a resumé written by a professional liar?

If the applicant is a man, the employer must ask only one question: did the applicant go to TCU?

If the applicant is a woman, the employer may simply ask: does she have a tongue that can lick the paint off a dormitory wall?

POSITION PAPERS

People who write position papers often find themselves in an enviable position. They are hired to write papers for both sides of the position.

A good position paper will have many words in it like "superincumbence," "egress," and "plurification."

You will not often find the phrase "lightweight dropcase limp-wristed motherfucker" in a serious position paper.

Charts and multiplication tables should always be included in position papers. They should look complicated enough to make Albert Einstein stagger across the room for a Tylenol.

A good position paper will never underestimate the value of a semicolon.

SEMINARS

Seminars may be held by anyone willing to rent a room on the mezzanine of a Sheraton.

A successful seminar may be held at very low cost. The seminar-holder can get the job done quite nicely by hiring only two assistants.

First, there must be an artist to draw the colored graphs that will be displayed on the easels. The graphs may go up or down, depending on the artist's whim.

Second, there must be a speaker. The speaker can use moderately big words at the morning session, then wear a wig to disguise his identity and use extremely big words after the lunch break.

There is the occasional piece of sound business advice to be learned at a seminar. A speaker named Tommy Earl Bruner once stated:

"If it flies, floats or fucks, rent it, don't buy it."

Herb Macklin's tip club was going to be an antibiotic for business pestilence. His club was going to be grounded in trust, honesty, mutual respect and good fellowship.

In the bar, Herb said, "It's like you've heard me say a hundred times, Juanita. A business deal is no good for one side unless it's good for *both* sides. I serve good food and good drinks. The customer pays his money. He's happy, I'm happy, and it don't require a phony handshake."

Juanita poured herself a mug of coffee.

"Everybody's got something to sell," Herb continued. "You might be selling used brick and I might be selling toilet paper, but we're both in the selling game."

"How are those things related?"

"You know a bricklayer who don't shit?"

"No," Juanita admitted, "but I think I can find a sales rep for a paper company who doesn't wipe his ass on the corner of a school building."

Herb had decided that the charter membership of his tip club would be limited to two individuals from the same business. In other words, there would be only two house builders, two electrical contractors, two restaurant owners, and so on.

"Who's the other restaurant owner?" Juanita wondered.

"Shorty."

"*Shorty?*" Juanita laughed. "Shorty Eckwood hasn't been up for breakfast since he played the bugle!"

She asked a favor of Herb in return for having to be at work the next morning.

"Would you include Lee Steadman? Doris is pressuring me. She knows you're having a club meeting. She thinks if Lee joined, it would help him make some friends."

"I got me two floor-coverers," said Herb.

"He really doesn't have many friends."

"Lee's not from the South Side. He's from the East Side."

"It would be a nice thing for him. Do it for me?"

"Well, all right. Tell him to get his ass over here."

"Thanks, Herb," Juanita said. "Doris already invited him."

That evening at Herb's, Juanita got a call from Doris Steadman about a more urgent matter. Doris panted excitedly, "Turn on Channel Five, quick!"

"Why?"

"Do it!"

"What for?"

"There's a big party going on in Westover Hills and they're televising it. Good-bye."

Juanita switched on the large color Sony and fine-tuned the picture for an audience consisting of herself, Slick, Foster Barton and Shorty Eckwood.

The first thing they saw was Beecher Perry's wife, Edna, dressed as a Persian princess sitting on a gold throne being held aloft by four black slaves.

"God in Heaven," Juanita mumbled to herself, quickly mesmerized by prime time TV in a way she had not believed possible.

Shorty Eckwood almost never stayed awake watching television, even if young girls in bikinis darted through the streets of Honolulu on mopeds trying to escape a gang of fat chinks with ray-guns. But Shorty was alert to the sight of Edna Perry, and he said:

"They's gonna be some harelips if them niggers drop her."

Next on the screen came an exterior view of the mansion where the social event was taking place. A wide-angle shot established the fact that the party-giver, Loyce Evetts, Jr., would find it horribly inconvenient not to live under a roof supported by twenty huge white columns. The mansion was guarded by dozens of statues on the lawn, mostly Venuses and discus throwers.

A TV commentator appeared and Juanita expounded on the commentator's *tall* hair, essentially saying you couldn't dent it with a hammer.

The commentator signaled for someone to join him. Loyce Evetts, Jr., meandered onto the screen. His costume encompassed leotards, a frock coat, a neck brace and a jeweled crown. He was surrounded by three tuxedo-clad violinists playing "Fascination." When he moved, the violinists moved.

The commentator said, "With me is Loyce Evetts, Jr., one of the most prominent citizens of Fort Worth *or* Texas. Mr. Evetts, we understand this is a coming-out party for your daughter, Laurette, *and* a housewarming for this fabulous home you've built."

"Yes, it is, Kel," said Loyce Evetts, Jr., "and I want to thank you and Channel Five for accepting our invitation to be here. We couldn't invite everybody, you see. Television seemed like the best way to let the rest of our friends share the occasion with us."

"It's very exciting," the commentator said. "I must say those buffet tables whet my appetite."

"Stay as long as you wish, Kel. Make yourself at home. By the way, would you pass the word along to your technicians? There'll be hotdogs for them in the basement."

"Great, just great!" said the commentator. "Mr. Evetts, if I could ask a serious question. Everyone in Fort Worth has heard the wild rumors about the cost of your home. *Is* the eight-million-dollar figure pretty close to accurate?"

Loyce Evetts, Jr., motioned for the violinists to hold it down a little. "Kel, I'm glad you brought that up. All things are relative, aren't they? Look. I have a business that nets me . . . oh . . . around three hundred and twenty-five thousand dollars a week. But that doesn't mean I don't have financial obligations like everybody else. Kel, before passing judgment on a person, one must . . . *connaître le dessous des cartes* . . . so to speak. *Comprende?*"

"Right you are," the commentator said. "Your daughter looks lovely tonight, Mr. Evetts. I saw her a while ago on the dessert barge. Has Laurette selected a college yet?"

"Yes and no. Her mother's pushing Sweet Briar or Stephens."

"What about Laurette?"

"Well, she's applied and been accepted at TCU, but we don't take that threat seriously."

"I wonder if we can get Mrs. Evetts on the show?"

"Phyllis will be delighted," Loyce Evetts, Jr.,

said, looking around. "She's one of the Marie Antoinettes. I'm not sure at the moment exactly where she's . . ."

Viewers were taken inside the mansion, first to a living room where an actual old-fashioned oil pump —the "Daisy Evetts No. I"—sat in a massive circular wading pool. A fern grotto loomed in the background.

Indoors, the camera picked up Loyce Evetts, Jr., again—and the violinists, who had resumed "Fascination." The host was seen welcoming two Groucho Marxes and a Geronimo.

There were screen-filling glimpses of other rooms in the house. Not all of them looked like the interiors of cathedrals. Some were exhibit halls of natural history museums.

Three full orchestras and four combos were scattered about, each providing dance music for a galaxy of Supermen, Apaches, czars, queens, Hitlers, Fidel Castros, Moshe Dayans, Eva Perons and Madame du Barrys.

Unless Juanita were badly mistaken, one of the more self-conscious Roger Staubachs was Hank Rainey, the society carpenter. On a dance floor, Hank was trying to keep up with Ernestine McLaughlin, the oldest and most breakable-looking Farrah Fawcett.

When a chubby Scarlett O'Hara in need of better posture and a more flattering pair of eyeglasses came on the screen, no one had to guess whether it was Laurette Evetts.

The debutante was staring with disgust at a young man in a bow tie seated in a wheelchair, a long cigarette holder in his teeth.

"Quite a party," said the commentator, moving in. "What do you think about all this, Laurette?"

"It's okay, I guess," Laurette sneered. "It'd be more fun if Franklin D. Roosevelt didn't have *polio.*"

"What's the problem?" the commentator said. "He won't dance?"

"You got it," Laurette said.

"Hear that, FDR, old buddy? The lady wants to dance. It's *herrrr* night!"

The young man blew smoke at the camera and said, "The hand that held the dagger has plunged it in the back of a neighbor."

The screen was again lit up by Edna Perry on her gold throne. The black slaves lowered her into microphone range for the commentator.

"Mrs. Perry, your costume is magnificent! Congratulations on really getting into the spirit of things."

"It was either this or Joan of Arc," Edna Perry said in a voice which could only have attained its depth through many hard years of gin-drinking. "Ernestine McLaughlin and Phyllis Evetts talked me out of Joan of Arc. They're Catholics."

It was the commentator's understanding that Mrs. Perry had furnished the iron pagodas and the outdoor lighting for the party.

"That is true," Edna Perry said. "The lights will be donated to the Downtown Merchants Association. They will be used to supplement the Christmas decorations on our fine buildings. I don't know what you do with a used pagoda, frankly."

"Charitable deeds by Edna Perry are a legend in our city," the commentator said. "Incidentally, did I not read in the paper that you are donating three thousand *unopened* department-store packages to an orphanage?"

"I don't know the exact number." Edna Perry handed an empty Martini glass to a black slave. "I was cleaning out rooms. Things from various shopping sprees. It was nostalgic, actually, seeing all of the old wrapping paper they once used at Saks, Bergdorf's, Bloomingdale's, Neiman's, Sakowitz, what have you."

"And they *were* unopened? You have no idea what purchases you might have made in all those packages the orphanage will receive in time for Christmas?"

Edna Perry said, "Oh, I couldn't begin to guess. But I'm sure the little cripples will enjoy opening them."

In a crowd scene near the close of the telecast, Juanita spotted Beecher Perry, a rather slipshod Hitler. He was exchanging pleasantries with a fretful Cleopatra, who was unquestionably Tina Busher.

Juanita assumed no oil men or home entertainers would be represented at the tip club breakfast.

Chapter Eleven

"Doris said I wouldn't have to stand up and make a speech. She promised."

Lee Steadman spoke in an undertone the next morning as Juanita led him to a table in Herb's dining room at the inaugural South Side Breakfast Tip Club meeting —where breakfast was over.

"Sorry I'm late," Lee said. "I should have stayed on 121, but I had a hunch about 303 and came around on 820. You know what? I'm starting to think real serious about trying 360 to 30, and—"

"I can still get you something to eat," Juanita said.

"Thanks, anyhow. I had a bowl of Frosted Flakes at home."

Juanita seated Lee at a table with Doug Marquardt,

landscaping, Stubby Hinton, ceramic tile, and J. J. Burleson, lighting fixtures.

At the table next to Lee were Tommy Earl Bruner, used cars, Foster Barton, burials, Shorty Eckwood, barbecue, Dr. Neil Forcheimer, Nobels, and Slick Henderson, gas pumps.

Juanita carried a glass coffeepot.

Foster Barton asked for a refill. As Juanita poured the coffee, he said, "This the one that beat me?"

A day earlier, Foster had bet Juanita ten dollars the Mr. Coffee in the bar could brew a faster pot than the Bunn-o-matic. To be sporting about it, Foster had given Juanita her choice of coffee makers.

Watching his Mr. Coffee lag behind, Foster had said, "How'd you know which one to take?"

"I had a man at courtside," she had said.

Foster leaned over to Tommy Earl at the table in Herb's dining room, and said, "You got a tip today?"

"Fuck, no," said Tommy Earl, amazed, if anything, by the question.

"I do." Foster kept his voice low. "I don't know whether to announce it to everybody or not, but it's a hell of a tip. Alabama–Ole Miss come 5½. I look for it to go to 6½ by tomorrow. Good chance for a middle."

Herb Macklin sauntered to the podium at the far end of the narrow dining room, a room with booths along each wall. There were tables down the center, and the wallpaper caricatured poodles. The podium had been borrowed from a chapel at Barton's Funeral Home.

Herb took the cigar out of his mouth, and said, "I want to welcome all of you. This is a real fine turnout. I'll just take a minute to go over the purpose of our club. Say a word to you about the benefits and the fun we can all derive from this thing."

"Okay, the purpose." Herb cleared his throat. "Real simple. If old Buford over there says he's about ready to start building homes on them fifty-foot lots out near Crowley, then maybe old Roscoe here can give him a good deal on some asbestos tile. Buford and Roscoe would find out about it right here in this room."

Herb allowed the purpose to sink in. Then he said, "Now all of us get around the city pretty good. We hear things from one person or another about this and that. I know in my heart each one of us can come in here every week with a real good tip for a member."

"I got a tip for Shorty," said a man from the back of the room. "I'm tired of findin' corpuscles in his sliced beef sandwich!"

Shorty Eckwood didn't hear that. He was already asleep.

Herb said, "It's my feeling we ought to pay dues and elect officers. This is a serious organization. The dues will help defray the cost of our recreational activities and social events. Here's where all the fun comes in. I foresee our own golf tournament. We can take over Mountain Valley for a day and play a scramble."

"Can we use grease?" another man called out.

"For what?"

"Why, hell, you put some Vaseline on your clubface, you can whap that sucker into the next county!"

"We'll have a rules committee," said Herb. "Let me just get finished. I foresee a dinner dance. That'll keep the women happy. We might even want to arrange one of them charter buses with a bar on it. Take it up to Fayetteville next season for the TCU–Arkansas game. They's lots of extracurricular things we can do."

A man raised his hand. W. R. Chalker, dry cleaning.

W. R. Chalker said, "Herb, can we pick another game? I spent twenty-five years tryin' to get out of Arkansas. I wouldn't go back if they were sellin' pussy on the side of the road instead of grape jelly."

That drew a response from E. H. Sutterlin, roofing materials. E. H. stood up, and said:

"W. R., I'm not from Arkansas, but I have to say

this. I wouldn't go see TCU play football again if the ticket office gave Sophia Loren an upperdeck seat on my face!"

It took a while for Herb to restore order.

Now he said, "I'll lead off with the tips today, seeing as how I'm already up here. I assume all of you know the big Murdock home over there on Elizabeth Boulevard. I'm talking about the house old Gayle Murdock built when he was Mr. Meat Packer out at the stockyards. The house has been sitting there empty ever since his no-good son moved away. Went to Tahiti, I think. Or Fiji. Wherever it is you go to lay around and play with your crack. Anyhow, young Dicky Wheeler on our city council told me something interesting the other day. The property's been zoned commercial."

Herb puffed on his cigar and put it down in an ashtray near K. G. Hines, weatherstripping.

"According to Dicky Wheeler, that old place is going to be redecorated and overhauled and turned into a hellacious art gallery. Picassos . . . sculptors . . . needlepoint, the works."

"Picasso ain't worth a shit," Tommy Earl piped up.

"Why's that?" Herb said.

"Fuck, Picasso never finished nothin'. If you buy a Picasso, you got to hire somebody to paint arms and legs on it."

Juanita's laughter could be heard by most of the members as she circulated with the coffee pot.

"At any rate," Herb said, "the Murdock home's been leased to an art queer. Shelton. Milton. Something like that. Dicky Wheeler knows the name. You can check it out with him. It looks like a big remodeling job. Could mean contracts for a lot of you. I'm talking about wiring, walls, floors, windows, plumbing, ventilation—everything. Of course, you'll have to deal with a queer. But I think this is an example of a good tip."

Tommy Earl rapped on a water glass with a spoon and got to his feet.

"Here's my tip, Herb. That's all a pile of shit. Dicky

Wheeler has started every rumor he can think of—for five years—tryin' to unload that corner for his daddy's real-estate company."

"Now wait a minute," Herb said, looking soberly at Tommy Earl. "Are you sayin' to me and the rest of the men in this room—are you sayin' Dicky Wheeler made up a story about a queer? A city councilman did that?"

Tommy Earl said, "Two years ago Dicky Wheeler told everybody in town Clymer Milner was buying that whole block for his Lincoln-Mercury dealership. We saw how fast that happened."

"Clymer Milner came down with cancer!"

"Not on that *block*," said Tommy Earl.

Herb directed his attention to the other members. "Those of you who want to pursue my tip can call up Dicky Wheeler."

"Dicky Wheeler's the same jerk-off he always was," Tommy Earl persisted. "His daddy makes him walk around in enough shit to cover a tall Indian. He had his head up his daddy's ass the night we whipped Heights 20 to 6 for the city championship, in case nobody remembers. Dicky Wheeler ain't tackled me *yet*. Who the fuck put him on the city council? Anybody in here vote for him? I don't know anybody who voted for him. You vote for him, Foster?"

Foster looked up from a tout sheet where he had been frowning at *Score's* Lock of the Year, and said, "No, but I had a minor position on Heights that night with the 7½."

"I'll tell you one fuckin' thing," Tommy Earl said. "When Dicky Wheeler dies, it ain't gonna be hard to find pallbearers. A trash can don't have but two handles!"

Sitting down, Tommy Earl said to his table companions, "Am I lyin' to anybody?"

Judge Derrell Wishcamper, felonies and misdemeanors, took the floor, rapping on his own water glass.

The judge said, "Gentlemen, on behalf of the West Texas Chamber of Commerce, I want to congratulate you on this fine organization. Fellowship is the string

you tie around the bundle of life. The tip I have today is
nothing you'll be able to take advantage of immediately, but I want to put you on the alert. I'm working in my
spare time on a project for the Tourism and Travel
Development Committee of the West Texas chamber.
As many of you know, I dabble in oils and water colors.
A while back, I weakened and let the chamber talk me
into putting my pastime to a good cause. I'm sketching
what we call a Wonderful West Texas Fun and Adventure Map. It's coming along pretty darn good. When
it's finished, there'll be reproductions. The chamber
has this idea to sell 'em as gift items. I'm sure all of you
will want one hanging in your office or den. Don't ever
forget Forth Worth is 'where the West begins.' That's
all I wanted to say, Herb. The sausage was real good
this morning."

Shorty Eckwood woke up suddenly, and blabbered,
"Huh? Who? Whur'd they do? Am I caught?"

Then he went back to sleep.

C. L. Corkins moved to the podium when Herb
called on him.

A trim man in his mid-thirties, C. L. Corkins dressed
neatly in pastel suits, and his face shined in off-white
enamel. His thick red wavy hair was parted too low on
the side. The bulk of it unfurled across his head giving
him the look of an heir to a stately home in Scotland.
His wife, the former Emmajean Swearingen, a grizzled
veteran of Tri Delt rushes and Hell Weeks at TCU, was
getting very close to being asked to join the Fort Worth
Junior League.

At the podium, C. L. Corkins said, "I want to thank
Herb personally for including me today. Quite honestly, I see this as a thrilling journey for all of us. Thank
you, Herb, and God bless. Now . . . if I may pass along
to you a fact I've learned recently, I believe it can be of
value to every serious-minded individual here. I'm sure
all of you have your minimum life-insurance plans.
Some carry more than others, depending on how much
regard you have for your loved ones. Incidentally, I'm
not here to sell you insurance today. You can relax. It

so happens I've designed Herb's overall plan, and I can tell you Herb is very well covered, but that's neither here nor there. My reason for addressing you, to be candid, is to let you in on a new program literally blazing through my industry. I find the concept very intriguing, and I wouldn't be fulfilling my obligation to what I see as the charter of this organization if I did not share it with you. To put it as simply as I can—and I will be more than happy to speak to any of you privately about it when we adjourn—there is now a plan available to every citizen of this country which enables that citizen to combine, and I stress the word combine, life insurance with personal savings!"

Tommy Earl Bruner, on the end of a yawn, said, "C. L. why don't you sit the fuck down?"

C. L. Corkins looked wounded.

Sprawled in his chair, Tommy Earl said, "Either sit down or tell us about old Brenda up there in your office. I hear you been grudge-fuckin' her at lunch."

C. L. Corkins' off-white enamel face turned to crimson, and he said, "I . . . there is a Brenda in our office, but . . ."

"Tommy Earl!"

The yell came from two tables away. Jack Yarnell, banking.

Jack Yarnell said, "Is that the same Brenda old Beecher Perry used to bring around the Baboon Rocket? Tall? Eyes like a cat? Looks like a Miss Texas gone criminal?"

"That's her," Tommy Earl said.

"Hell, I been wondering what happened to Brenda. She's the one at Rankin Title who wanted everybody to eat Hershey's syrup off her tits."

"Are you talking about *that* Brenda?" said Don Leach, stock manipulations and bond straddles. "Brenda Ivy? I thought she married a Methodist minister."

"She's still married," said Tommy Earl. "What's that got to do with anything?"

Don Leach said, "Brenda Ivy's that good-lookin'

home-wrecker who said to Beecher one time . . . 'Oh, baby, put two fingers here and one finger there and call me bitch.'"

"Same Brenda," said Tommy Earl.

"I got my first peanut-butter job from old Brenda."

"I got ice water–Binaca."

"Aw?"

"Am I lyin' to anybody?"

There was a ten-minute break at the tip club breakfast during which Tommy Earl and a dozen other members figured out to their mutual satisfaction that Brenda Ivy had moved from Rankin Title to Cowtown Savings & Loan, then to West Side Printing & Engraving, and *then* to Corkins Insurance.

After the interlude, Dr. Neil Forcheimer of the TCU English department spoke to the group.

"I merely want to say here-here to Judge Wishcamper, the other creative person in the room," the professor said. "I think it well to applaud the individual who chooses *not* to sacrifice his or her art for measly bowls of porridge. Yes, Judge, we artists, I'm afraid, are trapped by our desires and must live like fish on a hook, moving through vain and frantic rituals. I, myself, am presently submerged in work on a rather protracted biography of Andrew Marvell. Publishable? One prays. Commercial? One hopes. Happily, I *am* sensing from the 'book people' among my friends that across America there just might be a great hidden interest in Cromwellian pamphleteers."

The professor, late for Modern Lit, excused himself.

As he exited, he found the aisle blocked by D. E. (Ebb) Coltharp, wholesale lumber, who wanted to shake the professor's hand.

"Damn fine," said D. E. (Ebb) Coltharp, a close friend of Judge Wishcamper. "I want to buy that book of yours. Where's it at?"

A man now stood up at a table by the main entrance. Herb didn't know who he was. Neither did Juanita, who was leaning against the wall near the cash register, smoking.

"My friends," the stranger said, "I can see you're a society with which I have much in common. I would like to begin by telling you that within this past week, in an area behind my home in the Tanglewood section, I have completed a thirty by thirty-six foot fallout shelter. It is abundantly stocked with water, dehydrated food, power generator, and all the essentials to survive a nuclear radiation fallout."

"*What?*"

Juanita was not a club member. The word just popped out. And the look on her face was as troubled as it was quizzical.

The man put his thumbs behind the lapels of his blue blazer. "I know what all of you are thinking. Elbert has lost his mind. Well . . . I can assure you I am of sound mind, and I hope and pray I will never have to use my facility for radiation fallout. Why did I build it?"

The speaker looked sternly at Juanita and continued.

"About three years ago, because I believe in the American dream, I started reading as many financial newsletters as I could subscribe to. I was looking for the best way to invest my money for my family. That's when I began to find out about all the things the Communist media in this country keeps hidden from us. I learned about the Communists who infiltrate our government. I learned about the subversive organizations in America that are working for one world government. General Motors, for one. U. S. Steel . . . RCA, ITT. The list is endless *and* frightening. I learned, not only about the Jewish conspiracy, but about the black conspiracy, the Catholic conspiracy *and* the Christian conspiracy. We are losing our treasures, friends, everything we hold dear. We are losing our freedom gradually but surely."

"Who *are* you?"

Juanita again.

"My name is Elbert Tripton. I have dined here with my family. May I complete my thought?"

"That sounds like a bargain."

Elbert Tripton said, "My friends, do you realize the

Panama Canal was given away despite the fact that ninety-one per cent of the mail to Congress was against it? Do you realize there is enough oil in our country to last over two thousand years but our government is preventing us from knowing it?"

Elbert Tripton opened a valise and put a stack of newsletters on the table.

"Do you realize," he said, "that our government gives billions of dollars to Communist countries under the guise of humanitarianism but refuses aid to other countries who *oppose* Communism because our government wants to keep those countries militarily weak? Do you realize there are textbooks in our public schools which teach that Communists like Roosevelt and Eisenhower were *not bad?* Do you realize the trilateral minds in control of Washington, D.C., are behind the lawlessness in our streets, our incipient dope culture, the pornography being thrust upon our youth?"

Juanita said, "Do you realize you need to douche out your *brain?*"

"Sadly, my dear, your reaction is *expressly* what they want." Elbert Tripton smiled, cordially.

He held up a newsletter: *The Spread-Eagleist.*

"This is the only truthful publication in America," he said. "If we all speak as One, we can drive them back across the Dnieper."

"What's that headline say? 'Slasher Nails Trilateralist'?" Juanita's arms were folded and her back rested against the poodle wallpaper.

Herb Macklin said, "Mr. Tapper, we've got to move along here. If that's about it for your tip today . . ."

Interrupting, Juanita raised her voice, "There are a lot of things wrong with our government, Ace, but none of 'em scare me like *you* do!"

Slick Henderson left his table and went over to the stranger and put a clamp on his arm. Using his free hand, Elbert Tripton showered the dining room with the newsletters.

"You've all been poisoned, I tell you! This is the only cure!"

Slick grinned as a person does when nothing is funny, or as a Texan sometimes does when he is actually looking for a fight, and said, "The lady don't want to make a donation, Elbert. We better get you back to your fallout shelter."

Slick quietly but forcibly squired the patriot out of the restaurant.

Juanita lit a cigarette and noticed Tommy Earl laughing at her.

Up at the podium, Herb said, "They's another stray in the room, but fortunately I know this one. Right over there, that's Lee Steadman. Lee's in the retail carpet business on the East Side, but his wife works on the South Side, so I asked Lee to be with us. Like I say, Lee's in retail carpet, but I bet he can work out a volume deal for somebody. What's going on out your way, Lee?"

Lee had been shrinking—visibly getting smaller—in his chair.

"Would you stand up, Lee? I'd like for everybody to know who I'm talking about."

Lee Steadman timidly made it to a stance. He blushed and waved at the unfamiliar faces.

Herb said, "Lee, I hear Brayton Sealy is getting ready to build some spec houses out near you."

"I guess I don't know Brayton Sealy," Lee said.

"What about that office building going up right there by the freeway? Who's in on that deal? Any friends of yours?"

"Office building?"

"I'm talking about the building under construction across the parking lot from your salesroom," said Herb.

"There's a building under construction?"

"Aren't you located in that shopping center with Tim-Tex Medical Supply? . . . Hammond's Bicycle Shop? That ring a bell?"

"Not really."

"How long you been on the East Side, Lee?"

"Oh, heck. Let's see. All my life, I guess."

"I meant your salesroom."

"Sorry. Uh . . . eight years."

"Same location?"

"Same old one."

"Are you sure there's no freeway near you?"

"Yeah, there's a freeway. That's how I go to work."

"But there's no office building under construction?"

"Mr. Macklin, I don't want to say there's not," Lee said. "It could well be."

"There's a twelve-story office building almost completed out there by Luther's Cafeteria. I thought it was close to you."

"*Luther's?* I know Luther's."

"You do?"

"Yes, sir! Luther's Cafeteria is next door to me. I eat lunch at Luther's all the time. You can take my word for it. Luther's is right there!"

Herb said, "Well, you keep us in touch with everything out your way, Lee. Pleasure to have you with us."

Lee Steadman waved again at his fellow members and sat down.

Tommy Earl rocked back in his chair and said to Lee, "You're funny, you know that? I ain't lyin'. You're a witty motherfucker."

Bobby Jay Keeney, crime, insisted on speaking from the podium.

"Just a few things," Bobby Jay said. "The dice and blackjack is movin' to Doyle Ewell's Sporting Goods. Maurice is servin' after-hours on Berry. So's Pauline on Hemphill. Clap doctor still hangs out at Jimmy's. Stay out of the Skyview Motel. Been ruint. Nigger deal. New whore at Reba's. Ask for Janie. Just turned her out. Eighteen. Clean. Don't run the meter. That's about it."

The inaugural meeting of the South Side Breakfast Tip Club ended as Bobby Jay folded his notes and put them away.

Chapter Twelve

The narcs were in Aspen. They were in the bars, the restaurants, the discos. They were in the shops, the sidewalk cafés, on the ski lifts, on the trails. They were on the bunny slopes, where Austrian instructors were shouting at them, and they were cartwheeling down Ruthie's Run in their rentals. The narcs stared at people constantly and conversed only with each other. Keala and Remillard, who were still sharing the ranch house with Candy and Dove, were spooked. They had the feeling they were characters in a horror film and their minds were being stolen by aliens. Dove said it was worse than that. Dove had the feeling he was in Aspen and the narcs had come to steal his flake and put him in the joint.

"We haven't ruled out paranoia, but we're pretty sure they're narcs," Candy said on the phone.

Candy was calling the night after the tip club meeting, the night before the Paschal–Arlington Heights football game.

Juanita said to her daughter, "If they *are* narcs, they won't do anything if you don't get caught selling the stuff."

"We're operating under tight security," said Candy.

"Tell Dove not to be crazy. Flush it down the john!"

"Momma, I don't think Dove wants to flush two hundred grand."

Aghast at the figure, Juanita said, *"Two hundred thousand dollars?* What in God's name does your house look like? People must be skiing in your living room!"

"They couldn't find it if they looked forever," Candy said. "That's not the thing we're worried about. Dove thinks we could be under surveillance. The house could be bugged. One of them's watching me from across the street."

"Where are you?"

"He's drinking cappuccino."

"Where are you calling from?"

"I'm in a phone booth," said Candy. "I'm on a corner. Keala and I are having lunch at The Sinus Problem."

"Why aren't the narcs in *there?"*

"Because they're sitting at a sidewalk café called Blizzard Conditions."

The thing concerning Candy and Dove most was the possibility of someone—a customer, even a friend—helping set them up. No one would want to do a terrible thing like that, but the narcs might put the heat on a heavy user, threatening arrest and public embarrassment.

"Dove's worried he's the one they want," Candy said. "Too many people know he's got the best flake—eighty-two percent. They know he keeps blocks of ice, he's not a street guy."

Juanita said, "Angel, may I remind you of something? Prison is what's at stake here. *I* know Dove's not a criminal. *You* know he's not a criminal. But narcs don't think like we do. *They* have the rulebook, Candy."

"I know. That's what gets us. They ought to spend their time busting the scum selling heroin to kids around elementary schools. All tooth powder does is get you through a seated dinner."

"May I ask you something? Does Dove always keep two-hundred-thousand dollars' worth around?"

"That's what it's worth now, Momma. It's been cut. This is the shipment Keala brought back from South America last week."

"Did Keala dissolve it in alcohol?"

"There was too much. Dove considered shipping it in a case of brandy, but he was afraid the bottles would get broken."

"I see."

"There are lots of ways, Momma. The easiest is to know somebody who gets diplomatic courtesy going through customs, but Dove's friend was busy."

"Dove knows a cabinet member?"

"Congressman."

"Well . . . I'm glad to hear about a politician who's good for *something*."

"Keala used the old life-preserver trick," Candy said.

Returning from Bolivia, Keala stashed the flake in the life preserver under her seat on the 747. When the jet landed in New York, Keala got off, leaving the cocaine on board in the life preserver. She cleared customs empty, safely. She then bought a ticket on the same aircraft to wherever it was going in the next hour, who cared? Keala reboarded the 747 and reclaimed the flake from the life preserver. But before the plane departed, Keala got a pre-arranged emergency message. Her mother was dying. A passenger-service agent rushed on board and took Keala off the plane and put her in a taxi. Keala had already *cleared* customs, see?

Juanita said, "Candy, have I ever told you what a fertile mind Dove has?"

"There's getting to be a problem with the life-preserver method," Candy said. "Certain flight crews are starting to check the life preservers. Dove knows this stewardess in New York who just paid cash for a twenty-two-room triplex on Park Avenue."

Juanita learned she was going to be receiving quite a bit of mail.

"I'm what?"

"We wanted to alert you," Candy said. "They'll look

181

like get-well cards. Christmas cards. Don't pay any attention to the return addresses, but *don't* throw any cards away, Momma. You'll be throwing away fifteen hundred dollars."

"You're not mailing me the dope, Candy. Did you hear me?"

"We talked it over. It's the safest thing we can do."

"Candy, you are *not* going to mail me any cocaine! I wish you were here right now. You could watch my lips."

"You don't have to open the cards, Momma. Put them away somewhere. We'll get them later. There'll be one little cellophane package inside each card, that's all."

Juanita hastily estimated that she was going to receive about a hundred and fifty get-well cards.

"Dove can bring it here himself. Think of the postage he'll save."

"He doesn't want to travel with it, Momma."

"I'll flush it down the john, Candy. I mean it!"

"Oh, Momma, you won't do any such thing. You never throw anything away. You've still got your movie star collection."

Juanita got drunk that night.

It was not a thing she often did, and never on the job. But the prospect of all the get-well cards arriving at her apartment encouraged her to pour herself some Junior as she worked the bar.

Juanita was not an argumentative drunk. Not a crying drunk. Not a drunk who would be likely to go off and leave her purse or sunglasses. She was not a drunk who complained about the year of the wine. She was not a drunk who talked about the good old days. There weren't any. She was not a singing drunk, not a confessional drunk. She was not a drunk who dug around for a truth she wouldn't remember the next day. And she would never—it was unthinkable—drink alone.

At the bar, Doris and Tommy Earl continued to deal with the dilemma of Old Pink. Lee Steadman had left that morning for Colorado and the carpet convention. Doris was cut loose. A perfect time for Doris to hit on Tommy Earl, if he were on her list. Tommy Earl acted as if he were still interested in seeing Old Pink before it returned to its natural state of wire mesh. Foster Barton was there, studiously searching his football tout sheets for illuminating facts. Slick was in his corner.

Juanita laughed at something. Slick watched her glass overflow with Junior. She had thought of the get-well cards and the Christmas cards and the Easter cards and the happy birthday cards.

Would she need a Snow-Kat to move from her living room to the kitchen–breakfast room–den? She was going to be a lady with a mink coat and $200,000 worth of illegal goods but she couldn't afford a single item in Neiman's Christmas catalogue. That's what she was laughing at.

"What's so funny?" said Slick.

"Life itself," she said. "It's a good thing the South invented the sense of humor after the Civil War."

"Nobody laughed before the Civil War?"

Juanita swirled her Junior. "Of course not. Everybody was working too hard. They were trying to grow a potato and keep a Mohican from stealing it."

She said, "The pilgrims could have laughed at their clothes but they didn't have full-length mirrors on their bathroom doors, so they missed the chance. They never saw their matador pants or their tap-dance shoes."

Juanita relaxed in her tall chair as she said, "The pilgrims were pretty busy, anyhow. They all lived in Cape Cod and they spent most of their time trying to figure out what would happen if you ate a raw oyster. Otherwise, the pilgrims had a good deal, what with all the beach-front property they owned."

The pilgrims were white, all but one, a janitor, who had sneaked on board the Mayflower. If there had not been a janitor on the Mayflower there would never have been any slavery. The janitor's name was Kareem Abdul Eugene. His descendents later invented NBA basketball.

There were other stowaways. That's why the American Revolution began. The British found out a bunch of Americans had stowed away on their ships. The Americans won the war with nonviolent demonstrations. While the British froze in the winter, the Americans stayed in their log cabins and wrote pastoral couplets.

A long period followed the American Revolution when the pilgrims went off in many directions. They had heard these tales about farm equipment . . . cocaine . . . innocent young daughters . . . prep schools. They decided to explore the land. Thus, they became cowboys, soldiers, ranchers, farmers, physical-education teachers, and statesmen.

"There weren't any women statesmen until Kitty Wells sang 'It Wasn't God Who Made Honky-Tonk Angels.'" Juanita said. "That's what got women out of the kitchen. Loretta Lynn helped later on when she wrote 'The Pill.' Thanks to Kitty and Loretta, women found out they could cheat like their husbands."

Slick went behind the bar to help himself to a Budweiser and Juanita wrote something on her legal pad as she sat in her tall chair. Slick made Doris and Tommy Earl a drink while Doris removed Tommy Earl's hand from a sensitive area below her bosom. Foster accepted another glass of gin from Slick.

Behind the bar, Slick said to Juanita, "I didn't realize Kitty Wells and Loretta Lynn were that important to American history."

"They weren't until a minute ago," Juanita said. "I just thought of a song." She made another note and put down the legal pad.

Two strays seated at a table were gaping at Juanita with expressions ranging from appalled to alarmed.

Returning to her history lecture, Juanita said, "The Civil War didn't start over the slavery issue. That's a myth. The Civil War started because some Eastern bankers wanted the South for a resort development."

Doris said, "I think you're drunk, Juanita."

Juanita said, "The South could have won the Civil War if there hadn't been so many gentlemen around. Robert E. Lee had the whole ball game in the palm of his hand when he walked into the Holiday Inn at Appomattox."

What Lee should have done, Juanita said, was take along a few Israelis and ERA's.

Lee could have walked into the Holiday Inn and said, "Hi, Ulysses, how's your Mom and them? Can I borrow your Pentel to sign these surrender documents you got here?"

That would have thrown Grant off-guard just long enough for the Israelis and the ERA's to mop up. It would have broken the North's spirit.

Aside from fighting much too fair, Lee and the other Confederate generals spent far too many hours going to balls and jumping their horses over hedges.

"Once the war was lost," said Juanita, "there was nothing for the Southerner to do but laugh. He'd lost all his hired help. The Northern armies had stomped on his vegetables and slaughtered his cattle and stolen every expensive chandelier he owned. His wife had to pick up her own dress off the floor. It was terrible. His daughter married a Yankee and moved to Connecticut and started hanging out at regattas. His son went to California and started wearing pants without a belt. The Southerner turned to his wife one day and said, 'Fuck it, Louise. I don't know about you, but I think I'll try laughing at all this shit.' "

Juanita revealed to the room that laughter did not spread to the rest of the country until Southerners began to travel. People laughed pretty much everywhere now, except for rich women, of course—and except for people in San Francisco.

Nobody laughed in San Francisco because the people out there thought they should have been the first pilgrims and they were still pretty angry about the country starting at the other end.

"Actually," Juanita said, "it's better to have started out in the middle of the country. You got to miss a lot of that covered-wagon business, and you saw better football games."

Foster Barton looked up and said, "What do you think about Arizona State, Juanita?" He marked something on a tout sheet.

"I hear they give good cactus."

"Arizona State's got the fastest spades," Foster said, "but I say you have to go with USC when it's stink on stink."

When she went home that night Juanita wrote her Lib song, a song inspired by her American history lesson. She titled the song "Kitty and Loretta."

> *Thank you, Kitty and Loretta,*
> *For what you did for me.*
> *I was slaving in the kitchen*
> *The day you set me free.*
>
> *Makin' beds and feedin' kids*
> *Seemed like my lonely plight,*
> *Then you sang the songs that helped me*
> *Look out and see the light.*
>
> *Now I'm a honky tonk angel*
> *And I'm taking the pill.*
> *This liberated woman*
> *Is looking for a thrill.*
> *Can't remember how it sounded*
> *When I heard those wedding bells.*
> *Thank you, Loretta Lynn,*
> *And thank you, Kitty Wells.*
>
> *I'm a liberated woman,*
> *Creating a scene,*
> *Laughing at the nights I stayed home*

To cook and clean.
I'm a liberated woman,
And I don't drink alone.
I'm as single as my husband is
When he's on the road!

Yeah, I'm a honky tonk angel,
And I'm taking the pill.
This liberated woman
Is looking for a thrill.
Can't remember how it sounded
When I heard those wedding bells.
Thank you, Loretta Lynn,
And thank you, Kitty Wells.

After finishing the song, Juanita, still a little drunk, crawled into bed and stared up at the ceiling. She sang the song as she lay there, and then she rolled over and said, "Take that, you macho motherfuckers."

Only Foster Barton among Herb's regulars went to the Paschal–Arlington Heights football game the following night. His investment on the game was, as he had put it, "three large."

Everyone in the city must have read about the game on the front page of the *Star-Telegram,* however, for surely nobody could have resisted a story under a headline which said: HIGH SCHOOL COACHES FACE INDICTMENT.

The story read:

Fort Worth Police Chief W. S. Cotter said he may ask the Tarrant County grand jury to indict the head football coaches of two local high schools in connection with a riot that occurred last night after the Paschal–Arlington Heights game at Farrington Field.

"It were a terrible thing," Chief Cotter said. "Sports is supposed to be left on them fields of friendly strife."

Facing possible indictments for inciting a riot and inflicting injuries on Fort Worth police officers are Paschal Head Coach G. F. (Germ Free) Johnson and Arlington Heights Head Coach Jim Ben Hulsey. Each man is serving in his first year with the Fort Worth public school system, and both replaced beloved figures in the schoolboy coaching ranks.

G. F. (Germ Free) Johnson took over the Paschal reins this fall when B. B. (Bitty Bottom) Everett abruptly announced his retirement after his name was linked with a scandal involving a car-wash business. Jim Ben Hulsey succeeded Bill (Blubber) Lindsey last spring after Lindsey perished in a freak hang-glider accident.

Both Johnson and Hulsey were arrested last night and held in jail for 90 minutes before posting bond of $1,000 each.

Fisticuffs broke out near the Paschal and Arlington Heights team buses after the football game—won by Paschal 16–14—when an apparent Arlington Heights touchdown on the final play of the game was nullified.

Police are still looking for an unidentified Arlington Heights fan who may have started the melee by hurling an empty bottle of gin at the window of the Paschal team bus, believing the game officials were on board.

The coaching staffs of both schools and many fans took part in the riot, but witnesses said the Paschal and Arlington Heights football players all remained on the buses with their transistor radios.

Two police officers, R. T. Zachry, 27, and Pete Shepperd, 31, were hospitalized with bruises and rib injuries. Both are reported in critical condition.

"No charges have been filed," Chief Cotter said. "The charges will depend on the condition of my officers. I will turn all my information over to the grand jury. I realize tempers was runnin' high because the city championship were up for grabs, but them coaches hadn't ought to have kicked R. T. and Pete while they was down."

Arlington Heights suffered a bitter loss in the game. The Yellow Jackets led 14–0 through three quarters on two long runs by fullback Rusty Woodruff.

The Paschal Panthers stormed back in the fourth quarter on the passing and running of quarterback Billy Boy Bobbit, who was held in check most of the evening and seemed to be limping. Bobbit engineered two quick touchdown drives after fumble recoveries. Each drive was aided by pass interference penalties against Arlington Heights.

Paschal recovered fumbles at the Yellow Jackets' 11- and 16-yard lines and moved to a first down on the 3- and 4-yard lines after the interference calls.

Billy Boy Bobbit scored both touchdowns on the same run-pass option play around end and he accounted for each two-point conversion—the ultimate difference in the game—on the identical play.

An incident unrelated to the post-game riot occurred near the Arlington Heights bench only seconds after Paschal scored the go-ahead conversion. A Yellow Jacket player, defensive end Jonathon Sterling McLaughlin III, after coming off the field, was pushed, shoved, slapped and spat upon by Coach Jim Ben Hulsey and two assistants.

With time running out, the Yellow Jackets' Rusty Woodruff broke loose on a dazzling 65-yard run, and it appeared Arlington Heights had won 20–16 when Woodruff dashed into the end zone and two officials signaled a touchdown. A wild celebration took place among the Heights players, coaches and fans.

A minute later, a similar celebration was set off on Paschal's side of the field when referee Gino Sanducci came running up waving his arms and pointing to the flag he had thrown, ruling holding against Arlington Heights.

Both head coaches said they were proud of the

110 percent effort they got from their kids in the game, and they predicted the media would make a big thing out of the riot.

Everyone in Herb's Cafe read the story and speculated on whether Foster Barton might be "the unidentified Arlington Heights fan" who started the trouble after the athletic contest ended.

Foster was a likely suspect. The holding call which erased Arlington Heights' touchdown on the final play couldn't have been more costly. Not only would Foster have covered the 3½ with that touchdown, he would have won the Over. But he lost everything, and Heights lost "the whole game," as he would say.

When Foster came in the bar, he removed all speculation about his possible role in the riot with a surprisingly cheerful attitude.

It was the most fun he had ever had at a football game, Foster said. He had gone through every emotion. For most of the night, he had a three-thousand-dollar "laugher" going. He was even telling jokes to strangers. Then it began to slide away with the first pass-interference penalty. But it went slowly, inevitably, the cruelest kind of torture. Finally, it was gone. And just the right way. The zebras. Then suddenly, unexpectedly, miraculously, it came back on the last play of the game. Unbelievable. A bizarre moment of triumph, an almost obscene gift from fate. Then a final flag, the most heinous of crimes against humanity. Down again, everything lost—and this time for keeps.

"It was beautiful," Foster said, buying a round of drinks. "The fourth quarter was what it's all about. Actually, I wasn't surprised the zebra dropped that last flag. Hell, it weighed three grand."

Chapter Thirteen

Two days later Juanita found herself at Old Jeemy's radio station in a room she could have sworn was a laboratory where creatures with antennas in their heads, knobs for eyes, jagged arms, and dangly legs conducted experiments on the bodies of dead vocalists.

Old Jeemy ushered Juanita to a swivel chair on a platform where she was surrounded by these creatures and the vanload of trunks in which they came to this planet.

"Sit here, Darlin', while Rooster gets a level. Sorry your Martin don't have a pick-up."

An amp pick-up. Juanita's guitar was not rigged for sound. But the problem was solved. There was a Stratocaster available. She could borrow it. The electric guitar belonged to a rhythm player in the band of Rev. Buddy Jack Grady. The reverend was doing Old Jeemy's Music for Mourners live that afternoon, and his roadies had been hauling in equipment all day.

Juanita sat in the swivel chair and tuned the Stratocaster while Rooster, a sound engineer, roamed around twisting knobs on the black trunks. The trunks were large enough, it seemed, to hold all the beach apparel anyone might need on a trip to the Seychelles.

The trunks were the amplifiers.

Rooster, a man graying at the temples who wore a short-sleeve safari jacket, painter's pants and Pumas with holes in them, changed the cords on two amps, plugged in others, unplugged some, and moved two trunks six inches apart.

"What kind of sound do I want?" Juanita casually picked the same note on the electric guitar. "I'm not really into high tech."

"I'm giving you a bridled antithesis," said Rooster, starting to adjust a miniature crane.

Juanita watched a chrome-and-charcoal rod crawl up a wall, journey across the ceiling, and lazily bend down to her nose. It was the microphone.

Slick Henderson came over from a corner of the laboratory and placed a binder filled with yellow legal pad on top of a twin reverb near Juanita's brown Famolare sandals. She was dressed for her performance in her spiffiest pair of jeans, boys' size 28, and a pale green cable-knit sweater, 50% lambswool, 40% angora, 10% nylon, made in the Philippines. Her auburn hair touched her shoulders and it was still in a Lib frizz.

Slick returned to a cane chair and reached down for a paper cup of coffee sitting on the floor.

Old Jeemy relaxed in a director's chair. His three-tone boots rested on Rev. Buddy Jack Grady's two banjo cases. This day, his Western-cut Ultrasuede suit was a vision in camouflage lime and olive. "Old Jeemy" in silver lettering was spelled out on the band around his black gunfighter's hat.

"Darlin', you get comfortable and go at your own pace. This ain't no audition for Fred Rose."

"I may have to stop and start over."

"Hell, the army had a name for it. Strategic withdrawal. Anything you want to do is fine. Your voice sounds good from over here."

"Sure does," Slick said. "Old Rooster must have bridled the precious out of those cataracts."

"Antithesis," Juanita smiled, running a scale.

Rooster left the room, saying, "We'll need the studio

in forty-five minutes, James. Don't explore the history of music back to Mozart, okay?"

Juanita said, "I'll start off with a slow one. I guess you could say a rich friend of mine was responsible for this song. It's about a man who likes his steel-bellied airheads. I call it 'Foolin' Around and Hangin' Out.' A man's supposed to sing it, so I'll try to sound husky."

> *Foolin' around and hangin' out ain't easy.*
> *It takes a lot more than time.*
> *I've got to know what girls need pleasing,*
> *Who tells the truth and who's lying.*
>
> *I've been learning it all since my teens.*
> *I know my Debbies, my Sues and Charlenes.*
> *I know Tina's the prettiest yet,*
> *But she costs more than three times my rent.*
>
> *Foolin' around and hangin' out ain't easy.*
> *It takes learning games they play.*
> *I've got to know Kitty likes teasing,*
> *And how Lisa just likes buying suede.*
>
> *I've been learning it all since my teens.*
> *I know my Brendas, Dianes and Marlenes.*
> *I know if Tina's not handled just right,*
> *She'll cost me my kids and my wife!*

Juanita sighed, took a deep breath.

Old Jeemy said, "Now that right there, that can use some polish, but you got yourself the framework of a song, is what you got."

Juanita picked an exercise on the Stratocaster. "Can I have some coffee?"

Slick hopped up and went out the door.

"I don't know about the appeal," Old Jeemy said, conversing with himself. "Might be narrow. Tune's not bad, though."

Juanita strummed a melody, and said, "Here's a song about a jukebox. Everybody's written a song

193

about a jukebox. I thought I would. Let me see if I can find the key."

"What'd you say the name of it was, Darlin'?"

"It doesn't have a name. 'E-6 Blues,' I guess."

> I won't play E-6 tonight.
> I'm too sad and blue.
> I'm gonna change my life.
> Get rid of E-6, and you.
>
> I plan on staying late,
> But not with you know who.
> Think I'll try R-8.
> See what that'll do.
>
> I don't care how much money
> I leave in this saloon.
> I'll find a new honey
> And find a new tune.
>
> I may take a chance
> Out there on the floor.
> See if I can dance
> To that crazy G-4.
>
> I'll wind up with a prize.
> There's others here like me.
> Hell, the whole room cries
> When they hear J-3.

Old Jeemy walked around the room. "If I had a gun pointed at my head and I had to pin down your voice, I'd put it somewhere halfway between Tammy and nobody I ever heard before."

"Loretta?"

"Don't have the hard-knocks she does. It's more sassy. It's got a little of Tammy's harshness, but the pronunciation's more refined. I hate to use a word like 'refined' when I'm talking about country music. Don't let 'refined' get out of this room. Step on it before it starts crawlin'."

"Dolly?"

"Lord, no. Dolly's a hummin' bird in baby clothes. I'm not sayin' she ain't great. I didn't say that."

Slick came back with the coffee and delivered two paper cups to Juanita on the platform. "What's wrong with sounding like yourself?" he said.

"Nothing. If I knew what I was doing. I've never had a voice lesson."

She pretended to pull a puppet string out of the top of her head, and chirped, "Mimi was her Mother's merry miss!"

"What else you got, Darlin'?"

Juanita picked another exercise, and said, "Well . . . I'll try this. The melody is what you basically call fuzzy. It's another song about a friend. He happens to be in the room."

She smiled at Slick. "You haven't heard this."

She strummed a longer than usual introduction. Then, looking at Slick throughout, Juanita sang:

He wore a longneck in his hand and he hardly ever grinned.
His Exxon patch explained just where his life had been.
He'd straighten up a little with strangers in the bar,
But if they wanted conversation, he said nothin' for a start.

He told most everybody he expected nothin' big
From a world that put you places you really hadn't picked.
He said he had a knack for spendin' a lot more than he made,
Said he never knew a wife who didn't take more than she gave.

He had wisdom in his corner, old fillin'-station Slick.
His answers came out better than the questions people raised.

195

*Once I heard a woman try to see what made him
  tick,*
*Thinkin' there was somethin' deep inside him he
  had saved.*
*So she said, 'What do you think you might amount
  to, Slick?'*
He just smiled and slowly answered, 'nothin' big.'

*He'd now and then meet women who were some-
  thing of a flirt.*
*He'd seen all kinds, he said, and knew just how they
  worked.*
He'd let 'em make a move and then he'd fine'ly say:
*'You in love with my inheritance or my grease-
  repellent shirt?'*

I can't count up all the hours I invested in my youth
*Hanging 'round that barroom and listening to the
  truth.*
*But the thing I learned for certain from old fillin'-
  station Slick*
*Was that the world sure likes to tempt you, then give
  you nothin' big.*

Slick went to the platform and gave the lady in the
swivel chair a kiss.

"I was saving it for Christmas," Juanita said.

Old Jeemy took off his hat and began pacing again.
"Now that song right there . . . I'll just say this . . .
that song would only need to be produced properly—
with a few changes in the lyrics, and we'd have us . . ."

"What changes?"

Juanita's voice intruded thunderously. She pushed
the mike aside.

"Darlin', it's nothing a professional songwriter would
need a search warrant for. Very minor."

"What?"

"Well," said Old Jeemy, "if you want me to get
clinical, the thing about it is, you got you a song about
this fellow I'm sympathetic with. But then you come in

there with that line about a 'grease-repellent shirt,' was that it? Now he's a smart aleck, don't you see? That's all I'm talkin' about. Good collaborator can fix it in no time."

"It's the key line in the song."

"You're talkin' about reality, aren't you, Darlin'?"

"I don't know. Maybe."

"See, I'm talkin' about a commercial song."

"The line is essential to the character's personality," Juanita said. "It says everything about his wisdom . . . humor . . . attitude."

"Darlin', it's things like this you argue about with a producer after you been shipping triple platinum before your albums are released, if you catch on to what I'm saying."

Juanita smoldered, staring at an amp.

Old Jeemy said, "I don't want us to get side-tracked from why we're here today. Let's leave it like this. You *re-think* the lyric. That's all I ask. How's that?"

Juanita pulled the microphone back toward her. She sang four more numbers, concluding with "Baja Oklahoma."

Juanita, Slick and Old Jeemy walked together to the main lobby of KOXX. At the front door, Old Jeemy said, "Don't let this scare you, Darlin', but I can see how it could, comin' from me. You could go up on a stage, Juanita. I'm talking about in front of an audience. You could entertain—and there wouldn't be no flies to swat anywhere around you."

"I just want to write a song and get paid for it."

"Darlin', that's exactly what I'm gonna try to do for us. I'll get a letter typed up and sent to you. Sign it and mail it back. It'll be the standard agent-manager gobbledegook. Same thing you'd sign with anybody else in the business. It'll spell out how you and me will participate in the income I generate."

Slick said, "Agent gets ten percent, isn't that it?"

Old Jeemy had a strapping good laugh.

Those were the old days. Now, the split was more like 40–60, 50–50, 60–40. Which was as it should be, if anyone stopped to think about it, he said. Old Jeemy pointed out that the agent-manager might be forced to spend a ton of money on demos, musicians, rehearsals, studios, equipment, travel and entertainment in order to get a song published.

"Shows you how much I know about it," said Slick. "I thought in the case of a songwriter, you just sent off a song to somebody to see if they wanted to sing it."

"Hey, podna!" Old Jeemy draped his arms around Juanita and Slick both. "When we hit our home run, there'll be so many greenbacks, we'll be sailin' 'em out the window like paper airplanes!"

They went outside. Old Jeemy strolled with them to Slick's LTD. They stood for a moment and Juanita looked up at the theater-type marquee on the radio station, a two-story building. The marquee said: IF YOU DIDN'T EAT IT, OLD JEEMY DIDN'T COOK IT!

"Darlin', I don't know if you noticed, but I had a tape goin' in there. I'll send you a cassette. You can hear how you sound with a bridled antithesis."

"I'd like to have it," Juanita said. "Thank you."

"I still want to take you to dinner one of these nights," Old Jeemy said. "We haven't ever seriously talked music. I got lots of stories."

Slick was invited, too, of course.

"I think the two of you ought to go alone," said Slick. "I couldn't contribute anything. I just found out today what an agent makes."

Juanita said she would check her social calendar and choose an evening for dinner that wouldn't conflict with anything the maharani had planned.

As Slick drove away from the radio station, Juanita said, "Did you notice when I got arrogant?"

"What do you mean?" said Slick.

"Singing."

"While you were singing?"

"Yes."

"It looked like the longer you were up there, the more you liked it."

"I mean when I *really* liked it."

"Well, I could tell you liked doing it there at the end."

"It was right before I did 'Baja.' In the middle of 'Too Many Midnight Songs.' Then all through 'Baja.'"

"You got arrogant?"

"Yep," Juanita giggled. "That's when we had a winner in the hair-tossing contest."

Juanita reached Lonnie Slocum at the Mad Dog Music Co. in Nashville by leaving the urgent message that Dove Christian had called. Within an hour, Lonnie returned her call at Herb's.

"Where's Dove? Is he in Fort Worth?"

"Where's my cassette?"

"Shit, Juanita, I thought it was something important."

The cassette was there, but Lonnie had been too busy to listen to her songs.

"You're kidding, of course," Juanita said.

"Show biz is taking an awful toll around here," Lonnie said.

"You've had the cassette three weeks! I've been expecting a call from you, Lonnie!"

Lonnie said, "We're trying to make an album, Juanita. You've got to understand artistic temperaments."

"I'm supposed to have a song on the Goddamn album!"

"Hey, that's right," Lonnie said.

"You know what, Lonnie? You've suffered permanent brain damage, I'm serious."

"I wouldn't quarrel with that diagnosis, but I *am* your friend and I'll listen to your tape, I promise."

"Before or after you finish the album?"

"Pretty soon."

"Did you tell me to write you a song or did I dream that up?"

"Juanita, you don't know much about a man and his art. I've been preoccupied. I've still got a spot for you on the album. Did you write a good song?"

"Go fuck yourself."

"Come on, Juanita."

"Three Goddamn weeks. I mean, gimme a break, Lonnie."

"What's the song about? Is it a love song?"

"Yeah, it's a love song. A man falls in love with a spoon he can't get out of his nose."

"We're coming to Fort Worth, did you know that?"

"I heard."

"Playing warmup for Willie. That's why we're so busy. I want to get the album finished before we come down there."

"Good-bye, Lonnie."

"Wait a minute, Juanita. I promise I'll listen to your tape. Next week."

"Don't bother. I don't think the song's right for you. I'm sending it to Barbra Streisand."

"We've got a Deering now. It ought to speed things up around here."

"A what?"

"A grinder."

"Have you added an instrument to Dog Track Gravy?"

"It's for that smart stuff in your pocket. Makes your old heart swell up to see how much you have after you run it through the grinder. Gives you a whole new attitude about art."

"Go with God, Lonnie."

That evening in the bar, a planning session was convened to discuss a social event. The TCU-Texas football game coming up held the promise of enormous gaiety if Herb's regulars were to have a proper kind of tailgate party.

Doris Steadman volunteered her resourcefulness, which would insure that it wouldn't be a crass affair. No styrofoam containers or Kentucky Fried's extra crispy.

"We'll do it right," Doris said. "I'll bring my card tables and chairs and my pink linens and napkins."

Doris further announced that she would make her special jellied chicken salad and peanutty pork chops.

Vera Satterwhite would bring the clam dip and the candied Vienna sausages on colored toothpicks.

"I'll try to talk LuAnn Hodges into making a ladybug cake for dessert," she said.

Tommy Earl Bruner said, "I'd like to put in a request for something decent."

"Yeah," said Hank Rainey, the society carpenter. "Why don't we just bring some food and beer?"

Herb Macklin took Doris' position. "Let's step up in class. Do it right for a change."

"Herb, what's clam dip?" Shorty Eckwood asked. "Ain't that what I had at your July the Fourth picnic?"

To the rest of the group, Shorty said, "I think clam dip's what it was. I thought I'd climbed inside a sea turtle."

"Lee will be back by Saturday," Doris said. "I'll send him out to the stadium early to hold those parking places by the pecan trees. It'll give us more ambience."

"I don't care what it gives," Tommy Earl said. "Long as there's something to drink and Sheila keeps the kids off my ass."

Herb said, "I like the way it sounds. Anybody else got any ideas? How 'bout you, Foster?"

Foster Barton had been writing in his pocket diary. He said, "Okay, here it is. TCU, take the 34½. I like Baylor, give 3. I love A & M, give 12. I like the Over on Arkansas-Rice. I'm teasing the Aggies with Alabama and Army. Oregon's the West Coast saver. I'll probably go with the Under on TCU-Texas."

"We were *discussing* the tailgate party, Foster!" Doris was making her own notes on pink stationery.

"Talk about parties all you want to," Foster said, amiably, "but Saturday's a day at the office for me."

Beecher Perry and Tina Busher came in later and Slick said he would esteem to buy them a drink.

"There's an old rule," said Beecher. "Richest man in the room buys the whisky and that's me."

That wasn't the rule Slick had been taught by his father.

"My daddy said if you hung out with smart fellows, some of the smart would rub off. If you hung out with dumb fellows, some of the dumb would rub off. But if you hung out with rich fellows, you'd go busted picking up their dinner checks."

"Your daddy must have spent time in the East," Beecher Perry said.

"No, he was just an old wildcatter who never hit," said Slick. "But he helped make all those Cosdens rich, trading oil leases for groceries."

Juanita invited Beecher Perry to the tailgate party Saturday. Beecher said he was flattered, but he had already accepted an invitation to another pre-game party—if all of his old Kappa Sig brothers from the University of Texas didn't have midair collisions in their Lears and G-2's.

"I'm afraid the game's going to be a familiar story," he said. "Burnt-orange touchdowns and 'hook 'em, Horns.'"

Juanita made two hook 'em signs simultaneously with her hands, that sign being a gesture in which a person raises only the forefinger and pinkie. "What's this mean, Beecher? 'We're No. 4!'?"

"Number four's ass," Beecher said. "We're so No. I right now, our second string's I-A."

Tommy Earl said, "Beecher, if you got any influence down there in Austin, you better tell 'em to invite one of them Marylands in the Cotton Bowl. They're talking about Notre Dame. Notre Dame'll shit in your hat and hand it back to you before you get to the scrimmage line."

"Not if we play football."

"Listen to that *we*," said Tommy Earl. "You never heard any of that *we* crap from the Texas alumni when TCU had Sam Baugh and Davey O'Brien and all them motherfuckers!"

"That's been TCU's problem, hasn't it?" Beecher gave Tina Busher a hug to let her know he was aware of her presence in the room. "They haven't had any of those since hamburgers cost a nickel."

"We've had others," Tommy Earl said. "Lindy Berry . . . Jim Swink . . . Bob Lilly . . . B. C. Puckett. *Me*. I took us to the Radar Bowl."

"What was that?" Beecher said.

"Game we played against Penn State in a blizzard," said Tommy Earl. "Our team plane should have crashed just tryin' to get there. They won, anyhow."

"One thing about Austin," Beecher said. "Football program's still on sound footing. We're still building character in our athletics. I get inspired just reading the signs on the dressing-room wall down there at Memorial Stadium. They tell you what's important about life itself."

Beecher Perry spoke slowly, deliberately.

" 'What I *Saved*, I Lost . . . What I *Gave*, I Kept.' That's my favorite."

"It is?" said Tommy Earl.

"Think about it for a minute."

"Hell, I'm tryin' to, but I ain't got a fuckin' philosophy professor to help me. Goddamn, a kid from San Saba would be a *senior* before he figured out that shit. Am I lyin' to anybody?"

Tommy Earl pushed his glass toward Juanita for more Junior.

"I wish you luck, Beecher, in case you get hold of Notre Dame on New Year's Day. You know there's only three things a Texan's scared of, don't you?"

"What might those be?"

"A nigger with a knife, a Mexican with a driver's license—and a priest with a football!"

Juanita and Beecher traded gossip about their daughters.

There were now six people living with Babs Perry in the tree house near Lake Austin. Babs, Loraine and Heidi had taken in Gina, Vanna and Duncan.

Duncan?

Beecher was not to be concerned about the presence of a man in the tree house. Duncan wasn't into girls. Duncan wasn't into boys, either. Duncan was into Self.

Duncan was the most intelligent person Babs had

ever met. Not only did he have a master's degree in economics, he had been an artist who sculpted with styrofoam and chemicals—until the chemicals ruined his hands. Which was the thing that drove Duncan to found SELF. Duncan was teaching the practices of SELF to Babs and the other girls so they could become SELF-ettes and go out into the world and convert other lost souls.

SELF placed all of its emphasis on body contortions, not the hands. Never the hands. SELF stood for Sinewed Ecclesiastics of Legs and Frame. It also stood for Screw Everybody Like Francine, but that was Duncan's private joke. Francine was Duncan's ex-wife, who apparently had been notorious for her avarice around drugs.

Beware of the hands. That was Duncan's fundamental message.

If the hands could be eliminated from most human endeavors, a person would live a more tranquil life, a life less affected by hoggishness. A person must learn to go with the rhythmic temperaments of the body-turns, the artistic designs evoked by the arms in motion, the ever-emergent vibrations within the torso.

Beecher Perry said, "I had a golf pro tell me to go with my body-turn instead of my hands. He said if I went with my hands, I'd wind up with mustard on my shirt."

In the woods near the tree house, Duncan was twice a day holding training sessions at which Babs, Loraine, Heidi, Gina and Vanna practiced their body contortions in the nude. The sessions were being filmed. Duncan was a strong believer in film study as an aid to learning.

Babs had used up last month's allowance to buy Duncan two things the SELF movement needed desperately. A Trans Am and a Hobie-Cat.

"Well, who's to say?" Beecher grimaced. "If Babs had gone to Wellesley like Edna wanted her to, she'd probably be in the penitentiary now for trying to assassinate the Shah of Kuwait."

Beecher got off the barstool, handing Juanita the usual hundred-dollar bill, half of which would be a tip.

"You better call," Tina Busher said, reminding him of something.

"Right," said Beecher. "Where'd I go today? Am I in Los Angeles or Houston?"

Tina took Beecher's arm and pressed against him.

"Just tell her you're calling from the outskirts of Ecstasy, Texas."

When they were gone, Tommy Earl said to the room, "Beecher's the most thoughtful man I know. He'd do anything to keep from hurting his wife. He's always careful to avoid the No. 1 evil in the world."

"What's the No. 1 evil?" Juanita said.

"Needless veracity," said Tommy Earl. "Tops on the list. Been proved."

Chapter Fourteen

There were eighteen get-well cards in Juanita's mail the next day. Each card bore the name and return address of "Butch Hoot, General Delivery, Medicine Dock, Alaska."

Juanita squeezed the envelopes and held them up to the light. She shook them and tried to guess their weight.

The envelopes were only slightly thicker and heavier than those oblong types which contained a greeting card guaranteed to amuse Doris Steadman, the card with a cartoon illustration of a penis and balls bearing the incredibly witty sentiment: "All three of your friends miss you!"

Juanita tucked away the envelopes in a binder, a song file, on the countertop in her kitchen–breakfast room–den. Then a day later she received twenty-seven more, these from "Michelle Silhouette, Box 729, Secret Harbor, Calif."

If all estimates were correct, Juanita now had $67,500 worth of cocaine in her apartment. Therefore, she began to give serious thought to two things. First, where was she going to store it when the song file spilled over? Candy was right. Juanita never threw anything away. The other question was, should she open any of it?

If she never looked inside an envelope, she would not know what the contents were. She would not be a dope-hider. She would only be an unopened-envelope collector, which was certainly not as strange as being a bird-watcher. As far as she knew, bird-watching had yet to be declared a felony.

She would have a legitimate alibi when the narcs busted the Sans Su South. "Well, you see, Lieutenant, they kept stacking up on me before I could get them back to the post office."

The reason Juanita opened an envelope was because she could not resist seeing what the stuff looked like.

Coffee-mate.

A tightly wrapped cellophane packet of Coffee-mate. One packet approximately 1½ by 2½ inches in size, mashed flat, Scotchtaped inside the card—$1500. Here's wishing you a speedy recovery.

Juanita did not open the cellophane packet. One step could lead to another. She might try it and decide she liked it, and then she would have to write "Stardust" twice a year to support her habit.

The most evident thing was, she needed a good

hiding place in the apartment. That would require careful study.

The day the second onslaught of cards arrived, Candy phoned her mother at home to make sure Juanita was getting well and having happy birthdays.

"I have a great idea for Dove," Juanita said to Candy. "Tell him to sell Coffee-mate. I bet Coffee-mate will make your nose drip and your eyes water as good as anything—and it's legal."

"That's what a lot of dealers *sell*."

"Oh."

"Momma, it's spookier than ever out here. The narcs are still around, but we can only feel them, we can't see them. Dove says it's the worst possible sign. They're getting ready to hit somewhere."

"Are you being careful?"

"Yeah, we're cool. Remillard and Keala aren't so cool, though. They're acting pretty radical. Remillard shaved his mustache and got a crew-cut. Keala's taking so much speed to stay alert, she's pouring drinks before she picks up a glass. Last night she fixed a vodka stinger for a customer and said, 'That'll be three-fifty, please.' But she served him her empty hand!"

Candy wanted to know if the sympathy cards had come from "Joey McSurf, c/o The Rat and Fin Restaurant, Hanalei, Hawaii."

Not yet.

"There'll be thirty of those," Candy said.

Dove had a plan for getting the rest of the tooth powder out of Aspen. He was going to climb in the MGB with Candy and the last bundle of cards. He would drive as fast as possible into town. When the car reached the middle of Aspen, he was going to spin it, have a minor collision with a brick wall, the side of The Sinus Problem. This would create a diversion for the hidden narcs, enabling Candy to leap out of the car and jam all of the envelopes into a mailbox. They would be clean.

"That's the stupidest idea I've ever heard in my life," Juanita said. "You can get hurt, killed. Jesus!"

"Momma, it's not that dangerous. You can't drive that fast. There's too much snow, the streets are too slick. It'll be Dove's side of the car that hits the wall. He's been rehearsing the spin. Dove says if there are too many people on the sidewalk, he'll go to Plan B."

The backup plan was for Dove to stall the MGB in the intersection near the mailbox. He would then divert the attention of the hidden narcs by toppling out of the car and suffering a bizarre epileptic seizure while Candy raced to the mailbox.

"Tell Dove I like that better," Juanita said. "Tell him Plan B is immortal."

"There's only one drawback," Candy said. "Dove will really have to come up with a convincing epileptic fit. That's the way most people in Aspen act normally."

Grace and Mrs. Grimes were having lunch at a table in the community room when Juanita visited her mother at the Trinity River Nursing Center later that day.

Juanita took a chair at the table as Mrs. Grimes was saying, "I'll bet it was arteriosclerosis. That's what they thought I had before they found out I'd been eating too much starch."

"No, it was catalepsy," Grace said. "Lord, I couldn't move a muscle. Oh, it was so painful."

Mrs. Grimes said, "Well, I thought my arteriosclerosis was painful until I got conjunctivitis in this eye."

Mrs. Grimes showed Juanita her right eye.

"I had that," Grace said. "My word, you couldn't believe the eyeball, how inflamed it was."

Grace and Mrs. Grimes were wearing robes and slippers and eating breaded veal cutlets, mashed potatoes, and pinto beans.

"It caused embolisms up and down my body," Grace said.

"What did, Momma?"

"That pain."

Mrs. Grimes said, "You don't know what pain is until you've had hyperglycemia. It sneaks up on you. All you can do is sit down under a tree."

"Oh, I know what you mean," said Grace. "Hyperglycemia was how I found out about my spinal curvature."

Mrs. Grimes patted Juanita's arm, and said, "She's back on her elimination schedule, but they sure had a time with her."

"They did?" Juanita looked at Grace.

"I was vomicose," Grace said. "Oh, I wanted to see a toxicologist so bad."

"What was it?"

"Land's sakes, I just don't know. I'm in such poor health all the time." Grace scooped up some pinto beans. "I think it all goes back to my cardiovascular problem."

"She was as bad off as I was last week," Mrs. Grimes said.

"Oh, I was in more pain than you," said Grace.

"Mine were the hardest little pellets you ever saw," Mrs. Grimes said.

"Well, you can just go ask Boteet!" Grace said. "They had to take mine manually!"

Juanita left Grace and Mrs. Grimes to ride shotgun on their own bowel movements.

Doris arranged the "double date" that night, a Thursday, and Juanita went along with it, figuring it would be better to have other people around in case Old Jeemy proved to be The Glaze King on the subject of music or anything else. Doris' date was Tommy Earl Bruner, but it had to be handled delicately. Tommy Earl was going to meet the three of them accidentally at The Tonga Rain Forest.

The Tonga Rain Forest, which Doris had selected for dinner, was on the penthouse level of the Evetts Tower, a new skyscraper in the city. The Evetts Tower looked like a beast on stainless steel legs walking away with an armload of mirrored boxes.

The Evetts Tower was supposed to signal the start of an effort to restore beauty and vitality to the downtown area, which had lost many of its inhabitants to the suburbs. Hunks of steel sculpture surrounded the Evetts Tower, all of it done by an artist overly fascinated with the comma and question mark.

The downtown Fort Worth of Juanita's youth had seemed an exciting place, often dazzling, she thought, even when the wind tunnel of 7th Street would catapult her from the Hollywood to the Worth to the Palace theaters, once the grand first-run movie houses of the city.

There were times when Juanita longed to have downtown back as it had been in the days when she considered it an adventure simply to wander around in the big department stores, The Fair, Stripling's, Meacham's, Monnig's, Cox's, stores which seemed of immeasureable size then. They were stores owned by local families and they held an atmosphere of refinement and charm with their old-wood interiors, carpeted floors, wide aisles, promenades, tearooms, soda fountains—and sales people who worked in the stores for so many years they looked as familiar as celebrities or cousins.

Juanita wanted all of the downtown restaurants and night spots back as they had been when going out to dine or dance led revelers to places like The Clover Club, The Den, The Pirate's Cave, The Westbrook Grill, The Seibold Cafe, The Delta, places which had been there since the days when people drank pocket hooch and all the pretty dresses used to scratch.

Doris was waiting for Juanita and Old Jeemy when they stepped off the outdoor glass-enclosed elevator and into the restaurant's foyer. Doris was standing by the spear of a South Seas warrior. Among the other features of the Tonga were waitresses in sarongs, Mexican busboys dressed as voodoo doctors, a hundred dinner tables under bamboo shelters, a stereo thunderstorm every twenty minutes incorporating a deluge of rainfall and a fireworks display of lightning, and, in the center of it all, a barge surrounded by a murky pond.

An indefinable animal's head represented the bow of the barge. Dining facilities for an elite twenty-eight

people were under an awning. There was a small dance
floor and a stage for a combo, where a male vocalist in a
Hawaiian shirt was letting it be known he was going to
rely heavily on "What Kind of Fool Am I?" and "I Left
My Heart in San Francisco."

The barge was cleverly constructed on an underwater
hydraulic cable which allowed it to drift slowly and
moodily away in the pond and then drift back again to a
walkway over which enchanted travelers boarded the
craft and disembarked. Dining on the barge was the
"in" thing, for the passengers could sail about twenty
feet toward Abott, Texas, and sail back again.

Doris was wearing a pink flowered-chiffon poncho,
pink pajama pants, and pink suede sandals. Her eyes
were freshly painted murals of battle scenes, and she
had dipped her head in a vat of Breck super-hold hair
mist.

Juanita wore a dark gray skirt and jacket with a light
gray turtleneck and her stacked-heel Margaret Jerrolds,
having selected the outfit to offset both Doris and Old
Jeemy, whose Western-cut Ultrasuede suit was now
canary.

As lightning crackled across the ceiling and the
rumble of thunder blended with the sound of a down-
pour, Juanita contemplated the Tonga specialty she
would be having for dinner.

Fat-ka-bob.

Old Jeemy arranged for a table on the barge by
shaking hands with Kamehameha the Great.

"That's what you call 'the international slide,' Darlin'," Old Jeemy said, counting his money to make
certain he had only given the maître d' a ten-dollar bill.

Doris ordered a Hong Kong Slurp.

Juanita prevailed on a waitress in a sarong from the
isle of Hurst-Euless to explain what a Hong Kong Slurp
was.

"Ma'am, I don't really know," the waitress said. "I
think it's three kinds of rum, gin, brandy and bourbon,
and a bunch of gook that makes it look like a milk shake
had a head-on with a can of sliced peaches."

Juanita ordered a white-wine spritzer and Old Jeemy a stinger rocks.

Over the first round of drinks, Old Jeemy produced a letter of agreement for Juanita to inspect.

He said, "Darlin', the quicker you sign this, the quicker somebody in Nashville is liable to open up a satchel and start throwin' money at us. We may have to put a rock on your head to keep you from gettin' so tall in the music business."

As near as Juanita could determine from the legalistic wording of the letter, it proposed a fifty-fifty split between the artist and the agent/manager.

She *did* recognize the sentence permitting Old Jeemy to steal every penny she might ever earn. It read:

"The agent/manager agrees to pay all income due the client on a prompt quarterly basis after deducting such expenses as may be deemed necessary in helping the agent/manager generate said income, the sum of these expenses not to exceed a figure common and acceptable in the trade."

Juanita studied the last part of the sentence, then underlined it with the pen Old Jeemy had given her.

Handing the document back to him, unsigned, she said:

"Podna, if I wanted a hemorrhoidectomy, I'd go to a hospital."

Old Jeemy roared with laughter.

"This is just the first draft, Darlin'. We'll get it right. Hell, life's negotiable."

"I've got a motto of my own," she said. "If fine print wrote it, Juanita didn't sign it."

What with the intermittent rains and thunderstorms, an hour passed quickly. But Doris Steadman drank three Hong Kong Slurps, and she had developed a loud voice by the time Tommy Earl Bruner, acting surprised to see them, joined the table on the barge.

Tommy Earl sat close enough to Doris for their legs to touch.

"How many hard-ons you got left?"

Doris' question attracted stares from a couple seated nearby, a gray-haired gentleman who might have been the chancellor of a university and a woman who might have been the head of the Religion Department.

"Women don't get hard-ons," Doris said. "We get doughnuts."

Doris tittered and missed her mouth with the straw in her Hong Kong Slurp.

"We get doughnuts and you have to look for 'the little man in the boat,' right, Juanita?"

Juanita ate a crab puff and rooted for a roll of thunder.

Doris nuzzled Tommy Earl, and said, "If you can't find 'the little man in the boat,' then you don't have no business on the lake!"

Doris lifted herself up from the table by bracing one hand on Tommy Earl's shoulder and the other on something behind her—which happened to be the head of a three-year-old boy in a highchair spitting out sweet-and-sour pork.

"I want to dance," Doris said.

The vocalist in the Hawaiian shirt was singing "Vaya Con Dios."

Doris pulled Tommy Earl to the dance floor, bumping into the table where the chancellor of the university and the head of the Religion Department were trying to open fortune cookies.

Doris slugged the chancellor on the arm, and said, "Stick around, Newt. We're all gonna boogie."

Juanita's box score had Doris only falling down twice on the dance floor, once to "Tie a Yellow Ribbon" and once to "Waikiki Moon." Each time, Tommy Earl helped her up by the bosom.

Returning to the table, Doris said, "I got to go pee."

"Me, too," said Tommy Earl.

"Where is it?"

Doris' eyes were blurring.

"Fuck, I don't know. Go to Bangkok and take a left."

Tommy Earl followed Doris toward the walkway leading from the barge to dry land, but he made the mistake of lingering too many paces behind her.

A thunderstorm struck as Doris started across the walkway.

With lightning flashing and a torrent of rain falling, the Hong Kong Slurps led Doris to the edge of the walkway. For a split second, she did a high-wire act.

Doris Steadman then bombarded the pond and sank into the fathomless deep of the Tonga.

Juanita and Old Jeemy rushed to the bow of the barge and got there as Tommy Earl, who had bravely dived into the water, was cruising beneath the surface.

Peering into the water, Juanita thought she saw Doris and Tommy Earl grappling around on the ocean floor among rocks, fish, plumbing and what appeared to be an Adidas sneaker.

Doris came up for air three times and Tommy Earl once, and finally they came up together and waded out of the pond in water only five-feet deep.

Doris was an easy winner in the Tonga's wet poncho contest.

People applauded and assembled around Doris and Tommy Earl as they climbed out of the pond. Girls in sarongs and South Seas warriors wrapped Doris in tablecloths. Two men shook Tommy Earl's hand. Kamehameha the Great asked Doris to sign a piece of paper releasing The Tonga Rain Forest from any responsibility for whatever injuries she may have suffered.

In the middle of the activity, a shockingly familiar voice, that of a man, came from somewhere in the crowd, and Juanita spun around.

"What happened? What's going on? That looks like my wife!"

It was Lee Steadman, wriggling forward, excusing his way into the inner circle.

"Jesus," Juanita said, fully prepared to surrender and divulge the location of all the artillery and airfields.

Doris was missing one false eyelash and her hair had

214

begun to slacken and spread wings, but she sprang rapidly to the attack.

"What the hell are you doing here?" she screeched.

"Me?" said Lee. "I came home from Colorado tonight."

"I can *see* that!"

"I went to the house but nobody was there."

"That's because I was here having dinner with Juanita and her agent, helping her make a business decision. This is Old Jeemy Williams. You might say hello! He's a celebrity!"

"Oh, yeah," Lee said, shaking Old Jeemy's hand. "You're on KTIX."

"KOXX," Old Jeemy said. "Don't matter, podna. We're in the same alphabet!"

"Why in God's name are you in this place tonight?" Doris said to her husband.

"Well," Lee said, "there wasn't anything on TV. I knew some of the fellows from the convention were coming here. They talked about it on the plane. They said they weren't expected home till tomorrow."

"So you thought you'd come in here and gawk at these sarongs, *too*, is that what you thought?"

"I wouldn't have come if 'Hawaii Five-O' had been on."

"What happened to it?"

"They put on a news special instead."

"A *news special?* I hope you called the TV station!"

"You're soaking wet," Lee said.

Lee looked at Juanita, who was marveling at Doris, and said, "Doris is soaking wet."

Doris said, "Would you mind telling me what was so special about the news that it couldn't wait until 'The Today Show'?"

"I never found out," Lee said. "'Hawaii Five-O' came on for five minutes. A sniper started picking off paddlers in an outrigger canoe race. Then all of a sudden one of those guys who's not Walter Cronkite showed up with a big map behind him. It could have been Dub Rather but I think it was old Bob Sheetser.

Anyhow, whoever it was started talking about Russians and Chinamen and Arabs and Jews gettin' into something, so I came on over here."

Lee noticed Tommy Earl. "You're wet, too."

"He jumped in the water to save me from drowning," said Doris, shoving on a wing of her hair. "It was an act of heroics if I ever saw one."

"Nothin' to it, Lee," Tommy Earl said. "You'd have done the same thing."

Lee said, "How in the dickens did you wind up in the water, honey? That barge didn't run into something, did it?"

Lee strained to see if the Tonga's barge looked damaged as Doris said, "What I was doing in the water is what any wife would do if she cared about her wedding ring!"

Juanita turned away from Lee and bit her lip.

Doris said, "My ring slipped off my finger while I was walking over that gangplank. I went right in after it. That ring never has fit the way it should!"

"I don't think anything could have stopped her," said Tommy Earl. "Octopus or nothin'. I don't want no credit for what I did. I just happened to be the closest one to her, sittin' over there as I was, entertaining my customers."

"I got my ring back, that's all I care about," Doris said. "Take me home, Lee, before I get bronchitis."

Doris tugged on Lee's arm and they started out. Lee paused to wave aloha from the banks of the Tonga.

Tommy Earl searched his hair for seaweed.

"That's $400 I got comin' from Foster," he said.

"What for?" said Juanita.

"Foster laid me two to one I'd never see Old Pink. Underwater counts, don't it?"

Tommy Earl departed through a private dining room, the Kalawao Village, which, were it still on Molokai, would be the leper colony.

About thirty seconds later, Juanita and Old Jeemy were approached by a couple who looked wholly unfamiliar to the barmaid. The man and woman came

216

up behind Old Jeemy. The woman was not unattractive, given her seething anger. The man was overweight, his red sport coat too small, his tie loosened.

Looking coldly at Juanita, the woman said, "Did he tell you I was dead or incurably ill?"

Old Jeemy whirled around. "Hey, podna! What a surprise! Hale maki ooki pocki ha! Alooooooha!"

"Asshole," said the woman.

"Podna!"

"Jerk," said the woman. "Fool."

Juanita said, "Excuse me, but . . . are you . . . *Kathy?*"

"No, I'm Nancy Drew." The woman nudged the man with her. "Tell him."

The hefty man took out a notebook. "At 6:14 this evening, Mr. Williams, you picked up a female companion at the Sans Su South apartment complex. You and the female companion, Caucasian, proceeded to the Evetts Tower and were seen entering The Tonga Rain Forest at 7:19. At 9:29 . . ."

"Whoa!" said Old Jeemy. "This is a business meeting, podna! Ain't that right, Juanita? Sweetheart, this is Juanita Hutchins, my new client!"

"Aren't they all?" Kathy Williams said.

"Darlin'! Podna!"

Old Jeemy looked to Juanita for assistance. "Make my old podna here understand, Juanita. She's got this all wrong!"

Juanita said, "I'm trying to think of what to say, but I'm just so happy to see Kathy *alive*, I don't . . ."

Juanita let it go at that and retreated ambiguously into a dense jungle of palms.

Chapter Fifteen

The following day Juanita became a seamstress.

She first locked and bolted her doors and closed every drape in the apartment. She then spread all of the little cellophane packets across her bed. This included the batch of thirty from "Joey McSurf" which came that morning along with twenty-five more from "Smiley Dunlap, Rt. 4, G. D., Roach Grove, Ore."

After spreading them out, she tediously began Scotchtaping several of them together, making different patches.

She pieced all of the cellophane packets into singularly odd strips and blocks.

Next, she stitched the strips and blocks onto patterns she cut from yards of pure silk. The strips and blocks were covered with another layer of silk and then a layer of satin on both sides, like so much quilting.

And this was the lining with which she replaced the old lining in Aunt Bernice's full-length mink coat.

When Juanita took over from Thurlene Nix behind the bar that Friday afternoon, she had the momentary feeling she had just been freed from a time capsule. It wasn't Wednesday, but a full compliment of South Side B & PW's were there, and they seemed to be unanimously calling for the impeachment of Judge Derrell Wishcamper.

"What's everybody picking on the judge for?" Juanita was mopping up a work area behind the bar. It had become a creek of rum, coconut syrup and pineapple juice. The Business and Professional Women were drinking Piña Coladas.

Herb Macklin had no regular early-in-the-day barmaid. Business did not demand it. Waitresses alternated the task, and none of them liked doing it. The tips were almost nonexistent. That day had been Thurlene Nix's turn.

Thurlene Nix, as she was returning to the dining room floor, said to Juanita, "One of them ladies says she's been to the Caribbean and I ain't doin' these pint-of-clabbers right."

"LuAnn likes it creamier. If you add a little milk, that does it."

"She could have told me she wanted ice box pie," Thurlene said.

Doris Steadman, remarkably recovered from the night before, said, "Juanita, didn't you read the morning paper?"

Juanita had not, in fact, read the paper. Busy with the seamstress work.

What Juanita had missed in the paper was the story about Bobby Jay Keeney. Bobby Jay had been arrested after a hit-and-run accident in which a young black man had been killed. The accident had more accurately been a hit-and-stop, then run. It was suspected that Bobby Jay may have been looking for his victim. The black man had died with his boots on—also a blue velvet suit and a broad-brimmed white fur hat. Bobby Jay had gone to the trouble to write down his own name, address and license number for three eyewitnesses to the death of the rival pimp. Bobby Jay had then driven to Reba's Lounge where he got celebratively drunk and passed out. Reba's was where the police had apprehended him.

The thing which had so upset the South Side B &

PW's was that Judge Derrell Wishcamper had released Bobby Jay Keeney, now a known murderer, without bail.

Further, the judge had been quoted in the newspaper as saying, "Aw, old Bobby Jay was just drunk and havin' fun. He probably won't do anything like this again."

It occurred to Juanita that justice might best be served if Bobby Jay were turned over to Thurlene Nix.

One evening Bobby Jay had stumbled drunkenly into Herb's dining room and crashed into a booth and tried to order something to eat while fighting to keep his chin from puncturing a hole in his chest. Thurlene, in her usual convivial mood, had been his waitress.

Thurlene had listened tolerantly as Bobby Jay had said: "Gee a scrambly eggs two dap vanilla, grill grape sandwich, chockit keek onion rang, chicken farb sticky, mee shik mussard . . . lots cawky."

Thurlene had supervised in the kitchen and had brought Bobby Jay *exactly* what he had requested. The sight of the food alone had almost sobered him.

He had said, "Where'd this come from—between your legs? I'll show you what you can do with this shit!"

"Naw, I'll show *you*," Thurlene had said.

She had steamed into Herb's office and come back with Herb's .38 and stuck the barrel into Bobby Jay's neck and held it there, saying, "If I was you, I'd get after my dinner. If I pull this trigger, all I'll get is a citation for beautifying the city."

The gun had caused a commotion in the dining room. Two men wearing bowling shirts had dived to the floor and begun creeping toward the rear exit, and the woman with them had torn off her blonde wig and fallen to her knees in prayer.

Bobby Jay had been trying to choke down his grilled grape sandwich when Juanita had arrived and coaxed Thurlene into putting away the .38 and allowing Bobby Jay to leave. Which he had done—in a path of vomit.

Defending the manner with which she had handled

the customer, Thurlene had said to Juanita, "I wasn't gonna make him eat nothin' he didn't order."

Now in Herb's, the B & PW's talked over their options in dealing with Judge Derrell Wishcamper.

Vera Satterwhite said it wouldn't do any good to circulate a petition because people never signed their real names to petitions. When the club had circulated a petition to keep the city from widening the street that ran in front of Josephine McClure's house, most of the twelve hundred names on it had been Davy Crockett and Eliot Ness.

"She was going to lose those sycamore trees, anyhow," LuAnn Hodges said. "Two of them were already dead."

Doris said, "We ought to mobilize our effort before the next election."

"You can't get the old shithead voted out," Vera said. "He's a Shriner."

Vera opened her bag and went to work on a hot flash with her Oriental fan.

"How often do they come?" said Alma Roberts.

"This is my fourth in an hour," Vera said. "Feel the back of my head."

"It's too bad men don't have them," LuAnn said. "Men wouldn't have gone two hundred years without finding a Goddamn cure!"

"Have you tried hormone shots?" Alma asked Vera.

"Why hell no!" Vera speeded up the fan. "I'd rather have hot flashes than cancer. I'm starting on vitamin E."

"Well," said LuAnn, "at least you won't ever be constipated."

The course of action decided upon by the South Side B & PW's was for LuAnn Hodges, the current president, to write a letter on club stationery to the *Star-Telegram* denouncing a judge who would let a murderer walk the streets.

Had the women stayed at Herb's Cafe a while longer, they could have denounced the judge personally.

Judge Wishcamper carted a gargantuan canvas into the bar, his Wonderful West Texas Fun and Adventure Map, and propped the canvas on a table, leaning it against the casement window.

"It ain't quite finished yet," the judge said, backing away, standing near Slick Henderson. "I haven't drawed in Hardin-Simmons University in Abilene or the Permian Basin Petroleum Museum in Midland."

Juanita advised the judge to keep a low profile for a while. She had knowledge of citizens who were outraged at his handling of the Bobby Jay Keeney affair.

"When's Bobby Jay going to trial?" Juanita was eager to know.

"Aw, it won't ever come to that," Judge Derrell Wishcamper said, studying his painting. "It was just a nigger deal."

After the judge left with his Wonderful West Texas Fun and Adventure Map, Juanita said, "They ought to get the judge on TV. He'd be a great panelist on one of those shows where intellectuals discuss the New South."

Slick wanted to hear more about Juanita's evening at The Tonga Rain Forest. She got around to telling him, but not before she wrote the only straw-hat-and-cane number she would ever compose.

> *Salutary greetings to Bobby Jay Keeney.*
> *Oh, what a wonderful guy.*
> *Likeable, laughable,*
> *The gentleman type.*
> *He could really nail you*
> *With a heavy lead pipe!*
>
> *Salutary greetings to Bobby Jay Keeney.*
> *He's an American star.*
> *Charming and lovable,*
> *Out for a lark.*
> *He liked to roll the queers at night*
> *In Burkburnett Park!*

Salutary greetings to Bobby Jay Keeney.
Oh, what a beautiful sport.
Thoughtful, considerate,
Gave to the poor.
When he burglarized a Safeway
He'd leave half of the store!

Salutary greetings to Bobby Jay Keeney.
Always remember that name.
Now he's gone up for life,
Final-ly killed a guy!
Bobby Jay Keeney, hello!

Lee Steadman was punished Saturday for his unbargained for appearance at The Tonga Rain Forest. With the rear of his station wagon cleaned out of carpet samples and reloaded with card tables, folding chairs, linens, napkins, plates, silverware, drinking glasses, wine, beer, food and ice, Lee was dispatched to the pecan trees in the TCU parking area at 8 A.M. for the 2:30 kickoff of the TCU-Texas game and was instructed to seize the target and hold it at all cost.

If Lee failed for any reason to capture the pecan trees, his orders from Doris were to buy a tent or borrow one from an Arab. Doris was going to have ambience at the tailgate party.

Juanita and Slick were relieved to see Lee's station wagon parked by the pecan trees when they reached the stadium at 12:30. Doris' Granada was there as well. Doris was busily organizing the base camp.

Since Lee had been holding the pecan trees for four hours, Juanita was wondering how he had passed the time.

Lee had secured the pecan trees with the station wagon, then hiked up to University Drive, to a long block which had always been known as The Drag, even in the days when there was little else on the block but a corner drugstore that served the twofold purpose of a Student Union and Lettermen's Lounge.

If anything, progress had turned The Drag into a

blight on the campus and the neighborhood. The drugstore had been replaced by a bar catering to punks who carried knives, and the old TCU Theater, which once offered *Casablanca* regularly, now featured Bruce Lee films with Spanish dubbing.

On the modern drag, Lee had still managed to find a bean burrito and a Twinkie for breakfast.

He had walked around the campus. He had seen a girl in an evening gown perched on the steps of a building, playing the oboe; a young man reading poetry to another young man tied to a tree trunk; a group of scholars tossing textbooks on a small fire. From a group of Phi Kappa Sigs he had accepted a leaflet requesting arms, food supplies and medical aid for Northern Waco.

When Lee had reached a stark prairie known as the campus quadrangle, he wandered innocently into a picnic being held by a dozen members of the Class of '53. A woman in a smock and beret had said she did not recall Lee from her Interrelation of the Arts course. Nevertheless, she handed him a plastic cup of cider, and said, "I am B, the son of a tanner. I am a master of rhythmic line."

"Botticelli!" a man sitting cross-legged on the lawn had shouted, and Lee moved on.

He had toured the fieldhouse and peeked in the Athletic Department offices, checking to see if they might be needing new purple carpet. He had spoken to a lady who looked as if she might have some influence and had made an appointment to discuss the matter further. The lady with influence had worn a purple dress, white cowboy boots, a white bonnet with purple flowers on it, and she had proudly displayed a large purple and white button which said: THE FROGS IS OUT OF THE POND!

Lee had spent the rest of the morning listening to the car radio till the battery died.

Juanita and Slick had taken the precaution of bringing three pounds of ribs from Angelo's—not Shorty's—in case Doris followed through on her threat about the jellied chicken salad and peanutty pork chops, which she had.

Other guests must have had the same foreboding.

Tommy Earl brought a 21-piece barrel of Kentucky Fried, and Sheila Bruner brought her frozen yogurt. The Bruner children, little Sheila and little Tommy Earl, exploded on the compound with Rebel yells and flying tackles, twirling funsize bags of Butterfingers in their fists.

Sheila was a thin woman with boy-cut hair, and as she began assisting Doris with the food, she recounted the story of the gall-bladder operation her children had caused.

Herb Macklin and Shorty Eckwood were equipped with cold chicken-fried-steak sandwiches.

Hank Rainey, the society carpenter, had two sliced barbecue sandwiches from Angelo's, which he carried in a bag from Shorty's.

C. L. Corkins, the newly selected president of the South Side Breakfast Tip Club, came with a tuna on white, as did his wife, Emmajean, the grizzled veteran of Tri Delt rushes and Hell Weeks at TCU. Emmajean instantly sighted a Pucci getting out of an Audi and dashed over to say hello.

Dr. Neil Forcheimer of the TCU English department toted a corned beef sandwich from Chicotsky's and his Andrew Marvell manuscript.

"How's it going?" Juanita referred to Dr. Forcheimer's book.

"Mind you," he said, "I prefer *most* the very polished kind of writing, but I'm beginning to wonder how many people have to go *at* a book in order to savor the prose?"

"You can start with me," said Juanita.

"Precisely," the professor said. "I am on my twelfth draft and yet suddenly . . . this morning . . . I caught myself wandering about, almost convinced the majority of readers probably thirst for a well-plotted, fast-moving yarn with plenty of incident. I looked at myself in the mirror as I was shaving, and said, 'So do *I,* if you want the truth!' I would only say this to *you*, Juanita, but it is entirely possible that my respect for the arts is becoming incorrigibly less Continental! Oh, well. Starvation is against the American principle. I can always teach."

The professor sat under a pecan tree and began marking giant X's through whole paragraphs and entire pages of his protracted biography of Andrew Marvell.

Foster Barton did not bring any food, but he did bring along his two transistor radios, binoculars, notebook, and a first quarter score on Pitt-West Virginia.

The tailgate dessert had become a problem within the hierarchy of the South Side B & PW, so Doris diplomatically arranged for three desserts.

LuAnn Hodges made her famous carrot-and-raisin cake in the form of a ladybug, Josephine McClure made her famous pumpkin mousse, and Vera Satterwhite made her famous fruit fondue, which consisted of apple and pear chunks swimming in a pot of chocolate syrup.

As the women scurried about arranging the ambience, Shorty Eckwood caught a glimpse of Doris' jellied chicken salad.

Shorty's chuckling evolved into laughter which caused his eyes to water. He beckoned to Emmajean Corkins and pointed at the jellied chicken salad, and said, "I don't know who dropped this load, but he's crawled off and died by now."

Drying his eyes but still shaking with laughter, Shorty hollered across the compound. "Herb! We better get to the other side of town before this old boy farts again!"

The ambience was helped along by the weather. It was a gorgeous day. No wind. Far from cold but not hot, either. Only a severe critic would have considered the day too warm for the tight pink cashmere turtleneck in which Doris had sculpted her chest.

"Who are those for?" Juanita asked Doris, not expecting an answer.

"Randy and Skip."

Under the pretense of going to look for Alma Roberts, a lost B & PW, Juanita and Doris walked away through the other rows of parked cars.

Doris hurriedly told Juanita her plan. She was going to sit with Randy in the upperdeck on the West Side of the stadium in the first half of the game, and sit with Skip on the East Side during the second half. Randy and Skip knew the deal. Randy and Skip wouldn't care if the three of them sat altogether. Randy and Skip wouldn't care if the three of them did quite a few things together. But Doris was a no-frills girl. Group sex was depraved. She didn't know if she liked Randy best—or Skip. She hoped to determine that before the day was over. She would start out with Lee and everyone else in the South end zone, where the regulars always sat. But three minutes after the opening kickoff, she would get a virus. She would go scrambling to the rest room. Juanita would have to *pretend* to check up on her every fifteen or twenty minutes so Lee would buy the story. Juanita could go somewhere out of Lee's sight. She could stand in a portal and watch the game. Then Juanita could go back to the South end zone and say Doris was still squatting on the john with a cold rag on her throat.

"Who . . . are Randy and Skip?"

"Randy Gordon and Skip Pritchard," said Doris. "My new cutie pies. I haven't mentioned them? They moved into Mirage La Grande a couple of weeks ago."

"Together?"

"They are *men,* Juanita. I've seen their wives."

"What happened to the infatuation with Tommy Earl?"

"If you want my personal opinion, I think Tommy Earl Bruner needs sexual therapy."

"What happens after the game?"

"Well . . . now that Lee's battery is dead . . . I may go have a drink with Randy—or Skip."

"You'll be recovered from your virus?"

"I'll be feeling much better, thank you."

"Doris, I don't think I want to do this."

"Women stick *together*, Juanita, in case you don't remember the *code!* It's not like I'm asking a big favor, for God's sake!"

They had walked a fair distance from the pecan trees, and they realized they had come upon another tailgate party.

This one was ringed by Mark VI's, Sevilles and every model of Mercedes. A small white picket fence surrounded a country club veranda and two uniformed policemen guarded a gate to the party.

Five black men in chef hats and aprons were overseeing three charcoal grills. There were tables with white linens and candelabra. Other black men in tuxedos were pouring wine out of bottles leadened with mold and dirt.

An eight-piece Dixieland band was swinging the University of Texas fight song.

All of the men at the party wore burnt-orange blazers. All of the women wore burnt-orange pants suits, mostly Ultrasuede, and rather baroque sunglasses.

Juanita and Doris spied Beecher Perry in a burnt-orange blazer, white shirt, orange and white striped tie, and burnt-orange Tyrolean hat. He was standing next to a sullen, face-lifted, eye-jobbed brunette in a sable. Edna Perry.

Juanita, in her khaki whipcord jacket and corduroy jeans, waved at Beecher Perry. Doris waved at him in her pink sweater, a travel poster for the Alps.

Beecher Perry smiled at the women and gave them the 'hook 'em, Horns' sign.

Edna Perry tipped her head down slightly and looked at Doris' Alps over the top of her sunglasses. Calmly then, with a cultivated impassiveness, Edna turned to Beecher and emptied her stemmed glass of red wine down his shirt front.

Juanita and Doris scooted back to their own tailgate party.

* * *

They had no trouble finding their way because little Sheila and little Tommy Earl could be seen jumping up and down on top of Lee's station wagon.

"Oh, good," said Doris, as they neared the compound, "Randy and Skip are here."

Randy was a stout-looking man with a mustache and perm. His white leisure suit was a bit small on him, his red knit shirt a bit faded, and his white patent loafers a bit scratched. The cuffs of his jacket were turned up. He carried his mirrored glasses on the outer side of his breast pocket, hanging vertically, one limb stuck inside the pocket.

"Randy Gordon," he said, introducing himself around. "I sell big ones and little ones. If I sell little ones, I got to sell five thousand. If I sell big ones, I got to sell two!"

Then he would laugh.

Skip's white leisure suit was too large on him, his green knit shirt was new, and his shoes were white mesh-tops. He had a thinner mustache than Randy and his hair was short and combed forward in the style of a Roman senator.

He introduced himself around by saying, "Skip Pritchard, Tim-Tex. Whatever kind of catheter or walker you need!"

Only Tommy Earl commented on their matching white leisure suits saying:

"You fellows take the body to St. Joseph's or All Saints?"

Tommy Earl finished off a rib and pitched it into a pile of bones near Shorty Eckwood, who was asleep under a pecan tree, the opposite side from where Dr. Forcheimer was at work on his manuscript.

Doris led Randy and Skip to a table and joined them in a discussion of ways to improve the snack bar and game room at Mirage La Grande. Lee asked *where* the snack bar and game room were at Mirage La Grande.

Juanita sat with Slick, Herb, Hank and Foster. With his two transistors, Foster was listening to both the

Notre Dame-Georgia Tech game and the Army-Duke game.

Foster explained why the President of the United States had the best job in the world. It wasn't the President's own plane. It wasn't his own song. It wasn't even the free time. It was the Secret Service guy who walked around with the phone. The President, no matter where he was, could call Sports Line and get updated scores on all the games.

C. L. and Emmajean Corkins wandered off to see if they could find any of their friends from the First United Methodist Church, the Fort Worth Art Museum, the Van Cliburn Foundation or the Junior Woman's Club.

Tommy Earl went to speak to a TCU cheerleader, "the daughter of a good friend."

Sheila Bruner rested under the other pecan tree while little Sheila and little Tommy Earl plunged Butterfingers into her yogurt.

Shortly before the opening kickoff, Vera, LuAnn and Josephine served their desserts. Little Sheila endeared herself to most of the tailgaters by turning over the fruit fondue.

Chapter Sixteen

In the first half of the football game, Juanita went into the ladies rest room under the West Side stands, or somewhere near it, almost as many times as the Texas Longhorns went into TCU's end zone. She missed four Longhorn touchdowns, but she was certain there would be others. The score was 54 to 0 in favor of Texas when the Horned Frog band pranced onto the field at half-time blasting out the TCU fight song.

Lee Steadman had accepted the story about the virus.

"Are you sure I don't need to call an ambulance?" he said to Juanita.

"I honestly think she's a little better," Juanita said. "I'll check again in a minute."

Everyone's interest in the game had narrowed down to whether TCU could break the national collegiate record for the number of fumbles in a single game. The Frogs had lost 14 fumbles in the first two quarters.

Juanita was counting on TCU's star running back, B. E. (Belch 'Em Up) Bodiford, to break the record single-handedly. B. E. had accounted for 10 of the fumbles alone. He was publicized as the fastest ball-carrier in the Southwest Conference, but he had an annoying tendency. B. E. (Belch 'Em Up) Bodiford frequently ignored possession of the football in his unyielding search for the nearest sideline.

When the TCU band swung into a medley from *Man of La Mancha*, Juanita pretended to pay Doris another visit.

Lee tagged along. The concession counter was near the rest room and he wanted a Pepsi.

As they neared the swarm of people lining up at the concession counter, Doris came bruising her way out of the crowd, carrying three hot dogs and two Cokes in a cardboard box. Randy had not eaten at the tailgate.

Juanita and Lee ran headlong into Doris, and Juanita felt overcome with a fever. The jig was up.

"I thought you were *sick!*" Lee said, blinking at the hot dogs, blinking at Doris.

"I'm not too sick to feed hungry people!" Doris fired back indignantly. "You ought to see that poor old woman in the rest room. You know the one, Juanita? She sits out here in her rags and gives away religious pamphlets? Help me carry this."

Lee said, "Are you any better, honey?"

"Some," said Doris. "Luckily, I felt it coming on this morning and brought a tetracycline with me."

Juanita waited barely long enough to get inside the ladies rest room before asking Doris an incisive medical question. How was a capsule for a skin disorder going to help her virus?

"Lee doesn't know what a tetracycline is."

"I have another question. What if Lee happens to see the old woman in the rags giving away religious pamphlets? I saw her an hour ago."

Doris said, "Well, it will just have to be her Goddamn twin sister! That's the best I can do."

The score in the football game mounted to 76 to 0 before the end of the third quarter, and the University of Texas was substituting everyone but the Board of Regents. The voice on the PA system announced that TCU had, alas, established a new NCAA record for fumbles, the magic number being 24.

Following that announcement, the TCU band played the alma mater. Correspondingly, some TCU students in a section of the East stands produced an enormous purple-and-white banner, which said:

"WE'RE NO. 113!"

Clutching his transistors, Foster Barton jumped to his feet in the South end zone seats, and said, "I just had an all-time first! *Two* holding calls went in my favor in *two* different games at the same time!"

Foster sat back down, and said, "Can you imagine what it would be like to own your own zebra?"

Foster was behind in all games on all radio stations, but at TCU Stadium he was still alive on the Adjusted Under. At the half, he had found Puny the Stroller sitting with Circus Face, Jawbreaker, Little Mike, Spot, Boston and Scooter, and he had bet the total points in the game *now* would not exceed 85.

If the University of Texas coaches took out the Board of Regents and put in the Joffrey Ballet, he had a threadbare chance of winning the bet.

Juanita and Slick had no interest in the Adjusted Under, and no longer any interest in the game, now that the fumble suspense was concluded, so they talked about music.

Since Juanita's session at KOXX with Old Jeemy, Slick had taken it upon himself to find out some things about the recording industry. He had already learned more than he ever thought he would want to know by reading a few trade publications and some old magazine articles.

Juanita asked why he had bothered.

"In case something happens, I'd like to be able to talk about it intelligently," Slick said.

"You don't trust Old Jeemy?"

They both grinned.

"I found out one thing," Slick said. "If you ever get real lucky and have a choice, it's better to get recorded by an artist on a good independent label. You don't get lost in a computer."

She said, "I don't imagine I'd turn down Willie because he records for Columbia."

"No," said Slick, "but the problem with the giants is rock music. If you're country, you're at the ass end of everything, even though country's popular now."

A giant was a CBS, RCA, Warners or Polygram, for examples, and they had sales of six hundred million dollars a year, but it was nearly all in rock.

"The good part of it is, the giants have money to spend on new talent."

"I'm not talent," Juanita said. "I want to be a songwriter. *Talent* . . . is who records the songs. The big companies waste millions on rock groups nobody ever heard of except fourteen year olds. They want to discover another dope-head screamer and thumper from England who might make the kids buy records."

"That's the kind of thing I've been finding out," Slick said, as they both lit cigarettes.

Juanita said, "You turn to a rock station on the radio and here comes a teenage scum who sounds like the cheapest shit you've heard since your watch started running again, but you can read in *Variety* or *Downbeat* how he ships triple platinum for Elektra or Atlantic. That's Warners."

"It's hard to get anybody's attention in those big office buildings," Slick said.

"Remember the 'gold record'?" Juanita said. "Gold doesn't mean a thing any more. Gold was what they invented for a hit that sold 500,000. That got to be common so they invented platinum. Platinum was for hitting a million. The Beatles caused platinum, I think."

"Platinum sounds okay to me."

"Yeah, it's plenty okay in country music," Juanita said. "In rock, it gets laughed at. Have you ever heard of The Murderers?"

"Who?"

"The Murderers are four acne-faced punks from Blackpool in England. They claim they all killed their mothers and got away with it. They look like they weigh about ninety pounds and died two years ago. They can't play instruments. They can't sing. They can't write. But their last album sold eighteen million copies."

"What was it called?"

"*Gimme Some*. They had a hit single of that song, too. I listened to it ten times but I never heard those two words in the lyrics. I *did* hear a rhyme about 'dung' and 'hung.' Eighteen million copies."

"Why do kids buy that stuff?"

"Piss off their parents. Oh. And it's loud. They don't have to talk. Kids can't talk. Candy was the last kid who talked."

Slick said, "Got any idea how much The Murderers made off that album?"

"I can tell you roughly," Juanita said. "The average album retails for eight ninety-eight. Well, the other day it did, anyhow. But it's wholesaled to the stores for about four dollars. It's the four dollars the artists get their money from. Out of that four dollars . . . let me guess . . . the record company will get a dollar thirty-five, probably. Then you have to knock off all the costs for manufacturing . . . pressing . . . cover costs . . . copyright fees . . . promotion and publicity . . . studio recording costs. I'd say the artist gets around a dollar thirty."

"So the Murderers made a dollar thirty times eighteen million?"

"Right."

"That's . . . uh . . . almost six million apiece."

"On one album."

"I'd say that ain't bad," Slick shrugged.

"Not for spitting on people."

Late in the fourth quarter of the TCU-Texas spectacle with the Longhorns struggling to hold the score at 83 to 0, the voice over the stadium PA said:

"Ladies and gentlemen, may we have your attention, please? We have an emergency message for Miss Juanita Hutchins. Miss Juanita Hutchins. If Miss Juanita Hutchins is here, will you please report to the press-box elevator under the West stands? We have an urgent message waiting for you. Thank you."

Juanita came forward from a lounging position on an empty row in the South end zone, and clawed Slick's arm.

"Candy's been busted! No . . . she's been in a wreck!"

Slick said, "It's nothing like that. Who knows you're here today?"

"Dove!" Juanita said. "He played football at Texas. He'd know how to call a press box."

"If anybody got busted, Dove would know how to call a lawyer first and get sprung," said Slick. "If it was real bad news, somebody would wait till later to tell you. Calm down. I'll put my money on Doris."

Juanita and Slick scurried to the press-box elevator, and Slick pushed the button. They waited two minutes.

When the elevator door opened, they saw a coed elevator attendant in purple wool panties, white boots, a purple felt cowboy hat, and a white T-shirt proclaiming: FROG FEVER.

"I'm Juanita Hutchins. There's a message for me. Urgent, they said."

A clamor came from inside the stadium.

"Did those butt-holes score again?" said the elevator girl. "I'm supposed to go out with a T-sipper tonight. He can keep his hands to hisself, is what he can do!"

"Do you have a message for me?"

"I surely do," said the girl, untaping a piece of paper from a wall of the elevator. "Somebody took notes upstairs, but I think I can get it right. Miss Hutchins, your brother-in-law called from Nashville. Mr. Sloggett? Does that sound right?"

Juanita glanced at Slick with relief.

The girl said, "Not Sloggett. Slocum. Mr. Slocum says your sister Gubby was in a car wreck but she's not dead. She needs a transfusion and you are her only blood type in North America. Call Mr. Slocum at this number. You can use the phone in the maintenance office right over there. I sure hope everything is all right."

The elevator door closed, and Juanita said, "They've probably lost Dove's phone number again. That's the only emergency I can think of. I'll see what it is."

Slick went back to the South end zone to stand watch on Lee Steadman while Juanita called Lonnie Slocum in Nashville.

"Printers Alley Chart-Bustin' Country Ham and Redeye Saloon."

Lonnie Slocum sounded phenomenally straight, like a man who had not been near whisky or chemicals for two whole days.

"I know," Juanita said. "My cassette burned up in the fire, right?"

"Hey, Juanita, how you doin'? Are you still at the football game? What's the score?"

"Eighty-three to nothing."

"No shit? The Longhorns must be in shock. I thought Texas was supposed to win."

"Lonnie, what do you want?"

He said, "Listen, Juanita, you know that tape you sent?"

"Tape?" she said. "I sent you a tape? Oh, yeah. I remember. The one I mailed just after the birth of Christ. What about it?"

"You wrote a song, Juanita. That's what I called to tell you. I knew you'd want to hear the news. We settled it last night. 'Baja Oklahoma' is goin' on our album."

"Is this dope talk? What's PSX? What does that do to you?"

"I'm not jackin' around with you, Juanita. You wrote a song. I doctored the tune a little. That makes me a collaborator on the music, but the words are yours. Want to hear how it sounds so far?"

Juanita was numb but she listened over the phone to an arranged, orchestrated, mixed, dubbed, multi-tracked rendition of Lonnie Slocum and Dog Track Gravy doing her song.

"Jesus," she said. "It's music."

"That's why they call it Music City over here."

"I mean . . . it's . . . it's a *song*."

"Yeah, that's more or less how they refer to 'em. Songs."

"It's . . . Western Swing. Damn. Me and Bob Wills."

"What?"

"Lonnie?"

"Huh?"

"I think I just wet my pants."

Somebody from Mad Dog Music Co. would be contacting Juanita, Lonnie said. The company had to buy her song before it could be put on the album. Royalties were standard for writers. That would be taken care of when she joined ASCAP. But she needed an agent or lawyer. Someone to look after the other things: the cash advance, option clauses, escalations, subsidiary rights, foreign sales, so forth.

"That's what's goin' on when you hear somebody say, 'The Jews are fightin'.'"

"What should I sell the song for? How much?"

"Ask four times what they offer. Settle for times two. They like your song. I can tell you that much. Of course, that don't mean they think it's *good*. People in this business don't know if anything's good until it sells. Then it's good as far as they're concerned, even if it ain't worth a damn. Also, people in this business usually don't want to buy anything unless they hear somebody else wants it. You need an agent."

"I've talked with Old Jeemy."

"Juanita, give yourself a break. Old Jeemy would steal Denmark if he could figure out a way to get it home."

"What did you think about 'Too Many Midnight Songs'?"

"I liked it, but the producers didn't want to plug talent on other labels. Willie and Waylon are in your lyrics."

"Willie and Waylon are institutions! Their names

have already been in more lyrics than Mother and God!"

"Are you complaining already?"

"The producers are idiots!"

"I won't pass that along just yet."

"Lonnie, when you come down here for Willie's concert next week, we'll celebrate properly."

"Sit up on the stage with us, Juanita. Want to pick with us?"

"Thanks, sport. I'm not quite ready for fourteen thousand people."

"Well, it's like somebody puttin' that smart stuff up your nose. You never know what you're ready for in life until it happens to you."

Juanita walked exultantly to the South end zone, smiling at people she did not know, admiring the sky, the concrete, the asphalt, the litter, all the glories of the day.

She hugged Slick Henderson as she sat down.

"I'm a songwriter," she whispered. "'Baja's' on Lonnie's album. I'm getting a fucking *song* recorded."

"About time," Slick said without emotion, his eyes on the football field. "Write songs is all you've done since I've known you."

But he had taken her quivering hand in his, held it, and squeezed it affectionately.

Very few people were left in the East Side stands when Juanita was attracted to the flash of light. Then other flashes of light. Something flickering. A signal from a ship.

She borrowed Foster's binoculars and focused on Doris Steadman sitting between Randy and Skip directly behind the TCU band, not far from where little Sheila and little Tommy Earl were scaling the shoulders of two trombonists.

Doris was sending a message to Juanita with her compact mirror in the sun.

"May Day," Juanita said.

Events of the afternoon dictated that Juanita always

start toward the West Side john, wherever she might be headed, so to reach the East Side she was forced to go West and circle around and behind the North end zone.

This route at least enabled Juanita to be on top of the action when B. D. (Belch 'Em Up) Bodiford took a pitchout and retreated thirty yards into his own end zone and slipped down, thereby giving up the safety which made the final score 85 to 0—and blew the Adjusted Under for Foster Barton.

Doris was waiting beneath the East stands with little Sheila fastened to one leg and little Tommy Earl fastened to the other.

"You rang?" Juanita said.

Yes, Lee was to be informed that Doris had recovered to such an extent that she could drive her own car home, but Lee was not to worry if she was not home when he arrived. She might have to stop and sit on the john at service stations.

There was another thing Juanita could do for Doris. She could put little Sheila and little Tommy Earl in burlap sacks and drop them in the Trinity River.

Doris fought free of the Bruner children and kicked at them as they ran off to turn over trash containers.

"Oh, Juanita," said Doris. "Randy and Skip wanted me to ask you. They were wondering if you cared to join us? Just you, not Slick. Might be fun."

"Gee, it sounds swell, Doris. But tell Randy and Skip I just got the biopsy back. I wouldn't be any laughs."

Slick headed into the sunset on another of those Fort Worth streets with a name for which Juanita held great fondness. Camp Bowie Boulevard. Wonderful. The street was named for the World War I army base. Strolling along Camp Bowie Boulevard and sitting at the Café de le Argonne Forest. Slick continued west and worked his way north to Robert's Cutoff, not a bad street name in itself.

In another age Slick might have been taking Juanita to Inspiration Point, or on out to the lake, or over to a honky-tonk on the Jacksboro Highway—or even to the Old Crystal Springs pavilion.

Which was where Juanita insisted they go after the game that Saturday.

The Crystal Springs pavilion no longer existed. There was no fading board sign above the entrance which said:

CRYSTAL SPRINGS—DANCING & SWIMMING.

Now there was only a knobby plot of weeds and rocks where the old wood-frame dance hall had stood. In fact, a mobile home community was encroaching.

Slick stopped the car and they got out.

Juanita had last been to Crystal Springs on a night in the early 1950's when she had gone to the pavilion to hear Hank Williams. The place had looked the same then as it no doubt had on those nights in '31 and '32 when Bob Wills had invented Western Swing.

A dumpy old place, really. It had been built from the salvage lumber of Camp Bowie's army barracks. The ceiling was low and there were many roof supports—posts—which had to be avoided while dancing.

"The door was over here."

Juanita led Slick into the weeds.

"Pretty steep cover," she said. "It's seventy-five cents a couple, but they've got a fiddle player who can slur the blues and slicken your hair."

"Sure are a lot of people." Slick pretended to look around. "I think I see old Clyde Barrow and Bonnie Parker over there."

"They used to come here," Juanita said. "It was one of their hangouts. True. Know why it's crowded tonight?"

"Not exactly."

"Extra ladies get in for ten cents."

"You like your lore, don't you?"

Juanita assumed the pose of a lady who wanted to be invited to dance. Slick hesitated. Then he put his arm around her khaki whipcord jacket and took her hand.

Juanita moved in closer and held him. In the weeds and rocks, they began to dance—well, trudge—to music provided by Juanita, her head on Slick's shoulder, smiling. Softly and slowly, she sang:

"Oh, we never do brag, we never do boast . . . we sing our song from coast to coast . . . We're the Light Crust Doughboys from Burrus Mill."

Slick said, "I'd rather hear one of yours."

"Here's one I'm working on," Juanita said. "It's about all of us, everybody we know."

They kept swaying as she sang:

"They hadn't ought to have gone ahead and did it . . . like they went on and done it . . . because they knowed they'd did them kind of things before."

The dance ended with a kiss among the weeds and rocks in the place where the old Crystal Springs pavilion had been.

It was a kiss out of *From Here to Eternity*, but Juanita and Slick weren't caught up in any pounding surf. They could only hear the roar of a washer-dryer coming from somewhere in the mobile home community.

The LTD eased into the rear parking area of the Sans Su South, and Slick stopped in a space belonging to another tenant.

Juanita fumbled for her apartment keys as the two of them rounded a corner of the complex. That was when she looked up with alarm to see the lights on in Apt. 2-A, second floor, Building 3, East wing.

"It's a bust," she said.

"I don't think they turn on that many lights," said Slick.

They stood on the lawn near the hackberry trees and scrub oaks and studied the apartment. The drapes were closed but every room was aglow.

"What am I worried about?" Juanita said. "It's Doris Steadman's coat."

"It's Aunt Bernice's."

"Actually, it belongs to Roy Simmons."

"No. Actually, it's Dove's."

They entered the apartment through the front door.

In the living room there was evidence that the intruders had come from Taco Bell. The remains of an encherito was the only thing left on four aluminum trays. Three empty cans of Coors sat among wadded up napkins.

Just then, a voice carried from the kitchen-breakfast room-den.

"Momma?"

Chapter Seventeen

Juanita and Candy collided in the center of the living room, and after the hugging, kissing, weeping and laughing, Candy said, "Hi, Slicko," and trooped over to Slick Henderson. She gave him a smack on the cheek—and the high five.

Candy was chicly attired in dingy jeans, roughout boots, a man's unpressed shirt, and a U.S. Davis Cup Team warmup jacket. She wore no makeup. Her stringy hair needed the immediate attention of a one-day laundry service.

Juanita thought she looked wonderful and was still joyously tearful as the three of them gravitated to the kitchen-breakfast room-den.

"Yo, Mom."

Dove Christian was sitting at the butcher-block table. Juanita beat him to it. She rushed to embrace him.

Dove had brought her little girl home. When had a dope dealer ever done *that* before?

"That'd be your Slick," said Dove, standing up and shaking hands with Slick like an adult.

Candy and Dove had driven nonstop from Aspen. They had taken turns at the wheel of the MGB.

"Why didn't you let me know you were coming?" Juanita said. "We've been to a football game. I could have been here to fix dinner. I mean . . . one day I'm worried about plea bargaining, and the next day you're here!"

Candy's face brightened.

"Momma, you're not going to believe this. Like my mind is so *charged*, you know?"

"Mine's trashed, man." Dove was drinking instant coffee. He looked into the cup with a grin.

"They weren't narcs, Momma."

Candy waited for a reaction.

To speak of, there wasn't any from Juanita. Juanita looked blankly at Candy, then Dove. She looked at Slick, who was touching the kettle to see if it was still hot.

"They were *not* narcs." Candy broke into a big smile.

"They weren't narcs?" Juanita said.

"Not one."

"You're sure?"

"Positive."

"Were they anybody?"

"Oh, yeah!" said Dove. "They were somebody. They were real, and they were always around."

"*Everywhere*," Candy said. "The same ones. Leering at you. Hanging in corners. Weird groups of 'em. Keala got over-amped. This guy kept staring at her at the Coke-Palm. She *knew* it was a narc. He asked her a question about the bar in the Hotel Jerome. Keala started babbling about tourist attractions all over the Rockies. She poured the guy a Scotch and vodka and sprayed whip cream on top—and ate the cherry herself!"

Juanita said, "Who in the world were the narcs—I mean, the people?"

Candy and Dove looked at each other and burst into unmanageable laughter.

"Momma," Candy said, gaining control. "They were carpet salesmen!"

Juanita prepared the spare bedroom, Candy's room, for her houseguests while commenting at length about people choosing the type of life in which carpet salesmen could give them persecution complexes.

Candy and Dove had learned the truth about the non-narcs from another dealer. They had seen the dealer in Aspen with his arm lodged in a mailbox. He was trying to retrieve his sympathy cards.

The dealer had hired a private investigator to find out if the narcs *were* narcs. The guesswork had been driving him cuckoo.

The private investigator had solved the case quickly by eavesdropping on the strangers in town and picking up bits and pieces of information about shag, nylon and wool; modern trends in floor measuring; complaints about delivery from the mills; and why couldn't anybody get laid in a hot-shit town like Aspen?

Carpet salesmen? Colorado? Juanita was suddenly reminded to call Doris and see how it all turned out with Randy and Skip—and Lee.

By now, it was eleven o'clock Saturday night and Doris surely must have returned home from a football game that ended at five forty-five.

Doris was home safely, comfortable in her pink bed, and Lee was looking through the house for another tetracycline.

Doris had topped off the day's festivities by paying her respects to the Ramada Inn with Randy Gordon. Skip Pritchard had stayed at the Baboon Rocket to find out why his wife was there having dinner with a man named Sonny Hawkins.

"How was it?" Juanita felt like asking.

"Randy Gordon has a problem," Doris said.

"Doris, it's not true?" said Juanita. "Don't tell me Randy Gordon couldn't find the little man in the boat!"

"He might could," Doris said. "I don't know as though he'd be all that interested in it. He's just a fuckaholic, is all he is."

Candy and Dove were properly elated with the news about Juanita's song. Candy and Juanita hugged, kissed, wept and laughed all over again.

Dove was almost as pleased to hear that Lonnie and Dog Track Gravy were going to appear at the Willie Nelson concert.

He said, "Unless I miss my guess, the old convention center will be a good place to unload some get-well cards."

"By the way, Mom," said Candy. "Where's the blow?"

Juanita had not expected to be able to relish a moment like that. She said, "Kids, I've only had a hysterectomy and a quadruple bypass worrying about it. Now it's my turn. The tooth powder is somewhere in the apartment. You find it."

Dove began the quest for his merchandise with the cavalier attitude of someone trying to find a pint of French vanilla ice cream in the freezer at a market. He even acted as if he enjoyed the game for two days.

The third day, however, Dove started digging up trees, flowers, ferns, moving appliances out from their connections, loosening light fixtures, unscrewing wall sockets and panels, taking up floor tiles, rolling back rugs and carpet, gouging pillows, and tapping on sheetrock with his ear to the wall like a man exploring a tomb.

Toward the end of the week, Dove could have written manuals on carpentry, plumbing, electrical repair, unholstery, housekeeping and foodstuffs.

Dove assigned Candy to turn every page in every book, probe every sleeve of every record album, open every top on every jar, remove every cap from every tube, feel underneath every chair, table, counter, drawer and shelf, and to hold in readiness—as a last resort—crying in front of her mother.

Juanita knew all along she would give Dove the lining of the mink coat, but even she wasn't sure when that would be. It would *not* be in the style of a stupid parent striking a bargain. "Okay, here's your dope. Give me back my daughter." Many such parents probably never had a closeness with their kids again.

Candy had inquired about the mink coat and she had heard the history of it. She had tried it on and covered up with it on the sofa as she watched television. The coat had not rattled, a testimonial to the seamstress.

It was Dove who suggested a bargain in the latter stages of his search. One afternoon he said:

"Mom, what would you do if I told you Candy and I were gonna get married, and this was my last big score?"

"I wouldn't believe you," Juanita said.

"I didn't think you would," said Dove, pointing a flashlight into the flue of the living room fireplace.

During the days of the search, Juanita called Old Jeemy to tell him she had managed to get a song published despite the handicap of not having an agent/manager, but she *could* use his help in the negotiations with the music company.

Could Old Jeemy come to Herb's Cafe for a "business lunch" without a gumshoe?

"Darlin', I can't be there no quicker than you can say ten percent."

"Ten?"

"Hell, Juanita, there ain't nothin' lower than ten percent but Syrians or somebody!"

"How's Kathy's health?"

"That's all straightened out, Darlin'. She's fine. We're fine. I don't know what got into Kathy that night. She's had this mental problem for a while, and . . ."

"Jimmy?"

"What, Darlin'?"

"Cut the shit. All I want you to do is keep me from signing away my life insurance premiums to Mad Dog Music."

Juanita and Old Jeemy held their business meeting in a back booth of Herb's dining room.

Old Jeemy brought along a new letter of agreement for Juanita to examine closely and sign. Juanita looked over the letter while Old Jeemy savored his chicken-fried-steak dinner.

The chicken-fried-steak dinner entailed two generous chunks of round steak tenderized beyond recognition, soaked in egg batter, fried, and served on top of biscuits with French fries, all of it underneath a Niagara of cream gravy. The pinto beans and green salad came on the side.

The dinner had only changed in one way over the years at Herb's. Juanita had watched it go from eighty-five cents to eight-ninety.

Most of Herb's customers still considered that price a bargain, but most Texans were likely to consider any price a bargain for chicken-fried steak because once a week they required it, some intravenously.

Generally, if you saw a Texan running around performing acts which couldn't be printed in a family newspaper, the chances were that he or she had missed his or her chicken-fried steak that week.

Old Jeemy looked up from his batter and gravy, and said, "It ain't very good . . . but ain't it *good?*"

Juanita signed the agreement. It specified that Old Jeemy would receive 10 percent of Juanita's earnings as a songwriter and/or entertainer. His expenses for promotion and publicity on her behalf were not to exceed one-third of whatever figure made her kick furniture. The agreement between them could be terminated verbally at any time by either party.

"We got a break with Mad Dog Music on this deal," Old Jeemy said. "Mad Dog's with a good independent label. Arista. We got an up-and-comer with Lonnie Slocum. It's all in our favor."

"Who will you be negotiating with at Mad Dog about my song?"

"Probably old Marty Weinreb. I've fleeced him before. When I get through with Marty, he'll think he's run into a kitchen tool."

Old Jeemy said if Juanita's song attracted any kind of praise, there were innumerable benefits he could take advantage of.

He said, "I can schedule you into banquets, sales conferences, shopping-mall openings, supermarket weddings, all kinds of things. No big deal. You go in and pick and sing for thirty minutes. We scoop a couple of thousand and hit the silk. You and me may become a conglomerate, Darlin'!"

"I'm not a performer," she reminded Old Jeemy.

"Wait till your song comes out," he said. "That's when I earn my money. When Lonnie's album's released, I'll plug the shit out of it on KOXX. I'll get my old buddies all over the South to plug it. I've put a few saucers of milk on the floor in my day. They can do the same for Old Jeemy. It's back-scratchin' time at the old corral!"

"Is that how it always works?"

"Naw, not every time, Darlin'. Occasionally, somebody makes a good record."

Juanita's hair was critiqued by Rinaldo at Neiman's. While she was there, she went ahead and bought the ankle-length Indian-print cotton dress, and the turquoise-and-silver belt.

She rushed back to her apartment with only an hour to get herself together. Everyone was expected to be at Lonnie Slocum's suite in the Hilton Inn by six o'clock that night. The concert was to begin at nine.

Lonnie had authorized Juanita to invite anyone she wished to his party before the concert—or his party after the concert. Anyone who had a flak jacket and would feel at ease around eight hundred mental patients.

When Juanita sprinted into her apartment, she was welcomed by Doris Steadman doing a pirouette in the mink coat.

"I told Lee I was borrowing this tonight," Doris said. "It's the perfect occasion. There'll be celebrities there and who knows what all. I'm just sorry Lee wants to go. See you at the hotel."

Juanita subpoenaed Candy and Dove to the living room. The temptation was too much to resist. She stood at her living room window from which she could look down on the street.

"Come here," Juanita said to Candy and Dove. They walked to the window. Down below, Doris was opening the door of her Granada, the mink around her shoulders.

"There goes the tooth powder," Juanita said.

Candy and Dove were not people who clasped their cheeks and sputtered, or raised welts on someone's arm.

Candy placidly said, "The lining. Jesus."

Dove Christian said, "I'm out of it, nurse. Wheel me back to the room."

"There's a celebrity."

Slick Henderson referred to the young girl in the cowhide vest and clear plastic disco pants with nothing underneath either garment.

Slick, Juanita, and the others were inching their way into Lonnie Slocum's hotel suite before the concert.

Juanita had taken Lonnie at his word and infested the party with Slick, Candy and Dove, of course, and then with Doris, Lee, Tommy Earl and Old Jeemy, not that anyone would notice.

On their way to the living room, Juanita's group passed through a rodeo arena, a gymnastics class, a fuming sanitary landfill, and a chemistry lab, all of which, at one time, had been connecting bedrooms.

There was beer and tequila to drink. Individually or mixed into a "Texas Tornado." The beer was iced down in garbage pails in every corner of every room. Bottles of tequila were in crates sitting on dressers and chests, or they could be pried from the hands of the Egyptian mummies leaning against the walls. The Egyptian mummies were guests who had come too early.

Doors were open to other rooms across and down the hallway. These rooms belonged to the other members of Dog Track Gravy. No one was in any of the other rooms at the moment because all of the steel-bellied airheads were in Lonnie's suite, taking part in one activity or another, many of which were occurring in closets and shower stalls.

Lonnie had a grand mixture of friends at his party. The guests were comprised of:

Steer wrestlers.

Quarterhorse owners.

Little bearded men playing dressup cowboy.

Long-haired skinny girls in baggy jeans and drooping T-shirts.

Stocky guys in fatigue jackets and sneakers.

Shirtless Jesuses in mud-caked Levis and sandals.

Manchurian emissaries with opium pipes.

Delegates of good will from many African nations.

Men with tall hair and pendants.

Women with high hair and deep distrust of the men with tall hair and pendants.

Straight men in snappy sport coats discussing pussy and money.

Their nondrinking wives discussing children.

Peaceful young men in robes, bearing copies of the Koran.

Society matrons in fishnet mini-dresses and boots.

And two hundred others who were the normal musicians, soul singers, hookers, fags, pickpockets, actors, actresses, car thieves, dilettantes and dope dealers.

The girl in the cowhide vest and clear plastic disco pants was dancing on a radiator cover in front of the wall-to-wall, up-to-the-ceiling windows through which the Tarrant County Convention Center, only two blocks away, could be seen in the foreground of the downtown skyline. The skyline was outlined in Christmas lights.

Two members of Dog Track Gravy supplied the music for the girl in the cowhide vest and clear plastic disco pants, who in her own unparalleled way seemed to enjoy undulating with the window drapes.

Toby Painter was on rhythm and Jim Hensley was on bass.

In their more asceptic TCU days, Toby and Jim had dressed differently. Toby had never worn a derby and somebody's letter jacket from the 1940's, and Jim had seldom been seen in a Dallas Cowboy jersey and green tam, and they had nearly always worn pants over their jock straps.

Toby and Jim were chording an endless sixteen bars which were not familiar to Juanita, although the driving tempo was reminiscent of Jerry Jeff Walker's "Hill Country Rain."

Juanita asked a peaceful young man bearing a copy of the Koran if he knew the name of the tune.

It was a new thing Dog Track Gravy was working on, the peaceful young man said. It was called "Hold That Fucker in Abeyance."

Juanita found out from Doris that there were five people in the suite who were leading characters in TV shows, not the least of whom was Luke Renner, the star of "Duke Rentner, Honest Cop," a big hit as a comedy-adventure series on ABC. Juanita had seen the show once. "Duke Rentner, Honest Cop" was indeed a comedy-adventure series if you applied the comedy to the adventure and the adventure to the comedy.

Across the suite, Luke Renner looked as much like a steel-bellied airhead as any of the steel-bellied airheads.

"Luke's a good friend," Dove said to Doris. "I'll introduce you."

Quite a number of guests were apparently good friends of Dove's. They kept taking him aside for a chat.

Juanita and Slick pushed into a place to stand where

Slick could drink a beer and Juanita could drink a Texas Tornado. Slick adapted to the party as willingly as he would to the experience of being temporarily locked inside a movie theater running the out-takes of Ingmar Bergman.

Lee Steadman withdrew to an empty bedroom down the hall to watch television.

Candy may or may not have been stoned already. She curled up in a ball at one end of the radiator cover and became hypnotized by the Christmas lights on the downtown buildings.

Tommy Earl Bruner wedged himself into a vantage point from where he could review the performance of the girl in the cowhide vest and clear plastic disco pants. His latitude was a few degrees South of her navel.

The girl not too surprisingly became so moved by the merciless beat of "Hold That Fucker in Abeyance," she contorted out of her cowhide vest and slung it into the crowd, screamed like a pagan who had recovered her dildo, and indisputably shared an orgasm with downtown Fort Worth.

Tommy Earl took out a hundred-dollar bill, licked it with his tongue, and pasted it on his forehead.

A shirtless Jesus in mud-caked Levis and sandals peeled the hundred-dollar bill off Tommy Earl's forehead and gave him a tiny cellophane packet of Coffeemate.

Tommy Earl licked the cellophane packet and glued *that* to his forehead, and the girl in the clear plastic disco pants, now topless, fell into Tommy Earl's arms, hopelessly in love.

Old Jeemy had worn his rhinestone-and-denim suit that night, with epaulets on the pockets as well as the shoulders. Juanita observed the corner of the room where Old Jeemy had been crouching lower and lower with his hands on his knees, a tailback waiting for the snap. He was looking down and talking to Marty Weinreb of Mad Dog Music.

Juanita watched Old Jeemy and Marty Weinreb for twenty minutes. Most of that time they seemed to be highly concerned about the correct way to grip a golf club. Marty Weinreb would have trouble getting a jump-ball from a wire-haired terrier, but he was darkly tan and looked nimble. He was a man in his sixties.

When Marty Weinreb left the party with a steel-bellied airhead of perhaps nineteen, Old Jeemy bruised a trail over to Juanita and Slick, and said, "No problems, Darlin'. Marty knows I ain't tryin' to sell him a flu epidemic. We're in the same ball park."

Doris Steadman was not. She had been lured from the suite by Dove Christian and Luke Renner of "Duke Rentner, Honest Cop," and something like forty-five minutes had passed since her departure.

But the belt to her mink coat walked into the party at that moment. It was tied around Lonnie Slocum's waist.

"Hey, Juanita," Lonnie said. "How's the party? I was takin' a nap."

Lonnie gave Juanita a kiss, Slick a handshake, and Old Jeemy a nod.

"I've heard all the pickers," Old Jeemy said. "All of 'em. All the greats. But standin' right here, this is the greatest picker who ever picked. Yes, sir!"

"Wish I'd heard Attila the Hun," Lonnie said. "I bet that fucker could pick."

Lonnie had not shaved for a week. He was wearing his aged calf-roper's hat, dark glasses, sneakers with the toes out, and striped coveralls designed by the Pierre Cardin of stains, blotches and burned spots.

"Where did you get that?" Juanita meant the mink belt.

"This?" said Lonnie. "This is good luck. Somebody came in the room where I was hidin' and started gettin' it on with a woman and a animal. Old Dove gimmee this."

Before Juanita could ask which bedroom was Lonnie's, the rest of the coat was delivered.

Chet Woofter, pedal steel, came through the door with a mink sleeve on his left arm. Wendall Dacus, keyboard, had the mink collar hanging out of the fly to his jeans. And except for the other sleeve, which was missing, the remainder of the coat was being worn as a robe by Rob Stinson, drums.

"I knew that thing wasn't gonna die easy," Lonnie said.

Juanita examined the fur. No lining.

She urged Chet, Wendall or Rob to tell her in words of the English language where the struggle was taking place.

"I don't think you'd call it a struggle." Chet Woofter put an inhaler in his good nostril. "Looks more like love to me. They're down there in 406."

Dove Christian then wandered onto the scene with the contented look of a man who had brushed his teeth.

"Is Doris all right?"

That was Juanita's only concern.

"We don't have to worry about Doris," said Dove. "We might have to worry about Luke. I sure hope he thinks it's worth the sleeve I gave him. Part of the deal."

Dove was holding a blue paper bag of the kind hotels provide for guests who may want to send out laundry or dry cleaning. The bag was crammed full of sympathy and good tidings.

"Hope I marked this right." Dove grinned at a slip of paper. "Two pairs of slacks . . . one sport coat . . . six shirts, no starch . . ."

A procession got underway from the hotel to the convention center for the concert. Juanita stopped to rap on the door of 406.

"Doris? You there? It's me."

The door of 406 opened into an inch of darkness. The chain lock was on.

"We're going to the concert. Lee's in 410 whenever you're ready."

"Fine, hon," Doris cooed. "This won't take much longer."

The door closed on Luke Renner's death gurgle.

* * *

The architecture of the Tarrant County Convention Center was such that it made the lower downtown area look as if it were being visited by a colossal biscuit.

When the party-goers from the hotel suite paraded into the service drive behind the main entrance to the structure, they ran into five hundred other people with backstage passes.

Juanita, Slick and Old Jeemy, and Candy, Dove and the laundry bag hung in there behind Lonnie Slocum and Dog Track Gravy as the band pawed its way toward a room reserved for performers.

Tommy Earl and the girl in the clear plastic disco pants had stayed behind in the hotel suite.

The dressing room at the convention center was teeming with roadies, groupies and total strangers, all of whom were sticking their arms into more garbage pails of beer and ice.

The roadies, groupies and total strangers were chattering, gagging, fondling, whooping and guzzling.

Lonnie Slocum, Toby Painter and Jim Hensley stood coolheadedly amidst the holocaust and began tuning up. Lonnie's Martin Sunburst with an amp pick-up was strapped to his shoulder. Toby Painter and Jim Hensley had opted to wear trousers—jeans—and their electric Gibsons were strapped on their shoulders.

Chet Woofter, pedal steel, Wendall Dacus, keyboard, and Rob Stinson, drums, still bedecked in their mink, went ahead to the stage to check out their instruments and all the sockets and cords. They passed joints among themselves as they were leaving.

A Jesus in a sweatshirt now climbed on the back of a roadie in the doorway, and yelled, "Lon! You better come on! They're startin' to get rowdy!"

Lonnie removed a cellophane packet from inside his calf-roper's hat. He dipped the point of a Bic pen into the packet and medicated each nostril. He did the same for Toby and Jim—then Dove, Candy, and a sixteen-year-old girl who had gotten in line.

Lonnie took the lead and the entourage, which

included Juanita and the others, hacked, trudged and shoved its way to the stage entrance of the convention center, where four policemen were approving backstage passes.

A policeman said, "Got a cold, Lonnie?"

"Yeah, but it ain't real bad."

"Pick them licks, boy."

The audience of fourteen thousand burst into shrieking, whistling and stomping applause as Lonnie, Toby and Jim filed onto the stage. Additional strangers seemed to be squatting among the amps, lights and microphones.

A roadie found chairs for Juanita, Slick, Candy, Dove and Old Jeemy. They took their seats in the wings only four feet from where Jim Hensley began mindlessly thumping his bass.

Lonnie ambled into the middle of the band, a little out front, center stage. He turned his back to the throng and swigged from a bottle of tequila decorating an amp along with other tequila bottles and cans of beer.

He went to his microphone. He looked over at Toby Painter. Toby looked at Jim, Chet . . . Wendall . . . Rob.

And as unceremoniously as that, Lonnie Slocum and Dog Track Gravy began to perform.

Lonnie and the Gravy entertained for fifteen minutes —six numbers—before Lonnie condescended to speak to the audience.

"I want to thank all the relatives of Toby Painter for comin' out," he said to the mike.

Lonnie took another sip of tequila.

". . . and I appreciate the support I have here tonight from the Federal Bureau of Investigation."

Lonnie pushed the calf-roper's hat to the back of his head.

"Naw, uh . . . it's real nice to be back in Childress."

That got a chorus of boos.

"I'm just foolin' with you," Lonnie said. "I always know where I am."

He turned to Toby Painter.

"Where am I?"

Into his own microphone, Toby Painter said, "On the way to Seagoville, probably."

That got a laugh.

Seagoville, Texas, a town near Dallas, was mostly known for a detention facility where minor drug offenders often coexisted.

Lonnie and Dog Track Gravy then played continuously for an hour, working the crowd into a distemper for Willie Nelson.

The convention center aisles became dancing classes for devotees of the truckstop minuet. A fog smelling of the leading export commodity of Bogotá blanketed the audience. Flash attachments on cameras created sporadic light shows. Squealing girls formed untidy mounds of worship directly below the stage.

Lonnie was saturated with perspiration when he addressed the crowd again.

"We're gonna get out of here and turn you over to old what's-his-name," he said. "We want to leave you with a song that's kind of a treat for those of you who might be interested in life itself."

"I went to school with life itself," said Toby Painter in his mike.

"I was engaged to life itself," Lonnie said.

"Life itself can't be trusted."

"Don't ever turn your back on life itself. God only knows what'll happen."

"It's best to deal with it on a personal basis. Life itself."

Lonnie readdressed the audience, and said, "Anyhow . . . we're gonna leave you with a song that'll be on our first album. It's gonna be released pretty soon. This is a song called 'Baja Oklahoma.'"

In the wings, Juanita said to Slick, "I was hoping they'd do it. I didn't really think they would."

Now Lonnie was saying to the crowd, "This song got wrote by a pretty lady who's a good friend of mine. I'm gonna get her to come out here and sing it with us."

"Uh-uh," Juanita said.

"Get up there," said Slick.

"Go on, Darlin'," Old Jeemy said.

"No way," Juanita said. "Are we kidding here?"

Lonnie took her hand.

"Are you *kidding* me?" Juanita said to Lonnie, stricken with terror.

Lonnie dragged Juanita to the microphone at center stage.

"This is it, Lonnie," she was saying. "We're talking *Death Row!*"

Toby Painter placed the strap of his electric Gibson over the head of Juanita whose complexion was now tinged with scarlet but who nevertheless looked stunning in her long Indian-print cotton dress, turquoise-and-silver belt, high-heeled boots and Lib frizz.

Lonnie said to the crowd, "This is Fort Worth's own Juanita Hutchins . . . the mother of our country."

Polite applause, scattered. A few provincial yowls.

Dog Track Gravy ran through "Baja Oklahoma" instrumentally. Juanita strummed feeble rhythm, watching the band, refusing to look toward the audience. Toby added a harmonica to the sound.

Lonnie sang the first verse alone. Halfway through it, the mob began to stamp its feet and clap in tempo to the arrangement Lonnie had given the number. A groovy, intelligible beat. A blues with stirrings of Western Swing.

Juanita glanced at Slick . . . Candy, Dove, Old Jeemy. They were standing, smiling, keeping time.

On the second verse, she harmonized the vocal with Lonnie. Her complexion returned to normal, and it was as radiant as Slick had seen it that night in her apartment when she had written the song. A bright grin engraved itself on her face as she sang and finally did gaze into the crowd but saw nothing at all.

> *It's a skyline swiftly rising*
> *And poking at a star.*
> *It's a thicket's tangled branches*

Turning daylight into dark.
It's a breeze along the beaches
Where the Gulf is at your feet.
It's a lonely town imprisoned
By the dust and the mesquite.
It's a drive across the border
To the music and the sin.
It's the blue that's in a norther,
It's football games to win.
It's a roundup stirring mem'ries
Of the rough-and-tumble days.
It's a detour off the freeway
To see where you were raised.
It's the laughter you can carry
Through the years that turn you old.
It's "Baja Oklahoma,"
But it's Texas in your soul!

Lonnie gave a signal for Dog Track Gravy to swing into the finish again, but as they did so, the convention center erupted. A man strolled onto the stage with his own guitar hanging at his side.

It was the bandana knotted into a headpiece, the dark red beard, the flannel shirt, the faded Levis, the sneakers, and the expression of quiet merriment that made up the presence of Willie Nelson.

For two minutes, the convention center was occupied by fourteen thousand lunatics dedicated to the deafening of America. Willie acknowledged the outpouring with gracious smiles as Lonnie and the group vamped strains of "Baja."

Juanita and Lonnie shifted around at the microphone, making room for Willie, who joined them and picked and sang with them as they and the band hammered out a pulsating finish of "Baja Oklahoma" five more times while the hordes stomped, clapped to the beat, and two-stepped in the aisles.

It's the laughter you can carry
Through the years that turn you old.

It's "Baja Oklahoma,"
But it's Texas in your soul!

Gradually, then, Juanita was lifted away.

She spiraled into a vague cloud of rapture, that cloud of maddening bliss which had once thrilled a little girl hearing it for the first time as it came rising out of a college football stadium.

She soared up and beyond that cloud, to a place you could only reach if you had a love of people, a drive for working hard at the things you enjoyed, a gratitude for simply being a part of funny old life itself.

The mystifying cloud was suspended again, as it was that day over the football stadium—and in her joy and radiance she continued to hover above it. But if you were a friend of hers, or understood anything at all about the laughter you can carry through the years that turn you old, you knew Juanita Hutchins had always been up there somewhere.

Epilogue

Juanita Hutchins became a professional singer as well as a composer on that December night in Fort Worth, Texas, when Willie and Lonnie and the boys entertained from 9 till Overdose.

In early January, less than a month later, Juanita was invited to Nashville by the executives of the Mad Dog Music Co. She was accompanied on the trip by an Exxon dealer and a country disc jockey. They went along to look after her business affairs.

After three weeks in Nashville, she wrote a letter addressed to Herb Macklin, but it was meant to be shared by all of her friends. The letter read:

Dear Herb & the Chicken Frieds—

I was just sitting here in our motel trying on rhinestone eyelashes and I thought you might want to know what's been going on since we went off on that crime spree.

This town turns out to be like any other, if not more so. It's equally divided among people who took rich, and are somehow considered successful because of it, and talented people looking for work.

We could start our own silver mine if we piled up all the belt buckles we've seen. Nobody has an ordinary pair of boots. They're all made out of four kinds of unborn puppy dog. Slick saw an electric guitar he thought he remembered from watching the Daytona 500 on TV.

We've been to all the places you're supposed to go hear entertainment, like the Embers and the Carousel in Printers Alley. Everyone we've seen is somebody you've never heard of imitating somebody else you've never heard of—or somebody you're sick of.

As for the famous landmarks, the Ryman Auditorium where the Grand Ole Opry originated from all those years looks like a smaller version of old Paschal High. Lower Broad, the street where you'll find Tootsie's Orchid Lounge and Ernest Tubb's Record Store, is a good place to buy "adult books."

Music Row is out a way from downtown. It's a nice neighborhood where about a hundred music companies and fifty recording studios have moved in on a middle-income neighborhood. If you can imagine a bunch of little modern office buildings that say "United Artists Tower" stuck between TCU-type homes, that's it. But out there is where the Country Music Hall of Fame and Museum is, and I have to confess it's the greatest thing I've ever experienced.

It looks like a Lutheran church on the outside, but you go in and one of the first things you see in a glass-enclosed display case is Merle Haggard's pardon from prison. You wind up at Elvis' gold Cadillac. But in the middle is where I could spend a month.

I made Slick take a picture of the uncharred part of Dottie Newton's wig, which was recovered from the plane crash when she was killed with Whoop Collins and the Whoopers. Ferd Boady's fingernails are there, and Bambi McElroy's shotgun, and the blood-splattered sheet that was wrapped around Wirt Kincaid. I was pleased they saw fit to include a couple of Bob Wills' Roi-Tan cigars.

We've been to several business meetings at Mad Dog Music, which has a house near those office buildings on Music Row. I've heard a lot of talk about "artist rosters" and "pressings" and "risk-reward ratios."

Slick and Old Jeemy wouldn't let me sell 'em but one song, Baja. They say the others might be worth more after Baja comes out. Baja gets released this week as a single for Lonnie *and* on the album. Mad Dog says they'll give it "maximized P & D," which is promotion and distribution. Old Jeemy swears it's not a gamble. He says he invented "workin' between the cracks."

Whatever happens, the funny suits are interested in my other songs, and they want me to be an entertainer. Scares me to death, but I guess I'll try it. No wigs, though!

We're staying in a decent motel, even if the swimming pool is shaped like a fiddle and there's a life-size painting of Dottie Newton in the lobby. Mad Dog is paying for everything. Old Jeemy says this is "the honeymoon period." It's all been fun and exciting, but the room service here has about got me plastic-forked and Saran Wrapped into a coma.

Love everybody,
Juanita

When Juanita wrote that letter she could hardly have suspected she would be staying in Nashville another two months. The reason was the release of Lonnie Slocum's single of "Baja Oklahoma." It hit with a velocity that even impressed the Nashville record executives who had only a "blockbuster mentality," as Old Jeemy called it.

Lonnie's single was no pop crossover boffo platinum flattener, demanding confabs and pow-wows on the coast for a go-project movie by the same title, but it *did* become an instant C & W chart-climber.

Slick and Old Jeemy reacted quickly. They instructed Juanita to put on the eyeliner and the lip gloss and get out the old Martin. They whisked her into Marty Weinreb's office at Mad Dog Music.

Marty Weinreb's office was a four-wall record collection with a golf bag standing in the corner and a Watts line.

While Old Jeemy practiced his putting stroke with Marty's Ping, Juanita sang "You Dropped Out of the Game."

"That's the flip side of 'Baja,'" Old Jeemy said. "We got to cook while the stove's hot, podna."

To Marty Weinreb's credit, he agreed. He promptly picked up the phone and scheduled Juanita into Gip Hoover's Anti-Static Recording Studio.

"Of course," Old Jeemy said, "what she *ought* to do is, she ought to make her own album."

"Browse around the office," Marty Weinreb said. "Show me a catalogue of hits by Juanita Hutchins, and we'll do it."

Old Jeemy pointed through a wall of record albums, and said, "You know what's outside, Marty? You know what we got out there?"

"Two things," said Marty. "A market share—if she can get it. And Chet Atkins. Chet and me are late on the tee at Crockett Springs."

Marty Weinreb stood up, although it was difficult to be sure.

Old Jeemy said, "Marty, old podna, you named 'em yourself! What we got waitin' outside, all over the country, is a whole mess of them *vinyl a-ddicts!*"

"Good," Marty Weinreb said, leaving to play golf. "If she keeps the tracks on their arms, she gets the album."

Through some mixup, one of those show biz incidents occurred one morning at the studio where Juanita was learning how to lay her "Baja" vocal over the prerecorded sound of Lonnie Slocum's lead instrumental guitar, an eighteen-piece orchestra with strings, and a choral group.

Juanita was determined to lose the strings and choir. Thus, she spent much of her time at the studio arguing with the producers who claimed to have the loftiest artistic sensibilities since Michelangelo.

She did succeed in having her way with the pressing before it was over, but not until she had gone through many of those lengthy, bitter at times, and utterly useless discussions with the funny suits in which good taste most often lost out to their concept of reality.

It was during such a discussion that Patti Lou Springer barged into the studio.

Patti Lou Springer was the nearest thing to a hot property that Mad Dog Music and the Arista label had. Patti Lou had been a secretary at Mad Dog Music. That was when she had stolen a song from a session picker. She had left the guitar player half-crazed with the crabs, sold his song as her own, recorded it, and "Lil Levi Jane" had been a hit. She was now a star.

Patti Lou came into the studio, saying, "Okay, which one of the Jews fucked *this* up?"

Juanita had never met a female star before, but Juanita was not altogether shocked to find out that Patti Lou Springer's skin was gold lamé, her hair was sequined, and she fancied mini-dresses woven from chocolate doughnuts.

"I'm supposed to have this Goddamn studio today!" said Patti Lou Springer. "I didn't fly all the way in from Vegas to put up with this shit!"

A cluster of music executives tried to calm down Patti Lou with improved bonus clauses, but nothing worked immediately.

The star sprang on Juanita, and said, "I don't know who you fucked to get *your* job, honey, but either you haul ass or you'll see me kill more Goddamn Jews around here than Hitler! What do you think of *that?*"

"Well, I'm not sure," Juanita shrugged, holding a Winston. "Perhaps if it's tastefully presented . . . ?"

While in Nashville, Juanita kept up with the fun and frolic of the Trinity River Nursing Center by long distance. Too bad. For it was over the phone rather than in person that Juanita heard the heart-swelling news about Grace's colectomy.

It looked as if Grace were finally going to need surgery—after all the years of hoping. Part of a large intestine might have to be removed, though it wasn't entirely certain as yet.

Grace sounded bright and cheerful on the phone, more so than in years. A colectomy was a far more serious thing than the piddling hyperthymia currently troubling Mrs. Grimes.

"Hyperthymia, Momma?" said Juanita. "Isn't that when you're just overemotional?"

"Land's sakes," Grace said. "It sure wasn't anything like that when *I* had it that time! They couldn't believe my blood sugar!"

"Well . . . I guess hyperthymia doesn't require a colectomy, does it?"

"Oh, my word, no!" said Grace. "Juanita?"

"Yes, Momma?"

"We better hang up. Here comes my tray."

Juanita and Slick left Nashville only once during those two months. They made an overnight trip to Austin when Candy and Dove were married.

The ceremony was held in a modern and spacious redwood house in the hills near Lake Austin. Dove had rented the house with an option to buy when he finalized his decision to enter law school at the University of Texas. If he became a lawyer, Dove figured, he could fight the system from within.

Candy and Dove wanted a different kind of wedding ceremony, different even from those presently in vogue at which the bride and groom penned their own vows and recited them to the gathering, often glazing everyone over before the rings came out.

Therefore, Candy and Dove were married—legally, Juanita was assured—by a former football teammate of Dove's who had become an ordained minister by mail.

Just before the ceremony, Candy had said to her mother, "Hey, guess what? When Dove and I are married, you and Slick will be the ones living in sin. Cool, Mom."

The man who performed the ceremony was not only an ordained minister, he was, moreover, the founder of YOU, another of Austin's growing stockpile of religious sects. YOU stood for Your Own Urgency. The ordained minister, Rolf, had founded YOU when he had attempted to ride too large a wave at Makaha. Rolf had also left his flake on the beach with a shapely wahine. He had barely survived the wave, and the girl had simultaneously developed an allergy. YOU trenchantly opposed competition surfing and preached distrust of strangers.

The ordained minister was assisted in the wedding ceremony by a parakeet. After Rolf played the tenor saxophone and quoted passages from his untitled epic poem, which dealt with the theme of bacteria, he hugged both Candy and Dove, saying to those assembled, "This is really intense, man. We're not talking about a lame chick and a gnarly guy. We're talking about a couple of far-out dudes."

That was when the parakeet said, "Far-out dudes! Far-out dudes! Far-out dudes!"

And Candy and Dove were pronounced husband and wife and were dispatched to live happily ever after.

When Juanita and Slick returned home from Nashville after almost three months, they were met at the D/FW airport by Doris Steadman in her pink Granada.

It was a late afternoon in March, and by predesign they headed straight for Herb's Cafe. All of Juanita's friends knew she was coming back that day, and she was anxious to see them as quickly as possible.

Juanita and Slick also needed a chicken-fried steak and cream gravy. Country ham, the best thing about Nashville, could only get the job done for so long.

"You don't look different," Doris said to Juanita on the drive to Herb's.

"I'm not."

"Why, you are, too!" said Doris. "You're a star, Juanita. Your picture's been in the paper. Herb's got your record on the jukebox. You *ought* to be different!"

Juanita's single of "Baja" had virtually lapped Lonnie Slocum's on the C & W charts in only two weeks. It was moving at a terrifying pace toward No. 1. There were plans for Juanita to make her own album right away. She could do it in a week, Marty Weinreb predicted, because she was a professional, in contrast to most of the dope-sick invalids in the industry.

All of that was fine and wonderful and hardly even to be accepted as the truth by a sane person, but it seemed like it might play hell with life itself, Juanita thought.

"What's it feel like, Juanita?" Doris wanted intimate details.

"I don't know. I just hang on to Slick every time I see a little beard and an epaulet comin'."

Doris asked Slick if he had been operating his Exxon station by mental telepathy while he had been away.

"Same folks run it who always did," he said.

The major newsflash on the home front was that Doris Steadman was becoming president of the South Side B & PW. Doris said she hoped Juanita would be around for her installation in a month, but by then Juanita would probably be going on "all those Johnny Carson shows."

Throughout most of Texas, all TV talk shows were "Johnny Carson shows" regardless of the network, the host or the time period.

In the bar of Herb's Cafe that afternoon, those who were on hand to hold Juanita in abeyance were Tommy Earl Bruner, Foster Barton, Shorty Eckwood and Herb Macklin. Thurlene and Esther were there working. Juanita embraced them all endearingly.

"Thought you'd be wearin' an emerald mackinaw," Thurlene said.

Juanita's traveling costume consisted of a pair of pleated pants, sandals, a lightweight V-neck sweater with a gold chain, and a belted olive-drab raincoat.

"You look like you're goin' to the fuckin' K-Mart," Tommy Earl said. "I came here to see a celebrity."

Tommy Earl further observed that Slick Henderson looked as if he had done little more than tear off his Exxon patch.

"Them people take you seriously as somebody's manager?"

"They know I can multiply," Slick said.

Shorty Eckwood was awake for the occasion. He said, "Juanita, I don't care what anybody says. I'm happy you went out and did good."

Juanita and Slick ate their chicken-fried steaks—extra gravy—and they told a few Nashville stories. After a while, they stood up to leave, figuring they had better go check on their respective apartments to see if they still existed.

"Juanita, you haven't said anything about my new showstopper," said Herb Macklin.

No, Juanita had not. An opportunity hadn't presented itself, what with all the show-biz tales to tell. But Juanita had noticed the quiet young girl working behind the bar. A lovely creature, perhaps twenty-two. Tall, dark skin, slender, blue eyes. Brown hair that would be prettier if it were styled.

"This here's Robyn," Herb said.

The girl smiled at Juanita. "I sure do like your song, Miss Hutchins. Write some more."

"Thank you, Robyn. I'm trying. How's the job going?"

Foster Barton said, "Robyn doesn't know which coffee maker to bet on yet, that's the best thing about Robyn."

"Yeah," said Tommy Earl. "That and them legs that'd cut off your breathin'."

"Everybody's real nice," Robyn said to Juanita. "I miss my little girl, is all."

"How old is your daughter?" Juanita asked, buckling the belt of her olive-drab raincoat.

"Three years and eight months."

"That's a good age. But every age is. Take my word for it."

"My Momma keeps her when I'm at work," Robyn said.

"What does your husband do, Robyn?"

"He's in the penitentiary."

Juanita had not been altogether prepared for that response, but she tried to pass along to Robyn a look of admiration for Robyn's frankness and honesty, and she said:

"I'm sorry, Robyn. What exactly did he do?"

"Killed somebody."

"Oh?" Juanita said, suffering another mild surprise. "Well . . . I'm . . . sorry again, Robyn. Was it self-defense, I hope, or . . . one of those manslaughter things?"

"Naw, nothin' like that. C. M. just always had a real bad temper."

Ask a question, get back a plot—or a lyric. Juanita loved Texas, Goddamn it.

She smiled sympathetically at Robyn. She began moving around the room again to hug all of her friends, feeling, just then, that in so many ways she was the sum of what they were. She told everyone she would be in for a longer visit in a day or two, after resting up, before going back to Nashville—and on to wherever life itself had some more jokes planned.

Slick Henderson held open the side door of Herb's Cafe for the former barmaid, and she walked outside and into the late afternoon sunlight with the words of a new song already racing through her mind. Her music was surely going to take her away forever now, away from the old hometown, but Juanita Hutchins knew her heart would always be somewhere back there in that place called Baja Oklahoma.

The World of
JOHN IRVING

"John Irving's talent for storytelling is so bright and strong he gets down to the truth of his time."—New York Times

"John Irving moves into the front ranks of America's young novelists."—Time Magazine

Discover one of America's most exciting writers with these four books, all published in paperback by Pocket Books.

THE WORLD ACCORDING TO GARP
_____ 43996-0/$3.95
SETTING FREE THE BEARS
_____ 44001-2/$3.50
THE WATER METHOD MAN
_____44002-0/$3.50
THE 158-POUND MARRIAGE
_____44000-4/$2.95

- - - - - - - - - - - - - - - - - - -

POCKET BOOKS
Department JI
1230 Avenue of the Americas
New York, N.Y. 10020

Please send me the books I have checked above. I am enclosing $_____ (please add 50¢ to cover postage and handling for each order, N.Y.S. and N.Y.C. residents please add appropriate sales tax). Send check or money order—no cash or C.O.D.s please. Allow up to six weeks for delivery.

NAME_____

ADDRESS_____

CITY_____STATE/ZIP_____

169

POCKET **BOOKS**